EVEN
THE DOG
KNOWS

OTHER BOOKS BY JASON F. WRIGHT

The James Miracle
Christmas Jars
Christmas Jars Reunion
Christmas Jars Journey
Penny's Christmas Jar Miracle
Recovering Charles
The Cross Gardener
The Seventeen Second Miracle
The 13th Day of Christmas
The Wednesday Letters
The Wedding Letters
Picturing Christmas
The Christmas Jukebox

EVEN THE DOG KNOWS

A NOVEL

JASON F. WRIGHT

SHADOW
MOUNTAIN
PUBLISHING

Visit us at shadowmountain.com

Library of Congress Cataloging-in-Publication Data

Names: Wright, Jason F., author.
Title: Even the dog knows : a novel / Jason F. Wright.
Description: Salt Lake City : Shadow Mountain, [2022] | Summary: "A family's old, beloved dog joins his people on a road trip to help a man reunite with his estranged wife, helping all involved find forgiveness and healing."—Provided by publisher.
Identifiers: LCCN 2021049013 | ISBN 9781629729909 (hardback)
Subjects: LCSH: Dogs—Fiction. | Estranged families—Fiction. | Marriage—Fiction. | BISAC: FICTION / General | FICTION / Family Life / Marriage & Divorce
Classification: LCC PS3623.R539 E94 2022 | DDC 813/.6—dc23/eng/20211115
LC record available at https://lccn.loc.gov/2021049013

Printed in the United States of America
Jostens, Clarksville, TN

10 9 8 7 6 5 4 3 2 1

For Pilgrim
October 31, 2008–July 31, 2019

Because there were so many things that dog knew.

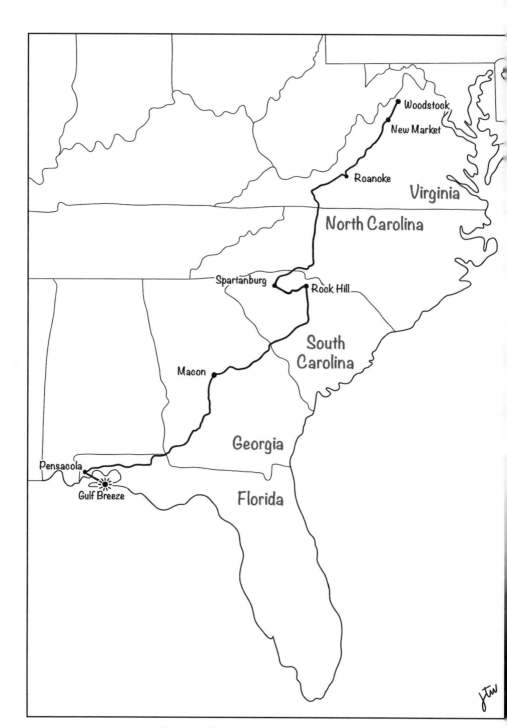

The Route from Woodstock to Gulf Breeze

PROLOGUE

Gary was sure the woman in the wool coat had whipped cream on her right earlobe. He watched as she cradled and sipped a cup of something—probably hot chocolate—at the fringes of the crowd gathered under the Washington Monument. He took a few steps toward her. "She can't be alone, can she?" Gary said aloud but to no one.

The young crowd bubbled and fizzed with excitement as the clock crawled toward the birth of 1951.

Gary moved even closer and memorized her features. Her hair was brown, sort of milky, like Hershey's chocolate but prettier. Like dozens of other women gathered to celebrate the New Year, the woman in the wool coat had styled her hair just like actress Grace Kelly.

Gary inched even closer until he stood just a yard away. He slid up the sleeve of his overcoat and checked the time. 11:57 p.m. As she took another sip, he studied her profile. A minute passed. Then another. *She's no Grace Kelly,* he thought. *This woman's much more beautiful.*

"Hello," the woman said.

"Oh, hello, hi. I'm so sorry."

"For?" the woman said. Her thin eyebrows rose. A smile did too.

"For being . . . distracted," he said.

Someone in the tightening, clamoring crowd began counting, and the choir joined in. "Ten, nine, eight, seven, six, five, four, three, two, one!" They cheered, a few hats flew into the air, friends and strangers kissed, and fireworks lit up the sky over the nearby Potomac River.

But for Gary Gorton, the New Year was no longer the most important event of the night. When the woman in the wool coat looked back at him, Gary grinned. "So, tell me. How long was I staring?"

She laughed. "Since 1950."

Gary laughed too, but at much more than the joke. He knew that if nothing else, he'd be hearing the sound of her voice in his head forever. "I have to say, I'm conflicted," Gary said, taking off his gloves. "Do I introduce myself before or after telling you I figure you have a dab of whipped cream on your right ear."

"My goodness! After!" she said with another laugh. Then, with her free hand, she wiped away the small spot of cream with her thumb and licked it clean. "And now I'm conflicted," she said. "Do I introduce myself before or after admitting that wasn't very ladylike."

Gary extended his hand. "Neither," he said. "Skip the apology . . . My name is Gary Gorton. And you are?"

"Slightly embarrassed." She winked. "But not really. I'm Meg Washington."

"You're kidding me, right?" Gary said.

Meg looked up toward the presidential monument. "Not that one."

Gary watched her turn and walk toward a trash can. She stopped a few feet away and tossed the cup like a basketball. It tipped the front of the can and dropped in. "Well done," Gary said.

As the crowd thinned and spread up and down the National Mall,

Gary and Meg sat on a cool metal bench and made small talk that grew up as the night grew old. "You're here alone? Really?" Gary asked.

"I am. I live across the river in Arlington, and none of my girlfriends wanted to come, so I said, Meg? You know what?"

"What?" Gary said.

"No, I was talking to myself." Meg giggled and rolled her eyes. "I said, Meg, you should go anyway. You've wanted to be down here on New Year's Eve, and you certainly don't need a companion to be there."

"And what did Meg say? The *other* Meg," Gary said.

"Well, she's here, right?" Meg's eyebrows lifted again until her entire face smiled. "What about you? Did you bid farewell to your boys tonight because you saw a maiden in distress?"

"I didn't know that whipped cream demonstrated distress," Gary said.

"Oh, Mr. Gorton, it does. In 1951 it surely does."

As the temperature continued to drop, Gary shared that he was from the nearby Shenandoah Valley in Virginia but had graduated from Holy Cross in Boston on a baseball scholarship and was hanging around the Northeast working as a mechanic during the winter and trying to play pro ball during the summer. He'd come with friends on the train for New Year's and then to spend a few days at home. What he didn't say is that if she'd let him, he'd gladly sit on that freezing bench until the train whistle blew that it was time to return to Boston.

Meg was also from Virginia and worked as a secretary on Capitol Hill. "I graduated from Hollins. Heard of it?"

He shook his head.

"It's an all-girls school down by Roanoke," she said.

"All girls? Sounds awful."

"Uh-huh."

Eventually they escaped the cold and walked to the famous Hay

3

Adams Hotel. They sat on a couch in the back of the lobby and talked about their families, their passions, Gary's father and his death, and the baseball dreams they had shared. He couldn't believe the honesty that gushed out. "I'm realistic. You know, about my talents. I figure I'm good enough maybe to hang around a small ball club somewhere, but I'm not the next Babe Ruth . . . I'm definitely not . . . *the one.*"

They talked for hours and slipped into the hotel's restaurant for breakfast when the sun came up. Later, they walked back to the Washington Monument. Only a few tourists mulled around, and park employees filled bags with trash and other remnants of the night before.

Soon they found themselves in the same spot where they'd met. Gary checked his watch. 8:18 a.m. "Your roommate must be worried about you," he said.

"Only if she worries in her sleep." Meg smiled. "I won't see her awake or sober until tomorrow afternoon."

Gary took his gloves off and for the first time took her hands in his. "This has been my favorite night of the year."

"Which year?" Meg laughed.

"Both," he said, and he noticed her hands were freezing. He pulled his large gloves back out of his overcoat pockets and slipped them onto her petite hands. "You know, we really were distracted last night. Came all the way down here to DC for the big moment and, well . . ."

"Well?"

"Hold on," Gary said, and he turned and jogged toward two policemen patrolling Constitution Avenue.

Meg watched him point back at her and seem to plead with his hands.

Seconds later, all three men walked side by side toward Meg in the shadow of the monument. Standing in front of her, Gary took her hands once again, looked at the officers, and nodded.

"Ten, nine, eight, seven, six, five, four, three, two, one!" they shouted.

Meg smiled, and Gary leaned in, his lips less than an inch from hers. "I figure now I'm really conflicted. Do I kiss you before or after saying 'Happy New Year'?"

"Both," Meg said, and they kissed for the first of a thousand times.

ONE

Woodstock, Virginia
Spring 1992

"Seven-zip." Gary tossed his wallet and keys on the chipped edge of the Formica countertop. "Seven. To. Zero." He punched the air with the numbers. "You hear me? Seven-zip. Another shutout. Almost made the boys walk back."

Only silence answered—the kind that gets louder as the sun sets on a lonely home.

"Where are you? Moses?" Gary walked down the long hallway of his brown-paper-bag–plain ranch home to the back bedroom. "Moses?"

Two legs poked out from beneath the California king that left no space for anything else in the room.

"You napping?" Gary bent over, his seventy-year-old knees creaking in unison with the wooden floorboards. He gently tugged on a warm, black paw. "Moses?"

The Lab panted, sighed, stretched.

"Come on, pal." Gary grabbed Moses's paws and pulled him forward until the Lab's large head cleared the edge of the gray metal bed frame. "Tough afternoon?"

Moses lifted his chin, and Gary heard the whack-whack of his tail thumping the floor under the bed.

"All the way out. Let's go."

On most days, Moses would have stayed hidden in the shadows, content to nap until the dry food hitting his metal bowl invited him to dinner. But today Gary's hands smelled like grass, peanuts, chalk and defeat.

Gary's eleven-year-old best friend followed him down the hallway and into the living room. "Up, up," Gary said, sitting on the cloth couch decorated with spring flowers and fresh ketchup stains. "We lost again," Gary said, stroking Moses's side. "Bats were dead, and that kid Dye can't pitch. Couldn't hit the Shenandoah River standing on the bridge. What a dope."

Gary Gorton ran nearly pitch by pitch through the latest loss for the Shenandoah Senators, his hometown minor league baseball team, based in Woodstock, Virginia. The ritual calmed him, and though Gary couldn't be sure, it seemed Moses enjoyed the recaps too.

Gary and Moses used to attend every game together, sitting in the same spot on a yellow, matted patch of grass up the first baseline. They knew most of the other regulars by name, and when Moses stopped tagging along, even the players noticed.

Moses stood, two legs on Gary's thigh and two on the couch cushion. He circled twice, licked his right paw and settled next to him with his head now resting on Gary's lap.

As the sun slid into the evening horizon, Gary kicked off his slip-on sneakers and sank deep into the couch. Shadows grew across the floor and the entertainment center that hadn't been dusted in three years. Moses was asleep again, breathing heavily, wheezing in steady rhythm.

Then, when dusk suggested to every other house in the valley that it might be time to turn the lights on, Gary sat in the dark with his memories.

This life wasn't his choice. At least that's what Gary would tell neighbors when his wife, Meg, packed her things for Florida. After thirty-eight years of marriage, the only girl he'd really loved met him on their front porch on June 2, 1989. She took a duffel bag of books she could hardly lift, boxes of crafts, two rolling suitcases, her maroon sewing tote, her favorite purse, her most current journal and a handbag of hurt feelings. Her sister, Sandi, sat in the driveway in her brand-new Ford Taurus, packed to the roof and engine running.

Moses watched through a living room window.

Now, almost exactly three years later, the conversation had become the show he never wanted to rewatch. But no matter how hard he tried to ignore it, the memory ran on every channel.

"I guess this is goodbye, Gary," Meg said.

"Goodbye?"

"Yes, goodbye. It's what we say when we leave."

"Leave?"

"Yes, Gary. Leave. As in, I'm leaving."

His knees locked. His stomach began twisting and wringing itself out. The taste of pretzels and salt rose up like heat off July asphalt.

"For what? Where?"

Meg gestured toward her sister's car and the Florida license plate.

"Why?" Gary said, still standing halfway up the front walk and facing her.

"Why?" Meg turned again toward the driveway. "He wants to know why, Sandi."

Her twin sister shook her head. "Why? Oh, come on, Gary," Sandi said, rolling her eyes with comic exaggeration. "Even the dog knows."

Gary absorbed the moment. The wool-thick Virginia humidity. The next-door neighbor watching from his garden. Moses's wet nose so close to the window that his breath left a foggy spot of breath and snot.

Another neighbor watched too but at least pretended to be busy repairing limping lattice on the side of his house.

"Gary, you cannot be serious. You just can't. How many times have we talked about this? Or around it, anyway . . . I've been hinting about Florida for what, two years? At least? And how many times has Sandi visited and asked me to come home with her. To create some space. To see what absence might do for us. How many times?" But the question wasn't really for Gary. Instead, it hung like a mirror in the air, and Meg studied it for a moment. "It's just . . . time. It's time for a fresh start."

Gary stole a peek at Sandi, then inched closer to Meg and whispered, "Honey, I figure we've talked about it. Sure. You wanting to be in Florida, close to Sandi, but I'm not ready. I just need time. I figure *we're* not ready yet. I need you here."

"No, Gary. You haven't needed me for years." A frown crept from Meg's mouth to her eyes. "Gary Gorton. Living together doesn't make us family. We're . . . *roommates.*"

The word hit him in the throat. And though he couldn't remember the last time he'd cried, he knew it was coming. His eyes filled with fat tears, and he turned away from her to face Moses in the window. A full minute passed, then another, and finally he looked back at Meg. The tears had leaked and had been caught like rainwater in the dark puddles under his baggy eyes.

"No. No, no, no." Meg caught her breath, and her voice squeaked at the edges. "No. Not now. It's time." She adjusted her purse strap and stood tall.

Meg stepped off the porch, turned toward Moses, blew him a kiss and walked toward her husband. Time stalled. Sputtered. Spat.

Inches from the eyes she'd fallen in love with, she smiled. "I love you. The day I said, 'yes,' I loved you. The day I said, 'I do,' I loved you. And every day since. I have loved you with everything I have." She paused, breathing back in her words as if saving them to remember later when the Florida days were lonely.

Then Meg placed her hand on Gary's stubbled cheek. She traced his jawline with her thumb, and a tear ran down the hump of his cheek. "But today? After years of wanting so much more of you? I need to do this. For me. Maybe for both of us. And I said goodbye, but goodbye doesn't have to be the end, does it? When we met you said forever." She pretended to wipe a dollop of whipped cream from his ear. "And it's not forever yet. It's only 1989."

Meg moved past him, walked across the uncut grass, loaded her remaining things in the car, and climbed into the passenger's seat. Before closing the door, she looked back at him and said, "Gary, you know where Florida is?"

He nodded.

"Then you know where to find me." As the car rolled back into the street and then pulled parallel to the only home they'd lived in together, the passenger window slowly dropped.

Gary's eyes lifted.

"Please take care of Moses," Meg said. "*Please*," she repeated, choking on the word and covering her mouth. "And yourself."

Again Gary watched the car pull away. Ten seconds later, the brake and reverse lights lit up, and the Taurus returned. Gary took three quick steps toward the road, his heart lit with a tiny spark, but Meg extended her right arm out the window and gave him a stop sign. "One more thing. There's a large box we can't squeeze in. Will you send it, please? It's in the corner of the living room."

Gary didn't remember nodding but knew he must have.

"Thank you," she added. "It's heavy."

Even three years later, Meg's final request rang in his ears. Gary looked at the box, unmoved and untouched in the corner of the room.

Guilt forced his eyes closed again, and he let the memory's final moments play out as they had thousands of times.

He saw the two sisters disappearing down the quiet street.

He saw himself standing halfway down the walk, whispering to the empty road.

"Please stay."

He could feel his legs carrying him back to the house and delivering him to Moses's side. His friend was still clinging to the glass, and Gary remembered thinking they must have both looked like inmates wishing for one more lap around the yard with their families and just one more breath of fresh air.

Gary looked out at the dark road. "Please stay," he said again.

Then he scratched Moses's head, both in the memory and in the moment. And Gary knew if Moses could talk, he'd be asking the very same thing.

TWO

Gulf Breeze, Florida
Spring 1992

The blue cloth recliner smelled like ginger ale. It had been a week, at least, since the spill, and Meg could still feel the sticky spot on the inside of the left armrest. The moment made her miss Gary and his habit of making messes one thousand miles and three years away in Virginia.

She balanced her newest leather journal on her lap and looked at her watch.

2:40 p.m.

Wheel of Fortune.

With her eyelids closed just enough for the ambient light to turn gray through her thin lashes, Meg pictured Moses and Gary sitting on the couch she'd picked out, staring at the obscenely oversized television across the room.

Meg's legs were sore and achy. She'd walked from her bedroom to the family room she'd shared with Sandi three times already since waking up late. "Oh, Sis." She sighed and glanced over at her sister's matching recliner. "Do you remember?"

Silence.

"Do you remember how many times Gary threatened to buy a baseball bus? I thought about it this morning, still in bed, looking up at the ceiling. Not sure why. Maybe the water stain from the neighbor upstairs . . . Was that back in January? I know . . . I said I'd call the superintendent . . . I'll get that looked at and painted over."

She looked again toward Sandi's spot and waited.

"I used to get so mad. You remember?" Meg allowed her arm to dip back into the patch of ginger ale. "I'm not sure he even wanted the bus, he just wanted to bring it up all the time. Like he was keeping score or something. All I wanted was to talk about it. That's all. Just talk it through. That's all I *ever* wanted."

This time Meg didn't wait for a response. "Of course you remember. You knew what it all meant, and I just . . . didn't. Not then." Meg pressed her palms down on her thighs and moved them toward her knees, pressing down, filling her lungs, and letting out long breaths. Her muscles asked for more, and she massaged the tops of her legs again with the heels of her hands.

Meg checked her watch again and knew exactly what was happening on the television in Woodstock.

2:55.

Pat Sajak walks the day's winner to the big wheel for the bonus round. He picks up an envelope. A few final letters chosen. Vanna turns the lettered panels. The contestant, maybe a teacher from Nashville, furrows her brow, maybe her entire face if the newly revealed letters are sparse, and time ticks down.

No winner, not today, Meg imagined.

But Gary and Moses? Well, they probably knew the answer. They were rarely wrong about game shows. Or life. Even when they were.

2:59.

Pat and Vanna wave goodbye, and the show credits scroll at a hundred miles per hour on the right side of the screen.

Meg's eyes opened and wandered to the window between her recliner and Sandi's. A gulf breeze snuck in and teased the leaves on the fiddle-leaf fig her sister had bought for their condo last year on Easter weekend.

Meg opened the journal, flipped past the daily entries to the next blank page, wrote the date and peeked again at her watch.

3:02.

Tears gathered courage in Meg's tree-bark–colored eyes, surrounded by wrinkles of grief and boredom. She gently rolled the tip of her favorite pen across the page. In cursive she wrote: *Still sick. Sick, sick, sick. And sick of it.*

She closed her eyes once more. "Thank you, Sis," she softly whimpered. "For listening."

Across the room, on a mantel next to a photo of the seventy-two-year-old twins, a black and burnt-orange urn sat still.

Sandi's memories said, *You're welcome.*

Her ashes said nothing.

THREE

The pads of my paws smell like Fritos, Moses thought. Not that he really knew, since Fritos were on the "too salty for Moses" list he'd heard about. But Gary had made the comparison often since Moses had come home from the shelter as a hyper puppy a decade earlier.

Moses lay on the couch and let the sun warm his thinning black coat. His head rested on the side of his right leg. His mind wandered, as it did most afternoons when Gary was at a game. *Moses,* he thought. *Moses, Moses, Moses, Moses.*

He hadn't always been Moses. Back in his shelter days he was simply "the obnoxious black Lab in cage four." Dozens of families had stopped to look at him during those weeks at the Shenandoah County Animal Shelter. But when Moses leapt onto the gate, excited, barking and growling and spitting and scratching, mothers pulled in their children and macho fathers cursed. "Git down, ya dumb dawg!" They'd kick or slap the fencing, sending Moses back to the corner to sulk until another family appeared and the act began anew.

Even with the daily disappointment, Moses confessed life at the shelter was better than the home he'd been rescued from on Back Road. The man who'd pulled him into his truck one afternoon as a puppy walking down Route 11 admitted he was using him to win back the girl from the gas station. Moses didn't know precisely what he meant by "win back," but he suspected it hadn't worked because the girl he'd seen only a few times left swearing and throwing what looked like engine parts.

Wait, Moses thought. *I did see her another time.* But she hadn't come in. She pulled into the driveway when the man must have been at work or drinking or both. When she left, Moses remembered the man's shiny black motorcycle had flat tires, cuts in the seat, and was lying down in the grass.

Moses was grateful when the man finally took him to the shelter early one morning before they were even open and tossed him out.

Weeks later, after the daily parade of sad eyes and rejection, Gary Gorton appeared in front of cage four. But this time, Moses didn't bounce up. There was just something about the man. His baseball cap. His large hands. His saggy khaki shorts.

Moses had stood, yes, and walked to the gate. But then he sat, stuck his snout through an open square section in the fencing and watched Gary in the same way Gary was studying him.

Maybe it was his eyes, Moses thought. A little lonely. Dark brown, almost black, like his own. His hair also black, but graying at the sides. His nose bumpy, and his ears a bit floppy for a human. His teeth white and clean, but also crooked.

Moses had looked even closer, pressing his nose so far into the opening his skin stung from rubbing the metal. *It's like I'm looking in a mirror,* Moses thought. But before he could bark his observations, Gary nodded and walked away.

Later that afternoon Gary returned, this time with one of the women who walked, cleaned and fed Moses and the other dogs. Gary carried a clipboard, and as they stood again in front of cage four, Moses already felt something growing inside him.

Before they were home, Gary had looked at his adoptee in the backseat and said, "You look like you know things. Do you know things?"

The grateful dog barked.

"You have answers?"

He barked again.

"I think I'll call you Moses."

When Moses began to feel overheated from his customary spot on the couch, he tumbled off and walked to their bedroom. It had been a long time, years he guessed, since Gary had asked the men with the matching T-shirts to deliver the giant bed. Even Moses knew Meg had been right all along—the room wasn't nearly big enough for a California king.

The day the bed arrived on the boxy white truck, Gary had moved the dresser, small desk and two nightstands across the hall to the other bedroom. When the new bed was in place and made with the new sheets and blanket, Gary looked at the skinny walkway remaining and swore.

Now Moses tucked his head and shimmied underneath. The wood floor and dark shadows cooled and comforted him. As the afternoon eased past, Moses slipped into a deep sleep.

He dreamt of Meg and her Sunday pot roast. Her perfume. Her impatience. The day they celebrated their grandson Troy's eighteenth birthday, his last birthday in their home. Meg had made a cake in the shape of a baseball field's home plate with a white ball sitting on top, which must have also been made of cake because Troy took a bite out of it. Meg had also made a small cake, and it smelled like bacon and chicken broth. Moses was nearly done with it before the birthday song ended.

Even lost deep in his senior citizen's nap, Moses's tail awoke and wiggled at the memory. He missed Troy. He'd lived with Gary and Meg even longer than Moses had, and the day he moved out to chase a career was almost as sad as the day Meg moved to Gulf Breeze.

"His dreams are coming true," Gary had said during another argument.

"His or yours?" Meg asked.

"Ours."

"But are they?"

"It's professional baseball."

"It's minor league," Meg said.

"It's *professional* baseball," Gary repeated.

"It's room and board."

Moses didn't remember much anymore. He didn't know who'd won *Wheel of Fortune* the night before or even what Gary had eaten for dinner. But he did remember that night in the living room.

"It's not even a single-A league." Meg raised her voice.

"It's baseball!" Gary said, his fists together as if pretending to hold a bat. "It's a chance to play with big leaguers who are rehabbing. It's what kids dream of. They pay his rent. They pay for meals. Fans ask for photos and autographs."

"Gary," Meg said. "You think Troy or any boy dreams of growing up and living in someone's garage apartment? Eating nothing but fast food? Riding a beaten-up bus from tiny town to tiny town? Just so they play?"

"Play what?" Gary asked.

"Baseball."

"Then yes. That's *exactly* what they dream of. It's what my own dad dreamed of when he got drafted, but not into the big leagues—into the war. Remember that? He carried a rifle instead of a bat. Never played again. Didn't even come home. Then it came my turn to be *the one*. To make it. To hit away the failures. Instead I was the best player in a small town and then the worst player on a college team that won despite me. I batted .142 at Holy Cross. That's sacrilegious."

"I know the numbers," Meg said. "And isn't that sad . . ."

"Meg. Troy's *the one*." Gary picked up an imaginary bat and swung it. Then he watched an invisible ball sail across the room and break through the front window.

A few days later, Troy had left to join a team in Texas, Gary left for a drive, and Meg left for a week at her sister's in Gulf Breeze.

Back under the bed, Moses waited for the game to end. For the bus to return home and to stop in front of their house. For Gary to come looking. For the smells. The recap. The scratches and strokes.

Moses stretched his aging body and knew just how Gary would expect to find him. He extended his back legs until they poked out from underneath the bed. Moses was no expert on why some dogs lived longer or shorter lives. But he knew he was getting old. And there were things he needed to do. His people needed him.

So Moses did what Moses did best. He waited.

FOUR

"Geez," Gary mumbled.

A man in basketball shorts and a snug polo was sitting in a red, ripped canvas camp chair in Gary's traditional spot. The chair's thin black metal legs bent beneath him, and as Gary set up his own chair some ten feet away, he secretly hoped the stranger's chair would collapse and strangle him. *That's too far,* Gary thought. *Maybe just trap him for an inning or two.* The image brought a guilty smile to his face.

The Shenandoah Senators were back home in Woodstock after a four-game road trip. They'd gone 2–2, and their bats had suddenly come alive. The season had another three weeks, and if they could get on a run, there might still be hope for the final spot in the league playoffs.

Nice crowd, Gary thought, surveying the outfield stands and the small section behind home plate. He had the ideal view in the grassy area away from the fans in the stands. When the team's manager had suggested it wasn't safe to sit so close to the field in foul ball territory, Gary said he'd take one in the forehead if it meant the guys were actually making contact at the plate.

The Senators played on the same field the local high schoolers used, and it didn't take many "rears in seats," as the announcer liked to say, for the place to look busy.

Buying and donating the retired county school bus had been a sizable gift, but if Gary really had money, he'd build them their own ballpark.

"Hi, Gary," a woman said as she walked between him and the fence on the first base side of the infield. She wore a Senators jersey, capris and a smirk that seemed to say, *You don't remember my name, do you?*

He didn't.

Capris, as he'd long referred to her in his game recaps with Moses, was just another woman in town who'd become friendly in the three years since Meg had moved to Gulf Breeze. Gary assumed she and the others knew he was still married. He'd taken off his wedding ring a dozen times since she'd left, but it never stayed on his dresser more than a night before finding his finger again.

Gary looked up at Capris. "Nice evening," Gary said, intentionally blurring the line between referring to the weather and signaling her chance to walk away and have one. Like a magnet, the ring drew in Gary's thumb, and he spun it around his bony finger.

She smiled and kept moving to her seat behind home plate with the other widows and divorcees who came to the games to do everything but actually watch baseball. He'd seen them knit, read books, play cards and write letters. He once saw them using a Bunsen burner to make chili.

"Gary Gorton, how are you?" a voice said from behind.

"That you, Greyson?" Gary said. His head turned just enough to make it look as if he cared.

"How 'bout them Senators?" Greyson said, coming into view and stopping between Gary and his neighbor in the dying camp chair. "Making a charge, huh?"

"Something like that," Gary said.

"Think they'll keep it going?"

"We'll see," Gary said. "I figure tonight they'll get some home cooking. They always hit better here."

"True, true," Greyson said. "Oh hey, how's Troy?"

Gary loved this question, even though he didn't always know the truth. "He's good. Still in Fort Worth. He's with one of the Astros' minor league clubs."

"Starting?" Greyson asked.

"Of course," Gary said. "You don't have control and a fastball that hits ninety-four without being a starter. Next year he'll move up the ladder."

"No doubt. No doubt," Greyson said. "What about Moses?"

Gary instinctively looked at the spot on the ground to the left of his chair. "He's fine. Getting old."

"He been to a game this year?"

"A couple, back around Memorial Day, opening week."

"Right, right," Greyson said, and the announcer invited the crowd to their feet for the national anthem. After the music ended, Greyson said goodbye and walked away.

Gary didn't have to watch him to know where he'd end up. Like the majority of the Senators' fans, he'd plant himself in the same spot he did at every home game.

Soon the mayor, Kensley Dalton, threw out the first pitch and waved to the crowd. She stopped at home plate and posed with the catcher for a photo bound to appear in the paper the next day.

The innings marched by slowly, just as Gary liked them. Neither team had much working, and the visiting team's pitcher was so slow the umps had given him two warnings. Gary wondered if the guy even wanted to be out there—or playing at all.

The stale pace gave Gary time to people watch. He enjoyed scanning the crowd and wondering what their stories were. Meg had teased him through the years about this habit, and with her living happily on the beach five states away, Gary gawked at strangers more than ever.

During the seventh-inning stretch, the man who'd stolen his spot didn't bother to stand. Gary watched him from the corner of his eye taking sips from a red water bottle and wondered what his story was.

In the bottom of the eighth, the Senators finally scored on a double that brought home two. "There we go! There we go!" Gary stood and yelled. "Moses'll like that."

In the top of the ninth, with the score still 2–0 and the Senators' manager taking his time on a pitching change, Gary noticed one of the valley's familiar silver Colonial cabs pull into the gravel lot near the concession stand.

A tall young man with just-above-the-shoulder, barely blonde hair got out of the back seat, reached in for a duffel bag, appeared to hand cash to the driver through the open window and turned to face the field.

Troy?

FIVE

"Step into my office," Gary said, pushing open the door of the Senators' team bus.

"You drive this thing even to home games?" Troy asked. He wore leather sandals, baggy shorts he knew Gary hated and a Montreal Expos baseball jersey.

"Why not? It's mine. And I figure it's great marketing."

"You've had it what, three years now?"

"About. Bought it right after you graduated."

"Right. So it was like a graduation gift? For you. You know you're supposed to get me something for graduating and leaving, right?" Troy teased.

"I did. I got you a ride to the airport."

"Whatever." Troy laughed and fell into a first-row seat. "You just bought this thing cause you like parking close and not having to walk from the outfield lot. Old man."

"Whoa. Watch yourself." Gary sat in a seat across the narrow aisle from his grandson.

"Good win tonight. They playing well?" Troy asked.

"They're playing. Well? I suppose. I figure they're on a bit of a roll. Won a couple road games last week."

"Playoffs?" Troy asked.

Gary raised his right hand, fingers crossed.

For an hour the men talked about the team bus and the new television and VHS player Gary paid to have installed, the Virginia weather, and the disastrous promotional free-taco night that nearly shut down one of the valley's most popular local food trucks. They discussed the Atlanta Braves, politics, movies and Moses.

When the conversation rolled to a lazy stop, Troy shifted in his seat to face his grandfather. "You're not going to ask?"

"Ask what?"

"Please, Pop."

Gary shrugged.

"You're not curious?" Troy asked.

"About what?"

Troy laughed and looked up at the off-white ceiling of the bus. "You're the worst."

"Thank you?" Gary said, and they sat long enough in silence that they both noted the parking lot had emptied. When the field lights were finally turned off, the bus fell dark. "I guess I just figure you'll tell me what you want to tell me, Son."

Troy had always liked being called "son" by his grandparents. They'd raised him for most of his twenty-two years, and although his birth certificate said otherwise, they'd been the only parents he'd ever known. Or at least remembered. "I'm hurt," Troy said.

"What?"

Troy stuck his right arm out. "It's my shoulder."

"Oh," Gary breathed. "How bad?"

Gary couldn't tell through the ten-o'clock darkness, but Troy had closed his eyes. "They cut me. I'm done."

"Oh," Gary repeated, though it now sounded more like an apology. "You were pitching well though, right? Aren't you under contract for one more year?"

"I was. They bought me out. Threw me some cash. I'm useless to them."

Gary let loose a long dry sigh. "I'm sorry, Son."

"I know. Me too."

"How long? To recover? It's your rotator cuff?"

When Troy didn't answer quickly, Gary pressed. "Surgery, I figure?"

"Yeah, not sure. I'll get an appointment soon."

"There's a new guy down in Charlottesville, at UVA. I hear he's the best. We'll get you in." Gary rotated his right shoulder out of a habit much older than Troy. "You know I had some shoulder issues when I played. I mean, you know I didn't pitch, but the outfield took a toll . . . And it healed. Usually does." He paused. "Son, you'll be fine. You will. You're still *the one.*"

"Haven't heard that in a while," Troy said. "Not sure I believe it anymore."

After another quiet beat, Gary reached across the aisle and slapped Troy's bare legs. "Okay, so how are these skinny things?"

"Uh, my legs? Fine. Why?"

"Because the grass at the house is tall."

"And?"

"And I'm old."

"Yes," Troy said. "Yes, you are." Both men laughed, and when the noise drifted and disappeared out the open bus windows, Troy turned again to face him. "So, it's cool then?"

"If you mow?"

"If I move. Like, move in."

"It's your house, Troy. You don't have to ask."

"Thanks, Pop. Can I ask something else?"

"Sure."

"Have you written Mom lately?"

SIX

"Meg? I'm here." Macy opened the front door of the condo and let herself in. She wore white knee-length shorts and a fitted T-shirt with the names and faces of a Christian music duo she was hooked on: the Freeman-Wood Project. Her jet-black hair was pulled back, and a playful ponytail bopped from side to side as she walked. She also carried her burgundy bag of books, puzzles and pills. "Good morning," she said as she appeared in the freshly painted yellow kitchen.

"Aren't you a sight," Meg said, sitting at the table and trying to stir orange juice in a glass pitcher. "The juice is winning today."

Macy set down her bag and took the wooden spoon. "Let me," she said. A moment later, the frozen concentrate packaging was in the trash, and Meg was sipping on a tall glass. "Good?" Macy asked as she took a seat across the square all-white wooden table.

"I mean I'm not a native of this place, but this has got to be a crime, right?"

"What is?"

"Frozen OJ," Meg said, taking another sip.

"Good point. Fresh on Friday?"

Meg raised her glass as if toasting the best idea of the morning.

"How'd you sleep?" Macy asked.

"Sleep? What's that?"

Macy's eyes narrowed. "It's what you do after Jay Leno signs off, unless you want to be a good girl and go to bed at a more reasonable hour."

"I love that you care about your clients like this," Meg said.

"Client." Macy's voice flicked the word from the air. "I loathe that you still think of yourself as a 'client.'"

"You prefer . . . patient?"

"I prefer Meg," Macy said, and she began unpacking her bag. "I brought the good stuff today. A new puzzle and that new book, the one by whatshername. Something or other Van Meter. Looks trashy if you ask me."

"One man's trash is another reader's treasure," Meg said.

"I also got another sample of a new antidepressant, another ten days, from Dr. Kimble." Macy slid the cardboard pill sleeve across the table to Meg. "I think he likes you," she poked.

"Please. He likes my insurance."

The morning breezed by, and the women covered the usual topics of their Monday-Wednesday-Friday sessions. Meg had resisted the idea of an aide when Sandi was alive because her sister so easily met their needs. The doctor's appointments, trips to the store and some light cooking.

But when Sandi died of cancer that no one knew she had until she was already plugged into life support, Meg finally made the call to the only name Sandi had ever given her. Macy was in her mid-twenties, and it didn't take long for both Meg and Macy to admit—at least silently—that the home healthcare relationship was more about companionship than meds and meals.

"You wanna talk about the letter?" Macy asked.

"Not really."

"You started it?"

"Not really."

"Is that the same 'not really' or a new one?" Macy asked.

"Same." Meg smiled. "I recycle."

"You're something else, Meg Gorton."

As Macy made a list of things they hoped to accomplish that day, Meg's mind left the room. It soared down the hallway of her condo. It swooped into her tidy bedroom. It hovered over the rolltop desk across from her neatly made queen-sized bed. Then her mind read the letter she'd been writing, tossing and rewriting for weeks.

Dear Gary—

SEVEN

Bacon. Is that bacon? Moses thought. *That's definitely bacon.* Moses lifted his head from his warm corner of the California king. *And something sweet. Syrup?* Moses sniffed the air and opened his big jaw. His long, red tongue stretched out and bobbed up and down. *Bacon.*

He rose, stood on the bed and took a long stretch. The sun was still low in the sky. Voices that seemed to start in the kitchen floated down the hallway and into the doorway. *Is that Troy?* Moses thought. *Is Troy home? Isn't he in—what's that place . . . Texas something. Or just Texas. Wait, did we move to Texas?*

Moses had lived long enough to have learned hundreds of people words, but he sensed emotions even better. He could identify thousands of them, he thought, if there were that many. Moses knew he was also fluent in body language and voice tones, and he'd gotten good at reading facial expressions too. But everyone knew his snout was still his best gift. Moses carefully lumbered off the bed and stepped into the hallway.

"You're kidding me, right? You're kidding me. You've never eaten more pancakes than I have. Ever."

That's definitely Troy's voice, Moses thought. He stood a second longer and felt the hair on his back end stand and salute the moment.

"Maybe not after I hit, what? Maybe sixty? But before then? Son, I could eat you under the table and out of Waffle House. Show some respect," Gary said.

Even Moses knew the words and the mood didn't match. The laughter, grunts and groans were unmistakable. When another flavor cloud of bacon smacked him in the face, Moses gave in and trotted down the hallway to interrupt their game.

"Mo!" Troy said. "You're up. Get over here."

But Moses was already there, head shoved into Troy's hands, his body leaning into Troy's muscular frame, his tail creating a breeze worthy of the Gulf.

"Hey, buddy. How's my Mo? Huh? You hanging in there?"

Moses answered with a lick and a nuzzle. He stared at Troy. Tall, tan, long hair. He wore a too-tight T-shirt with what looked like white stick figures saying something to one another. He also had on sweatpants. *Or maybe track pants,* Moses thought. *Same thing.*

"You want some bacon? Huh, pal?" Troy asked, and Moses didn't have to answer.

Troy flung a piece in the air, and Moses trapped it in his teeth and inhaled it. Then a second, smaller piece that was mostly fat was dropped in his dog dish by the door. *Bacon.*

After eating and a trip to the yard for his morning business, Moses lay on the floor in the wide doorway between the kitchen and living room.

"Mo doing okay?" Troy asked. "He's looking a lot like you—a senior citizen."

"He's fine, I think. He's eleven. In dog years for a Lab, he's practically dead. But I figure if he can still get up, move around, walk around the block a few times a week, he's fine."

"You taken him to the vet lately?" Troy asked.

Gary hesitated. "Been a while."

Moses listened intently, even though his eyes had fallen closed.

"Honestly? Sometimes I think he's faking the aches and pains for attention," Gary said, looking toward his friend on the floor.

The men took their time, like an unusually long inning with pitching changes and lots of runs. No hurry. No rush to be anywhere other than the table. They ate stacks of pancakes soaked in sticky syrup.

When their conversation curved back to baseball, Moses opened his eyes again and inched closer.

"What are your stats?" Gary asked. "I mean before the injury."

"They were okay."

"Still hitting mid-nineties with the fastball?"

"Sometimes."

"ERA? Wins? Losses?"

Troy pursed his lips and tapped his fingers on the table. Moses watched him leave the table and scrape half a pancake from his plate into the trash can near the counter. He rinsed his plate and loaded it into the dishwasher.

"Oh, wait," Gary said. "That doesn't work. Just leave it. I'll get it later."

As Gary finished up his bits of bacon and bites of scrambled egg, Troy wiped down counters and took inventory of the refrigerator.

"So how about those Braves?" Gary asked. "You following? They're 20–17, I think. Something like that. Third in the division."

"They'll be okay," Troy said.

Moses watched and listened to the familiar drone as the men debated the rest of the contenders—who was pitching well and who might be looking for trades. *I miss this*, Moses thought.

"You're still all about the numbers, huh, Pop?"

"I figure so. What else do I have?"

When the conversation left baseball and ballparks, Moses allowed himself to finish the slow stroll to deep sleep. There, in the crowded, colorful space of dreams of memories, Moses walked into the kitchen during another season and another morning.

"Mornin', Meg." Gary greeted her the way he had every morning since Moses moved in.

"Good morning, honey." Meg edged up to the counter and poured herself a cup of coffee. "You were up late."

"I know. What a game. Fourteen innings. I could have watched all night. It had it all."

Meg sat in her chair at the table and poured cream into her coffee. As she sipped and stirred with a silver spoon, Gary took her batter by batter through the game. Moses watched her face—the morning light painted it with a brush that made her look younger. Wrinkles blended away. Her soft eyes had sparks of life at their edges, and her hair shined. She wore a light blouse that Moses knew Gary liked. *At least I think that's the one,* Moses thought, still living in a memory from his younger years.

After the lengthy recap, Meg hugged her mug and looked at her husband across the table. Each in their place. Their corner. Their world.

"Gary."

"Yeah?" he said.

"Do you remember our first date?"

Gary looked up from his cold bowl of oatmeal. "Sure."

"Where did we go?"

"Uh, dancing. At that place in Winchester?"

Meg slowly spun her mug a full rotation, its bottom making a scratch-scratch-scratch sound on the tabletop. "No."

"No?"

"How about the night before you proposed. You remember that? The movie we saw?"

"Of course." Gary looked at his oatmeal, and even from across the room, Moses could tell he was fishing. "*Kansas City Confidential*. We loved that film."

"No."

"You sure?" Gary asked.

"It was *Singin' in the Rain*," Meg said without looking up.

"Right. Of course. I figure we must have seen *Kansas City Confidential* the day before."

"One more?" Meg asked.

"Why? What's happening, sweetheart?"

"Humor me . . . How many hits did Mike Schmidt have?"

"Easy. 2,234."

When Meg didn't respond, Gary stretched out his arms and hands as if to beg for his grade. "Well? Is that right?"

Meg stood and took her mug to the sink. When she finally turned after rinsing, washing, and rerinsing it, she turned and folded her arms across her chest. "I have no idea. One more?"

"No," Gary said.

"Last one, I promise."

"No, thank you," Gary said.

"Why didn't you tell her no?"

Nothing.

"Why?" Meg asked again. "Why not just say it? Why?"

Nothing.

"Gary, why is our sweet Mallorie dead? And why can't we talk about it?"

Sometime after the sun rose above the level of the front windows, Moses woke to the sound of ESPN on the television behind him. He rose, stretched, walked into the room, scaled the couch and wedged both his body and his brooding melancholy between Gary and Troy.

Moses sighed. *I'm so glad Troy's back,* he thought. And Gary is happy today, even if I can tell he's in one of those moods. Then Moses allowed himself to drift again. *But I hate secrets,* he thought as another nap arrived. *And we all have one.*

EIGHT

"I'll never stop saying that I can't believe you bought this thing," Troy said as Gary backed the team bus onto a dead strip of weeds and dirt next to their ranch-style home. Gary turned the bus off and engaged the parking brake.

"I know. And I figure you're not the only one who feels that way. I guess I just needed something. When, you know. When I had so much more time."

Inside the house, Troy headed to bed after another close Shenandoah Senators victory, and Gary called to Moses to meet him for a game recap. A rain delay had pushed the first pitch by almost two hours, and it was after midnight when Moses willed himself up onto the couch.

Gary turned on the television and flipped through the channels until he landed on a campaign infomercial for presidential candidate Ross Perot. As the Texan detailed his agenda for America, Gary described in even greater detail the team's 4–3 win. "We're making a real run at the playoffs," Gary said, but he wasn't sure if Moses was paying attention anymore.

"I know," he said. "It's late."

Gary continued rambling on about pitch counts, batting averages and the team's decision to hike prices at the already overpriced concession stand. If Meg were still home, Gary knew she would have long vanished to bed.

When the Perot ad ended at one o'clock in the morning, Gary lifted Moses's heavy head and slid out from underneath him. "Keep sleeping, bud. I forgot to check the mail. Be right back."

Gary took his time moving down his front walk to the barn-shaped, white-and-red wooden mailbox. The years hadn't been kind to the gift he'd given Meg back in the early 1980s. What Meg had asked for was a barn-themed shed for her crafts and storage. "I just need a place that's mine," she'd said. "A place to escape. It doesn't have to be big at all."

When he built the mailbox instead and put a bow on it for Mother's Day, he thought the gesture was both kind and hilarious.

She disagreed.

Now more than a decade later, Gary wished he'd simply built what she'd really wanted. Replacing the mailbox was on his endless to-do list. *If only I had more time*, he thought as he pulled down the door and reached inside.

The stack of mail was larger than usual, and Gary began sorting through it as he slowly walked back up the path toward the house. *Why do they waste their time on this junk?* he thought, counting the envelopes from campaigns and political-action committees. There were requests for his vote, his time, and his money. There were catalogues from Sears, JCPenney and two mail-order companies he didn't even recognize. Each was addressed to Meg, and he knew he'd never get them corrected. He wasn't sure he even wanted to.

At the back of the stack, he found a small, hand-addressed envelope with his name and address carefully written in distinctive cursive. He didn't need to check the return address to know who it was from.

He stopped, halfway up the walk, facing the house, in a familiar spot, and opened the envelope. She'd written every three or four months since leaving, mostly to check in on Moses. Gary had responded with short newsy notes, but only because Moses seemed to stare at her letters in the wicker basket by the couch as if he actually knew what they were and what Gary needed to do with them.

The porch light bathed the newest letter just enough for him to read the folded note on crisp, periwinkle-blue paper. It smelled like Meg's favorite lotion.

July 4, 1992
Dear Gary—

I've been through ten sheets of stationery already. It's funny, isn't it? This draft I'm writing now might not even be the one I finally mail. Your letters are never this hard.

I'm writing with a special request. More than that, really. It's a lot to ask, I know. I am trusting that a long life of living, loving, laughing and sometimes fighting under the same roof grants me the right to ask.

First, I suppose I should tell you Sandi died. Maybe you already heard from Troy, I don't know, but I should have told you myself immediately. And maybe you wouldn't have cared, I don't know. But she was in your life as long as I was, and even though you never believed it, she loved you like a brother. Even though she didn't always show it. Anyway, you deserve to know. I'm sorry.

Now I guess it's my turn. I'm sick, and I think I'm too tired to travel. They don't really know what it is, but I'm worn out. One doctor thinks it's all in my head.

Troy called me, which you might also know, to tell me Moses is declining. And quickly. I don't know what hurts more—my own body growing old or knowing his is.

Gary, I want to see him again. I want to see him before one of us dies. I miss him, more than I ever thought I would. I miss him so very much. These three years have not been everything I thought they'd be. Now with Sandi gone, my days are long and lonely. I'm old. Moses is old. How long do any of us have? I think of that question every day.

Gary, maybe you don't want to see me. I suppose I would understand. But will you please bring Moses to Gulf Breeze?

I know getting on a plane is out of the question, and Troy is busy with baseball. Perhaps you can drive or take a bus.

Please consider it. This is my final wish, the last thing I'll ask you—to see Moses. To say goodbye.

Sincerely,

Meg

P.S. You still haven't sent the box. I hope not anyway because it hasn't arrived. Maybe bring it with you? Please?

Gary read the letter again and looked up. There he stood, on the walk, facing the porch.

Moses was awake, his wet nose so close to the window that once again his breath left a foggy spot of breath and snot.

Only this time, it looked like Moses was smiling.

Gary walked inside, ignored Moses and bent over Meg's cardboard box in the living room. After staring at it like a hostage for three years, he peeled up an edge of packing tape and ripped off the long single strip across the top. He opened the flaps carefully and found at least a dozen of Meg's journals. No two were alike, but each had the year written in block-style handwriting so precise, the numbers could've been stamped on by a machine.

He fiddled through the box and was stunned to find a journal from 1989, the year Meg broke his heart in a Ford Taurus. *She left this one?* he thought.

He read for over an hour, including an entry from the night before she left. Then he cried into his hands.

NINE

"Sandi, I feel so paralyzed." Meg said the words aloud to the space around her that could not answer.

From her recliner Meg had watched the Florida Friday sun slowly rise. She'd spent the previous afternoon reading and journaling, then eaten dinner and invited a knocking neighbor carrying warm cornbread into her condo. Hours later Meg had fallen asleep under a Shenandoah University blanket—something she'd shoved into a crevice of the trunk of Sandi's car three years earlier.

Meg waited anxiously for Macy. Her young, effervescent aide had been hammered by a summer cold and missed both her Monday and Wednesday visits. Meg managed, of course, but the loneliness was thick. She had a few friends in the planned retirement community, but she hadn't moved to Florida for them. She'd come for Sandi.

The front door opened shortly after nine o'clock—Meg didn't remember the last time the condo was locked—and Macy breezed in with all the happy energy of the Gulf.

"Good morning!" Macy said, as more an announcement than a greeting.

"I'm here!" Meg answered. She might have tried to bundle up her excitement, but it had been a week, and she couldn't hide her enthusiasm that, at least for a few hours, the emptiness would be asked to leave like a pesky houseguest.

Macy appeared in the living room carrying her bag and wearing a pink Pensacola Beach T-shirt and white skirt. Her outfit, her brown-sugar hair pulled back into a ponytail, her white slip-on sneakers, her light lipstick and bright eyes—all of it advertised the kind of joy that Meg missed.

"I'm so glad you're here," Meg said. "You're better?"

"Sooo much so," Macy said. "I haven't had a bug like that in a while. It feels great to be on my feet." She knelt on the floor in front of Meg's legs. "And how are you? I missed you, you know. Been sleeping? Been moving?"

"So many questions," Meg said, letting a smile splash across her face.

"Fair. So start with the last one. Been moving at all?"

"Been trying."

"Define trying," Macy said.

"Well, I've walked to and from the bathroom."

"That counts! One point for each trip," Macy said. Still kneeling, she massaged Meg's tender calves, and the women caught up on their lives in the week since Macy's last visit.

Macy had finally finished *Men Are from Mars, Women Are from Venus.* "I'm not sure whether to be encouraged or not," Macy said. "Something still tells me men are just aliens, and women are . . . just perfect."

Meg had also finished a book, but she'd started it only two days before sliding it back onto her bookshelf. "Oh my, yes," she said. *"Bridges of Madison County* was every bit as good as I'd heard. I laughed, cried, bawled, sniffled and sobbed a little."

Macy laughed. "Maybe we need to switch books."

The women chatted about television—both had watched plenty while Meg had been home alone and Macy sick in bed. They giggled and gossiped, tossing back and forth the usual rumors and rumors of even more rumors. Then they laughed as they revealed how much they despised people who gossip.

Later, when Macy returned to the living room after cleaning up lunch, Meg offered a confession. "I wasn't totally honest earlier," she said.

"How so?" Macy sat in Sandi's old recliner, crossed her legs and let her body ease into the comfortable chair.

"I moved more than I let on."

"Go on," Macy said, playfully lowering her voice and eyeline.

"I walked more than I said."

"That's terrific! How far?"

"Outside."

Macy clapped her hands. "I love that! How far?"

"To the end of the street."

"To see someone?"

"Not really."

"Fresh air?" Meg asked.

"No, not that either."

Macy leaned forward. "Why do I feel like I'm missing something?"

Meg closed her eyes. "What's at the end of the street?"

"The community center."

"What's outside the community center?" Meg asked.

"Hmm. Mulch?"

Meg chuckled. "True. But what's big and blue and metal and boxy with a small door and rests in a patch of mulch next to the community center at the end of the street?"

Macy uncrossed her legs. "You didn't!"

"I did." Meg opened her eyes.

"You mailed the letter?"

"I did."

Macy stood, skipped the seven feet between their recliners and hugged her friend. "I am so proud of you, Meg Gorton. So proud!"

Meg whispered, "Thank you," and she felt tears tease her eyes.

"And now?" Macy asked.

Meg sighed. "Now we wait."

After a long game of checkers and two glasses each of raspberry lemonade, Macy excused herself and returned with a heavy leather-bound photo album. "Okay, my brave and marvelous Meg, is it now time for the photos?" Macy paused for an answer. When none came, she continued. "Please look stunned and mildly offended if the answer is yes."

Three blinks later, Macy placed the album on the table between them and sat. "Perfect," she winked. "I just picked one."

"You're much too much," Meg said as she opened the cover. She knew her friend was right. She'd been avoiding putting faces to the names, and if she'd been ready to write the letter, she was ready to let Macy into the memories that mattered.

Meg hadn't brought any of the photo albums with her when she left Virginia. She'd written Gary a few weeks after getting settled in Sandi's condo and asked for them, but he'd never answered. Ten days later a big brown box arrived, and Meg was pleasantly surprised that her husband had included a pair of shoes she'd ordered from a catalogue but hadn't come before she and Sandi rolled away.

Meg turned the pages gingerly, as if each represented one wound to open and another to close. Her hands and words moved cautiously, not wanting to scare the past. The photos, living safely under thick laminate sheets, coaxed the women into their colors, their moments, their memories.

Troy's second birthday—Gary dressed in a homemade dinosaur costume. Gary at his retirement dinner—wearing a suit he'd barked and balked about.

Troy in T-ball. Troy in Little League. Troy on his first travel team. Troy in high school holding an MVP trophy and standing on a pitcher's mound at the state championships in Richmond. Troy on the day he signed his free-agent deal.

There were family photos on the beach in Corolla, North Carolina, and in front of the White House and reflecting pool in Washington, DC.

More birthdays. Cake smeared on Troy's face. Troy at senior prom with his high school sweetheart.

"This is her," Macy said when Meg turned the page and ran her finger over a four-by-six photo trapped by plastic and time.

Meg nodded. "That's my Mallorie. When she was little." Meg giggled at the memory. "We called her Malweeweewawa."

Macy placed her hand on Meg's. "She is lovely," she said. "Like you."

Meg nodded again and seemed to study the photo for the very first time. She remembered meeting her daughter for the first time. Mallorie had been so little, just a tiny blip of a baby. But in the photo, she was all adult, standing alone by a Cessna 172 Skyhawk. Her smile was wide and real. She wore jeans, a baseball hat and an ocean blue windbreaker. Even in a photo and even two decades later, her eyes still danced. Excited. Ready. Anxious.

"She loved that plane. It wasn't hers, of course. I mean we couldn't afford that. But she saved her money, bought her time, and I think in some way she felt like she owned the plane and it owned her."

Meg traced the handwritten date below the photo—August 7, 1972.

"She looks so content," Macy said. "Doesn't she? Just those eyes and that countenance. Like this might have been the best day of her life."

"It was," Meg said, as the sting and weight of the words bent and snapped her voice.

Then she turned to face both Macy and the painful moment all at once. "It was . . . It was the best day. The very best day of her life . . . and her last."

TEN

Rain and hail pounded the metal roof of the team bus. "I figure they'll give it another hour—tops—then call it," Gary said. When the clouds exploded, he and Troy had fled for the bus while the players hunkered into the dugout. At Troy's insistence they'd also brought along Moses, and he lay down in the aisle between the seats near the back of the bus.

Troy had been home for three weeks, and the Senators were tied for the last playoff spot with a single game left. Hours earlier, the other team, the Charleston Miners, had lost a day game on their home field in West Virginia. If the Senators won that night's battle against the scrappy squad from Baltimore, they were in. But with an end-of-world summer storm unfolding across the Shenandoah Valley, it seemed likely the game would need to wait another day.

Moses stood, walked the length of the bus, sniffed the empty driver's seat, looked out the windshield at the line of marble-sized hail forming along the tops of the wipers, and barked.

"See what I mean?" Troy said. "Mo's glad we brought him. He wants his baseball."

"Could be," Gary said. "He's had more energy, I think anyway, since you've been back."

Troy whistled, and Moses half-trotted toward him. He buried his snout in his lap, positioning his ears for maximum contact with Troy's thick fingers. "That's my baseball boy right there, right, Mo?" He scratched and rubbed Moses's head as the Lab's tail whipped through the air.

"Hey, Moses," Troy said. "Can I ask you something?" He steadied Moses's head, and they locked eyes. "Do you think Pop should go to Gulf Breeze?"

"Oh, come on," Gary said, taking off his Senators ball cap and rubbing his scruffy face.

"What?" Troy smiled. "You told me I couldn't bring it up with you. Not my fault you're eavesdroppin' on my private conversation with Moses."

Gary whipped Troy's leg with the hat.

"So? Whaddya think, Mo? Should we road trip to Florida?"

"*We?*" Gary said.

"Well, yeah."

Gary ruffled his hair back into place and put his hat back on. "You've got a trip in mind, Son?"

"I do, in fact. And so do you," Troy said, and he gave Moses a pat on the rear sending him to the back of the bus. Troy watched him lumber away, tail down, looking over his shoulder once or twice like a child too young for an adult conversation. When he lay back down, Moses positioned himself with his back to them.

"You gotta go, Pop."

Gary let the quiet collect and settle between them. "Troy, it's not that easy."

"Fine," Troy said. "Then tell me why." He threw out the invitation, a fastball Gary ignored. "Look, I get that it's complicated. I've lived with you both pretty much my whole life. So yeah . . . But Pop, she's still your wife. Right?"

Gary nodded.

"Right. Exactly. Tell me why."

Gary crossed one leg onto the other to tie a sneaker that didn't need tying. "I figure there was no point in getting a divorce, making it all official. We're not looking for anything else. She's happy there. I'm happy. Mostly. She's better off."

"Really?" Troy asked.

"I figure when she left, we made a trade, you know? We traded hurting each other for a little loneliness. Like trading a so-so middle infielder who can't hit worth a darn for a relief pitcher who's good for about fifteen pitches. Not perfect, but there are worse trades."

"She's not a baseball player, Pop. She's your wife."

"When she left, she upgraded to Sandi, and I . . . I got Moses."

Troy's eyes went blank—a wet canvas that wouldn't hold paint.

"Plus we're old, Troy. Too old for it to matter." For a mile-long minute, Gary watched Troy's face, covered with patience and shadows. "Son, the separation wasn't my idea. You weren't there."

Troy continued to hold his words, like unborn secrets, and waited.

"I don't know what version of the story you've heard," Gary said. "But I didn't chase her into that car. I didn't pack her stuff. She chose to leave. She just wasn't happy with me anymore. With life. Troy, when you graduated high school, signed your deal and left, maybe it's like a piece of our marriage moved out with you. And then a couple weeks later she just . . . left. I figure she finally decided she was happier on her own."

Troy plucked at words he'd prearranged in his head. "Pop, when Mom left here, she still had Aunt Sandi."

"I know. I was there."

"And now? Aunt Sandi's gone. You think Mom would have ever just up and moved to Gulf Breeze alone if her sister had already died?"

"Maybe—"

"—No. You know that. She wouldn't. She needed a friend. And now she's down there alone, and I don't know how to help you see that you've got no choice . . . Pop, the game has changed."

Behind them, Moses snored and his feet twitched in his sleep. His mouth twisted with swallowed snarls and growls.

"Okay," Gary said. "Let me ask you something. I mean, I've tried since you've been home without being too . . . what would you call it . . . in your face? When's the last time you talked to her?"

"Mom?"

"No, Barbara Bush. Seriously? Yes, your mother. When was the last time you spoke?"

"Last Sunday."

Gary felt like he'd taken a fastball to the chest. "Sunday?"

"Yeah, why? You're surprised? You didn't think we talked? At all? She writes me letters too. You thought I kicked her out of my life when . . ."

"When what?" Gary asked.

"When she left."

"No. No. Of course not. I just. I just didn't realize you kept that close. I guess I figured you were busy with your career and whatever."

"Too busy for the woman who raised me?" The words clipped the air.

Neither man knew how much time had passed, but when they made eye contact again, the clouds were thin and quiet and the dying sun was peeking in the western windows of the bus. "Maybe we'll play this game after all," Gary said.

"Yeah, maybe."

"Son," Gary said, and he put a hand on the back of Troy's neck. "If we win, we're in the playoffs. If we win the division series? We move on. And shoot, I figure if we get hot, we could have another month of baseball."

"I know how playoffs work," Troy said.

"Even if I wanted to. And sure, a part of me does. I admit. But even if you and me and Moses all wanted to hit the road tomorrow, we can't. Not now anyway. I have responsibilities here. The bus, the insurance—it's mine. I drive these guys. I drive *my* guys."

"I get it."

"Troy, it's fine if you don't. I wish it were easy. Easy to just go. Make it all normal again—whatever that even is. But some things are too broken. And some people are too broken too. There's just so much . . ." Gary's voice pulled up, slowed down, caught its breath . . . *So much you don't know*, he thought.

The awkward atmosphere of regret and silence ended with a fist pounding five times on the bus door. "Let's play ball!" a voice said, and Gary knew it was Ben Kimble, the team's longtime and long-bearded pitching coach. "Game's on!" Ben shouted, and the men watched him jog back to the dugout.

Gary and Troy stepped off the bus and settled into the same camp chairs, in the same spot, armed with the same cheers. Moses lay next to them, his body stretched flat so every inch touched the wet, cool, comforting grass.

Three and a half hours later they said goodbye to the players and walked back to the bus. Game over. Night done.

"Seven-zero," Gary said as he dropped into the driver's seat. "Again? Geez. Seven. To. Zero." He inserted the key, pushed the comically large red start button, and adjusted the mirrors. "We'll get 'em next year, right?"

Moses barked from the back of the bus.

"Next year . . . " Troy said from a seat several rows back. "Let's go home."

ELEVEN

Moses slept late the next morning. His thick hips were sore, but his heart was happy. He'd drifted to sleep after the Senators' loss without needing Gary's usual recap.

I was there, Moses thought. *I rode the bus. I got love from the players. I found most of a chili dog under the seats behind home plate. No regrets.*

Moses stood on the bed—his stomach twisted and churned like Meg's old taffy maker. *Okay,* he thought. *Maybe a few regrets.*

He stepped down onto the bedroom floor and sniffed the scent of both brunch and himself in the Virginia air. He made the journey to the front of the house and found Troy on what had to be a phone in the kitchen. The front door was open, but the screen was closed, and Moses knew Gary must have left for his morning walk. He stood at the door until Troy let him out for his morning business.

In the yard he realized how much he missed his morning walks. He hadn't been up and down Water Street with Gary since before last Christmas—that is, if it's still called Christmas without a tree, wreath or gifts.

Moses stood near his dish and watched Troy make what looked like some potato thing in a frying pan. There was clearly an egg carton on the counter and a block of cheese so close to the edge that young Moses, as he recalled, could have easily helped himself.

Something's wrong, Moses thought. Troy was on the phone, obviously talking, taking turns, talking some more, listening. But the phone was still on the wall. *What's happening?*

"I know, Mom," Troy said. "He's thinking about it." Troy spun to grab the cheese block and spotted Moses waiting patiently by the back door. "All done, Mo? Hungry? Mom, I'm putting you on speaker—hang on."

Troy set the odd black phone on the counter and let Moses back into the kitchen.

Moses cocked his head for a better view. *That's not Gary's phone,* he noted. It was something new. It was very thin with no cords. *No cords!*

Troy put an extra cup of dry food in Moses's dish. Moses breathed it in and emptied the adjacent water dish like a skinny man ending his Sabbath fast. Then Troy returned to whatever mound of heaven he was making on the stove. "I'm back," he said.

"That was Moses you were talking to?"

Meg! Moses nearly lost his footing scampering toward the counter and following the voice.

"Yeah," Troy said. "Getting him some breakfast. Old man slept late today."

"Can he hear me?" Meg asked.

"Um, yeah? Phone is on the counter, and you're on speaker. But he is, you know, a dog."

"Moses? Moses? It's Meg."

Moses tilted his head, and his pulse raced to his tail and escaped through wild wags and whacks against the nearby trash can.

"I miss you, Moses," Meg said.

Moses barked. Seven, eight, nine times.

"Oh, Moses. I do. I really do miss you. Come see me in Gulf Breeze."

Troy laughed and threw Moses a jagged corner of the cheese block. "Never thought I'd see that. Mom and Moses talking on a cellular phone."

Moses sat and listened as Troy turned off the stove and heaped piles of potatoes, eggs and melted cheese onto two plates. "I should go, Mom. Pop'll be back pretty quick."

"I understand. You'll keep trying, though?"

"I will," Troy said.

"Promise?"

"Yes, Mom."

"It's . . . hard, Son. Being here."

"I know, Mom. I'll keep talking to him. You want to know a secret? He misses you."

After what seemed to Moses like a pause so long he could have napped and not missed a word, he could tell Meg had asked for one more thing.

"Troy?"

"Yeah, Mom."

"Will you tell him?"

"Sometime. I dunno."

"You have to tell him, Troy."

"I gotta go. Dad's coming down the sidewalk."

"Troy, tell him. Please. Please tell him the truth."

The truth? Moses mused. *What's that anymore?*

TWELVE

3AB, Gary thought. *Three days after baseball.* He couldn't remember the first time he'd tracked his summers that way. He just knew that summer meant much less when the Senators failed to make the playoffs or were sent packing in an early series. Within a few weeks he'd pretend to find other things to keep himself busy, and even he knew counting the days until the next season would qualify him as something much more serious than just a baseball nut.

Each year after the sting of losing was sopped up by the Virginia humidity, Gary took the team bus into Caden's Cars for a tune-up and he did his own deep cleaning. Gary freshened the paint and repaired seats worn and torn by cleats and miles of abuse by competitive young men. Gary also drove the bus regularly during the off-season because Caden—the only mechanic he would ever trust with the bus—once told him it wasn't good for the bus to sit idle for too long.

Gary hated to admit that the days after baseball mostly meant one thing—time. Time to think, time to remember, time to regret. As the games became memories and the players were long back in their hometowns or playing in some other league down south, Gary always surrendered to the past. It was never easy, but the reminder he was still broken always arrived like an unwanted subscription.

On day 5AB, Gary woke up just after six and slipped out of the house without bothering either of his snoring roommates. He sat in the driver's seat of the team bus, started it and pulled out of the makeshift grass parking spot next to the house.

"Let's ride," he said to the large steering wheel.

He turned onto Water Street and nearly hit Mr. and Mrs. McCarthy on their morning power walk. He honked and mumbled under his breath. Half a mile later he took a right onto Senedo Road. Then at one of only a few lights in town, he swung left and southbound onto Route 11, also known to locals as Old Valley Pike. It was one of the few roads older than baseball, and Gary took it as often as possible instead of the busier, faster and more dangerous I-81. The road was deep with history, and Gary easily imagined he was driving among the ghosts of wagons and war heroes, presidents and preachers.

The two-lane road was even quieter than usual for six thirty in the morning. He steadied at forty-five miles per hour and watched the light slowly dress the treetops. The morning's shy fog was gone before he passed the Shenandoah County landfill.

He stopped at a gas station in Edinburg and bought a ham biscuit, a carton of locally made chocolate milk and the day's edition of the *Northern Virginia Daily*.

"You're up early," the cashier said. He'd known Peggyrose for years, and though she wasn't a regular at the Senators games, she attended enough to talk baseball when Gary stopped in.

"Morning, Peggyrose. Just burning off some gas from that loss the other night." He regretted the choice of words before they'd even crossed the counter. "From the gas tank, you know. I figure it's bad luck to leave that fuel in there, right?"

Peggyrose smiled. "I agree. Fresh start. For the bus, the team, all of us . . . You need a bag, sweetheart?"

"No thanks," he said as he gathered up his items. "See you next time."

"Hey, Gary?" Peggyrose called out as he walked toward the exit.

"Yeah?"

"You going to go?"

Gary looked at the door and pushed the metal handle. "Huh?" he said, and his two bushy eyebrows gathered into one.

"I mean to Florida."

Gary gave Peggyrose what Meg would have called a "salty smile," half-waved, returned to the bus and made a mental note to chat with Troy later that morning.

He continued south to Mount Jackson and passed the apple-packing plant. It was already alive with steam and employees slinking out with sleep in their eyes and others walking in with McDonald's coffee cups in their hands.

Farther south he passed through New Market's cozy downtown, and he was tempted to turn west on 211, toward Timberville. He crossed under the interstate and after a few country miles and wide turns, he found himself parked once again in the lot at the New Market Airport.

He turned off the bus and wished Moses were with him. He'd dig his fingers behind Moses's black-and-gray ears and talk while he scratched. "What are we doing here? Huh, Moses?"

He'd stand, maybe, and move to a seat farther in the back and on the other side of the bus. "Right here, Moses. This is the view." Moses would jump on the seat next to him, and his eyes would point in the same direction as Gary's. "This is about where I was standing when it happened."

Another dog might have wondered what Gary was referring to. Not

Moses. He'd heard the story enough. The storylines were wrinkles on Gary's face. Even though Moses hadn't been there—or even alive—he could have told the story himself.

Gary looked at the window and saw what only time and grief could still see.

Lights. Red, blue, white.

Police cars. Rescue squads from three jurisdictions. Fire engines from four. An airport maintenance truck. Shenandoah County Sheriff Marin Murphy's sedan. The army of responders and their vehicles gathered near an angry heap of flame and black smoke.

Gary looked closer, squinting his eyes to see through the twenty years that separated that moment from his morning on the bus.

He saw himself gazing at the catastrophe, his breath consumed by fear and fuel on fire.

The wreckage was strewn nowhere near the runway. There were two craters and four wings. Arms of metal and fiberglass not meant to meet were twisted around one another, water gushed in three streams, and the steam and smoke were married into a color that Gary had never seen before.

Sheriff Murphy appeared, Gary didn't know from where, and reached up to put her delicate hands on his shoulders.

Then came two words that grabbed him, choked him, held him down late at night when his soul wanted to run.

"Mallorie's dead."

THIRTEEN

Gross, Meg thought as she stepped out of her condo into Florida's morning swamp air. *Sandi lied to me. It was supposed to be less humid down here in Gulf Breeze than up in Virginia.* Meg walked to the sidewalk and turned right. *Less humid my—*

"Morning, Meg!" Her neighbor across the street, Jessie Barton, was on her hands and knees in a tiny flower bed in front of her matching condo. "Lovely day!" she said, gesturing with a trowel to the high, wispy clouds.

"It sure is," Meg said. And even though her clothes were already clinging to her skin, she felt sorry for complaining about the thick air. "Be grateful," she whispered to herself.

"Excuse me?" Jessie called, head cranked around on a swivel.

"Just saying I'm grateful," Meg answered, and she resumed walking down the bright white sidewalk toward the community center. *She hears everything.* After a few more steps, Meg looked back one more time. Jessie was still gazing up, eyes closed, soaking up the sun, and Meg couldn't promise it, but it sure sounded like she was humming an Eagles song.

Meg walked on with the breeze at her back. She'd considered ditching her weekly LWCOGB, but she'd missed last week. She knew if she skipped too many, her place in the club would be taken by Nicavary, Jada or Julia. The nearly ninety-year-old triplets, three streets to the east, had long been lobbying to take a spot in the club.

Meg was first to arrive in Activity Room 2, inside the spacious, green-themed community center that served as the hub for the neighborhood. People came to mix, mingle, snack and sleep. It wasn't even nine o'clock, and Levi from Louisville was already asleep in a reading chair by one of the massive windows facing the courtyard. They came to dance, take classes, tell jokes and—more than anyone would admit—tell lies.

LWCOGB. Meg repeated the clunky acronym in her head, but her groan was audible. She'd hated it from her first day as a member. "Meg Gorton! We're so excited to welcome you to the Letter Writing Club of Gulf Breeze!" club president Veda Charlton had said at Meg's induction ceremony. The fact that there was such a ceremony would have scared off most prospective members. But Sandi had been a long-standing member, and it was "good fortune," she'd said, that Ron Elmer had croaked just a week before Meg arrived. He'd been the founder of the LWCOGB, and the other eleven members had attended the funeral service and placed handwritten notes in his casket.

Meg retrieved her stationery, pens and stamps from a cubby in the corner with her name on it. As she neatly arranged the items in front of her, the room began filling with the other club members. Silence was replaced by gossip, giggles and good news.

"Hi, Skye."

"Hello, Caleb!"

"Good morning, Kaleigh."

"Lili's here, ya'll! Let's write!"

The voices blended together, almost indistinguishable, like a small church choir of well-meaning singers who came together more for friend-ship than art. Meg greeted them, most with hugs, a few with dainty don't-break-my-fingers handshakes.

After Veda's usual opening, she announced the week's project. "My dear club members, I am so excited to announce that this week we're writ-ing orphans in Oman."

"Orphans!" Kaitie, one of the younger members, said. "I love or-phans!"

Oh, bless her, Meg thought.

Each club member received a three-by-five card with a name, age, address and international stamp. Meg studied hers, imagined the young boy—or girl, she wasn't sure—living in poverty in the Middle East. She wondered if the person had ever had a home and a family. *Are they alone in the world?* she wondered.

At exactly nine thirty, per club bylaws, the members broke for a snack and bathroom break. "How are you, Meg?" Kaitie asked. The women were the only two left at the table.

"I'm all right."

"You look really good," Kaitie said. "You know that?"

Meg's hands instinctively went to her hair, and she fluffed it up on the sides. "My . . . I mean thank you. I need to get this mop fixed."

Kaitie grinned. "You know, Meg. You're not like most of the people here."

"At LWCOGB?" Meg couldn't believe she'd said the messy pile of letters aloud.

"No, no," Kaitie corrected. "I mean *here,* in the neighborhood."

"Oh," Meg said, trying—and failing—to not sound curious.

"No, you're not like most of them at all. Sometimes I feel sorry for them. I know I shouldn't. 'Pity isn't pretty,' my mother used to say. I just look and see them sick, unhappy, like they're giving up."

Meg nodded along and pretended to care about how neat her letter-writing station looked.

"But you? I think you're better than most. I look at you, and I don't see someone ill. Someone always so sad. But we control so much of how we feel, at least that's what I believe. Positive thinking. We're as healthy as we tell people." Kaitie raised her hands as if to prevent an invisible opinion from entering the room. "I know, I know. They say you're not well. Last week when you were gone, the others had all sorts of theories about cancer, some mysterious nerve disease and maybe even a bad heart." Kaitie smiled. "You know what? I think your heart is good."

Meg said nothing, but her mind raced. *How long have I been this good at shielding my feelings? Hiding my heart?* When her thoughts had settled like words on a page, she noticed the room had filled again and the club was back at it. Their ideas, imaginations and prayers were all headed to Oman.

Not Meg's. Hers were standing in a front yard in Virginia.

FOURTEEN

Moses woke up thirsty and sore just after the sun. *Why am I on the bathroom floor?* he thought. The tile was cold and comfortable, and Moses had napped there before, but he'd never found himself in the bathroom in the morning. *Maybe I really am losing it.* He stood, took two steps to the open toilet bowl and peeked in. The water was clear and the porcelain surprisingly clean. He poked his parched snout in before yanking it back out. *Nope,* he thought. *I'm an animal, but not that kind.*

Moses wandered into the quiet kitchen and emptied his water bowl. Then he walked to the window and saw the bus gone and Troy outside in the yard. *He's on that phone thing again,* Moses thought. *In the yard!*

He watched as Troy paced up and down the sidewalk, pressing the Pop Tart–sized phone to his face with one hand and gesturing wildly with the other, like one of the humans on the television show that Gary called *Law & Order.*

The bus was gone again, and Moses wondered why Gary was taking so many early-morning drives. Moses meandered to his window and was grateful it was up. He felt the unusually brisk air sneak in through the screen, and his nose breathed in the dewy smell.

Before Moses had time to tune in to the conversation that had Troy so excited this early in the morning, the team bus pulled up and into its improvised space by the house. Moses couldn't see the bus's door, and it felt like three hours before Gary finally appeared around the corner and into clear view. Moses pressed his nose into the screen and pinned back his ears.

Gary stood in the grass and tucked his hands in his pockets. Troy pushed a button on the phone and shoved it into his right pocket. "Where you been?" Troy asked.

Gary looked back at the bus, then again at Troy. "Driving. Why?"

Troy nodded, pulled the phone from his pocket in his sweatpants and moved it to his left. "Pop, I'm going to Gulf Breeze. And I'm taking Moses."

Gary shuffled his feet, but he didn't look down at them like he usually did when he didn't want to talk. "Okay."

"Okay? That's it?" Troy said.

Neither man said anything for a long time. Too long, Moses thought. Then for the first time he saw Troy's bag and an extra backpack on the top step of the porch. Gary saw it too. "Like today?"

"Like now," Troy answered.

"In what?"

"Well, if you're not coming," Troy said, "I'll take the Miata. It'll be tight, but Moses and I will fit."

Moses watched Gary's face as closely as the window screen allowed with its tiny holes and support brackets. *Is that anger?* Moses thought. *Like when I used to destroy his shoes? Or sadness? Like when Meg left, and I had to remind Gary to feed me for a month.*

"All right," Gary said. "Even if I wanted to go and drag Moses however many miles—"

"—904 miles," Troy interrupted.

"So a thousand miles. Even if I could go, how do we know Moses could handle the trip? Or would even survive the trip?"

Moses moaned. *Keep me out of this.*

"I'm ahead of you, Pop. And you're right. I made an appointment with Doc Thompson. We get him checked out."

"You know how long it takes to get an appointment at his place?"

"Sure do," Troy said. "That's why I called the day after you got the letter."

Moses thought he might have heard Gary curse—like one of the big ones—but there was no time to lose focus.

"When's he going in?"

Troy looked at his watch. "Eleven thirty."

This time, Moses didn't have to wonder.

"So if we all go, we take the bus? That's your plan? You ahead of me on that too?"

"Pop, you drive that thing all over to away games, what, a few thousand miles a summer? More? It'll be fine. Plus we can sleep in the beds you built in the back. Save money."

"I'm sorry, Son, but I don't think this old school bus can make it to Florida and back. It would need a tune-up and checkup, at a minimum."

"Then you better go," Troy said, pointing at the bus. "Caden's waiting for you."

"He's almost as booked as—"

"—Be there by ten." Troy's smile was so big and bright, like a second sun on the ground in Moses's very own front yard. "You'll be in and out today."

Gary covered his face, rubbed his cheeks, as if moving his hands would somehow make the world different. Moses recognized the move; it was just what Gary'd done when he and Meg had disagreed.

"Here's the deal," Troy said. "If the bus and Moses both get a clean bill of health. If both are good to go, we leave this afternoon."

Gary looked up at the house, and it was obvious to Moses he was supposed to make eye contact. The two friends let the truth find and circle them.

Trapped, Moses thought, *like a runner between bases.*

Late that afternoon, after a huge early dinner, all three men walked out of the house and boarded the bus to Gulf Breeze.

Gary was secretly anxious. Excited. Hopeful. Troy was content.

The emotions bouncing off both men prompted Moses to wag, bark and pant with excitement. He sniffed the air as the bus rolled forward. He couldn't smell Meg yet, but something in his gut knew they were heading in the right direction.

FIFTEEN

Day One

The crew stopped at seven in the evening, just south of Roanoke. They'd traveled only 150 miles, but they'd started late that afternoon and Troy had agreed to keep the days shorter than he might have if he were driving on his own.

"I'm not a kid anymore," Gary said, pulling into a truck stop off I-81.

"I get it," Troy said. "Neither is the bus. This works."

They ate drive-through burgers and shakes, and Gary teased—with not-so-subtle edge—about Troy's diet. "Don't you want to stay in game shape? As best you can?"

Troy took six fries and plunged them into his gaping mouth. "I'm always in game shape," he said, fry guts spilling from his lips. Then he tossed a fry to Moses.

"I just figure when you're done rehabbing, you know, you'll want to sign someplace else. Pretty quick. Maybe a fall league if you're ready by then. Or a winter league in Arizona?"

Troy nodded as he took a long drink.

Later that evening, the men sat in camp chairs they'd packed near a small field designated for pets. Moses roamed the area, introducing himself to other dogs and letting strangers pet him as they came and went. Trucks barreled down the interstate, their drivers anxious to return home to warm beds and hot meals. One driver parked his semi near them and circled it a dozen times with the hood open, as if his laps would somehow resolve the smoke that billowed up.

Troy caught his father up on the latest developments in something apparently groundbreaking called dial-up internet, and Gary didn't bother hiding his uninterest. "How many fads are you latched onto, Son?" Later Gary refreshed Troy's memory on old neighbors and the football rivalry between Woodstock and Strasburg.

When Troy left to brush his teeth in the restroom, Gary watched Moses's eyes catch a golden retriever at the opposite side of the field. Moses stood and lifted his chin. *Is he preening?* Gary thought.

Moses shook his head, and the energy vibrated his neck and torso and escaped through the tip of his tail. "Moses?" Gary laughed the word more than said it. "You interested? You're old enough to be her father. Maybe grandfather. Easy, now."

Moses took high, long steps and moved toward the retriever. The dog's owner let them sniff, circle and wander off.

"What's going on over there?" Troy said, returning and dropping his toiletry bag on the grass next to his chair.

"Moses might be in love," Gary said. "Smitten, at least."

The men watched Moses and the retriever continue their supervised date across the field. It was after ten, and only a flickering parking lot light kept them from blindness.

"Speaking of love, Son."

"Uh, no," Troy said.

"Come on. Anyone interesting back in Texas?"

"Interesting, sure. But no. I'm not following anyone across the grass."

"So tell me about the interesting girls," Gary said. "Those kinds can lead to more, you know."

Troy leaned back and looked up at the sky. The stars weren't quite as brave and bright as they were two hours north in his hometown front yard. They sat quietly for a few minutes and watched Moses say goodbye to his girlfriend. They saw her climb into a Honda Accord, and it looked like she was gazing at Moses through the rear window as the car pulled out of the lot and merged back into the light southbound traffic.

"Hey, Troy, whatever happened to Grace?"

The name snapped Troy's neck around, and he faced his father. "Grace?"

"Yes, unless her name changed."

Troy leaned back again to stargaze, and Gary sensed his son hadn't thought of his first love in a baseball season or two.

"Haven't seen her around in a while," Gary said. "Maybe a year?"

Troy put his hands behind his head and breathed deep.

Suddenly Gary remembered. "At that Mexican place that came and went so fast. What was it . . . Zach's Mex Mix . . . that was it. How did that place fail? Their guac was Gold Glove caliber."

"Pop, I haven't seen her in a lot longer than that. She came to Texas. When I was playing. Stayed a month with a cousin there. Saw some games. We went out a few times. She wanted more than I was ready for and went home."

"My goodness," Gary said. "You sound like you're sending a telegram."

"Well, you're old enough to remember getting one," Troy said.

"So tell me, didn't she *always* want more than you were ready for? I figure since elementary school." Gary burst into a stream of staccato laughs. "What was that teacher's name?"

"I dunno, Pop."

"We laughed so hard, your mom and me . . . Miss Crouch! That was it."

"I'm worried you remember one of my elementary schoolteachers and I don't."

Gary continued, undaunted. "She caught you sending those notes and called us in. You'd stolen paper from Mom's basket, and Miss Crouch couldn't decide whether she was more worried about the theft or the love notes."

Gary leaned forward just enough to catch a smile daring to curl the corner of Troy's mouth. "You remember, don't you?" Gary said, reaching over and slugging his son's arm.

"Barely," Troy said, and the smile won.

"You know your mom and I thought you'd marry Grace. I figure we all did. Her parents would have let you get married in high school. Geez, after you won the state championship, I bet her dad would've driven you to one of those twenty-four-hour chapels in Vegas."

"It wasn't that bad," Troy countered.

"Maybe not, but you were the couple everyone in town rooted for."

"Everyone?"

"Everyone that mattered," Gary said.

After another stretch of silence, filled only by passing trucks and engine brakes, Troy sat up and looked at his father. "She's in Rock Hill."

"South Carolina?"

Troy nodded.

"Why?"

"She went to be some kind of nanny for a family she met in Texas. They were moving there for the guy's work, I think. I don't remember. I just know they hit it off, her and the family, and she went with them when we stopped . . . hanging out."

"Hanging out? Son, you'd been dating since . . . forever."

"Fine. When we broke up, ended it, she hung around a while and then moved to South Carolina. She helps with their home school and stuff too. I think. Honestly, I . . . don't . . . really . . . know." Troy's voice slowed and ran out of gas.

"You know what?" Gary said.

"What's that?"

"She's the one. She was always the one."

"Look at you, Phil Donahue. You need your own show."

"I'm serious. What could have possibly ended the best thing that ever happened to you?"

"You're messing with me right now, right?"

"Not at all," Gary said. "I'm just saying she was pretty special."

"She still is," Troy answered.

"Of course. But not to you?"

They sat and watched Moses's chest rise and fall with his heavy breathing. Then Gary stood up and excused himself to the bus. When he returned a minute later, he carried a large AAA road atlas.

"So I'm thinking—"

"—Wake up and run, Moses," Troy said, as he nudged Moses's back-end with his foot. "Pop's thinking."

"Hilarious," Gary said, and he sat again in his camp chair. "So yes, I'm thinking. And I'm thinking Rock Hill isn't that far off the road to Gulf Breeze."

"No, no, no." Troy jumped up, and the commotion put Moses on his feet too. "We're not making a side trip. We gotta get to Mom's."

"It's time," Gary said.

"Hold up. You have no idea how to fix things with your own love life, and you're giving me advice?"

"Son, some mistakes are young enough to fix." Gary unfolded the map in his lap and pulled a small flashlight from his pocket. "It's a couple hundred miles, maybe, from Knoxville. So just a few hours out of the way."

"No way."

"We stop by, say hello, let you catch up. Make things right."

"Make things right?" Troy said. "They *are* right."

"Are they?" Gary refolded the map and stood again. "You see this, don't you? I'm doing something that wasn't my idea—this trip to Florida. This whole mess of your mother seeing Moses again. But I'm doing it. I'm trying. I'm stepping up."

Moses spun around at the sound of his name.

"What did you tell me, Troy? That I needed closure or some other psychology term? Looks like you do too."

"Pop, it's late. I'm tired. Mo looks tired. Let's get some sleep. Leave early and put in a long day . . . And maybe on the way back, if we haven't pummeled each other, we'll make the detour."

"Moses," Gary said. "Go. Get on the bus." And he did.

"Troy Gorton. You want to see your mother? You want to make this trip in my bus? You want her to see Moses one more time before . . . before whatever?"

"You know I do."

"Then it's my turn to deal. Call it my curveball. You want this bus to go to Gulf Breeze, it stops in Rock Hill first."

Troy crossed his arms, and if he were still somewhere between a toddler and a teenager, Gary would have called it a tantrum. "And if I won't?"

"Then head north but don't walk on the interstate. Cops don't like that."

"You're being ridiculous, Pop."

"I know," Gary said, folding up his camp chair and walking backward toward the bus.

"But tomorrow afternoon, I'll be ridiculous in Rock Hill."

SIXTEEN

Meg opened her eyes to the soaring sounds of a light voice. Through the grog and the fog, she wondered if it was from a bird, a neighbor, the television. *Did I leave something on last night?* she thought. *I'm sure I didn't.*

She wiped sleep and bad dreams from her eyes and blinked away the blur until the alarm clock's tall red numbers appeared. 8:35 a.m. She sat up and slid her feet off the bed. Her legs felt good. Strong. More awake than the rest of her.

Again the voice broke in through the windows. *Who is that?* Meg thought.

She cut short her morning bedroom routine, stopped in the bathroom and walked into the condo living room to discover both the front and screen doors propped open. The sun spilled into the room, and the voice was louder.

"Amazing grace. How sweet the sound. That saved a wretch like me. I once was lost but now am found. Was blind but now I see."

Meg stepped through the light and into the doorway. Macy was sitting on a rolling garden stool pulling weeds from along the walkway to the street. "Macy, what are you doing? You know we have people for that?"

Macy spun around. "People for that? Who are we? The Rockefellers?"

"You know what I mean." Meg waved a dismissive hand and rolled her eyes. "We pay those fees, you know, for the land guys to do things like that."

"Land guys?" Macy laughed, stood and gave Meg a long hug. "I know. I got here a little early, and you were still sleeping so . . ."

"Peacefully?"

"Something like that," Macy said, skipping back to her stool and resuming the tedious task of pulling weeds that looked exactly like the neighbor's grass. "I opened the screens on the doors—hope you don't mind—for some fresh air."

"Not at all." Meg watched her aide move inch by inch, like a curious bug on the concrete. "Macy, dear, I didn't know you could sing."

"I can't," she said, grinning at the grass but not looking up.

"Nonsense. I heard you. It's lovely. Your voice is . . . quite beautiful."

"Well, thank you, Mrs. Gorton," Macy said, pretending to bow from her seat just six inches off the ground. "I've been singing my whole life, since the nursery, my parents said."

"How have I not known this? I thought we had no secrets?" Meg's voice was light, playful, forgiving.

Macy swiveled her head, smiled and bopped her thin eyebrows up and down. "Oh, sister. We have secrets."

SEVENTEEN

Day Two

Gary, Troy and Moses had truck-stop food for breakfast. Packaged do-nuts, granola bars, two bananas, milk for Troy and a Diet Dr. Pepper for Gary. They were on the interstate by 7:30 a.m., bound for Gulf Breeze via Rock Hill. As they'd fueled up the bus, Troy had again tried to convince his father that the detour would be costly and unnecessary. "I don't even know the endgame," Troy had said. "What am I even talking to her about?"

"I don't know, Son. But you've got a couple hundred miles to figure that out."

They hadn't said much since then, and the miles ticked by slower than a rain delay. Troy sat in the back of the bus with Moses at his feet. He'd made a list of things undone in Texas on a greasy notepad he'd found in the glove box. But it all seemed so unimportant given the direction of the bus.

> *Call landlord*
> *Call back team's PR guy*
> *Send check for utilities*
> *Send flowers to receptionist at gym?*

Have Samuel send books to Pop's
Find last cellular phone bill

He put the pocket-sized notebook back in his duffel bag and invited Moses to join him on the seat. Together they watched the shades of green change with subtlety as Virginia became North Carolina. Moses soon dropped his head on Troy's lap, and the trees and trucks outside became a screen for memories.

Troy saw Meg in the stands at his games. Cheering. With a foam finger almost as tall as she was.

He saw Meg at the table amid bills and stamps, hunched over a calculator.

With his eyes closed, he smelled Sunday dinner after church. The two of them had gone alone, again. The scent of roast beef and homemade gravy and hot rolls was so strong it refused to leave at the end of the night.

Sunday evenings.

His mother cleans and makes lists of her own for the week to come. Baseball is on, probably the game of the week. Troy sits with Gary on the couch. His dad has a scorebook he bought at Ben Franklin, and even though the stats are displayed on the screen, Gary tracks them by hand.

He manages the team on television from the couch. Calling pitches. Stealing signs. Complaining about umps and strike zones.

Mom goes to bed, but Troy doesn't know when. At the end of the night, Gary tells Troy he loves him and disappears down the hall.

Then it's morning. And even in his memories, years later, sitting in the back of a bus, the house feels like Monday.

• • •

Meg warmed up oatmeal and waited for Macy. Soon the women were sitting across from one other at the square, all-white table, hitting their usual conversational topics.

"You're caught up on meds?" Macy asked.

"Of course."

"You're going to your club tomorrow? The blahblahblah letter thing?"

"Be nice," Meg said, and she waved her spoon at her like a magic wand.

"Great idea. Terrible name." Macy winked. "What else? You talk to anyone since I was here Friday? Jessie across the street?"

"No, I think she's in Vegas."

"Really?"

"Just a rumor."

They covered a dozen other topics before Macy made an offer. "You want to talk about your friends in Virginia?"

"Not really."

"Or I could sing for you . . ." She let the words hang in the air like clothes on a line. They rippled with the long pause.

"Fine."

"So, where are they?" Macy asked.

"I'm not sure, exactly. I just know they left. Be here in a few days, I think."

Macy's eyes closed, and her head looked like it was on a spring—she'd become an adorable bobblehead. "So, how about this? Trip to the mall? Maybe a new dress? Something . . . hmm . . . saucy?"

"Macy! Absolutely not."

"Oh now, don't you dare pretend that you don't want to knock his socks off when he gets here." When Meg didn't answer, Macy's fingers crawled across the table. "Or maybe it's not the socks you're worried about?"

"Okay! We're done here," Meg said. She left the table and scrubbed her bowl until her wrist hurt.

"Was blind, but now I see," Macy sang, her voice rising and

expanding until it was so loud the neighbor Jessie might have heard it—
even in Vegas.

•   •   •

At lunchtime, Gary pulled the bus into a Taco Bell parking lot in
Spartanburg, less than an hour from Rock Hill. They fed Moses and
left him outside the bus for some sun and space while they ate inside the
restaurant. They ordered enough for six men and sat in a booth near the
window so they could keep an eye on Moses, even though he hadn't been
a flight risk in years.

As they inhaled tacos, Troy explained how his cellular phone worked
for his technologically disabled father. "Don't worry, Pop. Most people
don't really get these things yet. And not even a lot of people have them
yet. It wasn't cheap."

Troy showed Gary how to make a call, and he punched in the 800
number on the wall for Taco Bell's customer-satisfaction line. When
someone answered on the first ring, Gary panicked and dropped the
phone.

"Sorry about that," Troy told the woman on the other end. "It's a
phone, Dad. Just like any other."

They refilled their drinks, threw away their trash, and Troy stepped
into the men's room while Gary stood at the door. Moses was on his feet,
wandering in the grass, sniffing a stray piece of litter and leaving his mark.
As if you'll be back, Gary thought, and Moses stepped out of view.

Moments later Gary was sipping on his drink when he heard brakes
screech and rip in the intersection in front of the restaurant. He watched
as a pickup truck and a small car sped toward each other beneath red
stoplights.

The moment breathed, Gary placed his free hand on the window, the
cars hit, head on, and smoke and sparks exploded into the air.

Troy reappeared from the restroom and stood next to his father. "What was that?"

Gary's eyes were fixed on the street. Two vehicles married into one. Steel twisted, long arms around one another. Auto bodies crushed and bruised and bloodied.

Troy looked toward the bus, and his voice tore the words, "Pop! Where's Moses?"

EIGHTEEN

Meg didn't always admit it, but there was much to love about Gulf Breeze. The horizon, smells, sand and shopping. Her sister, Sandi, had bragged on their drive south three years earlier that Gulf Breeze and nearby Pensacola had more restaurant and shopping options within a few miles of their condo than everything within fifty miles of Woodstock. Sandi had been right about that, and nearly everything else.

Meg, hugging her journal against her chest, sat in a plastic chair next to the front door of her condo and watched the sun say a long goodbye. The only thing she loved more than Florida sunrises were her sunsets. Adjusting to life in Florida hadn't been as tough as she'd feared, and she attributed much of that to the views. Meg smiled at the light painting the tops of the palm trees. "This is one of those Bob Ross nights." She sent the words into the atmosphere and prayed they'd find her. "Sandi, do you see it?"

She sipped on a water bottle full of some strange vitamin powder Macy supplied her with every couple of visits. It tasted like dirt and mulch, but better to fight through it than to fight Macy when she checked in by phone that night.

Meg kicked off her flip-flops and gently swiped her toes left and right across the concrete. The sensation tickled and woke her feet. She massaged her thighs one at a time with the heels of her palms, bullying them into allowing blood to flow in and through her legs. Meg's circulation had improved recently, and she was walking farther than she had in months.

"Hi, Meg," a woman said as she trailed her St. Bernard down the sidewalk.

"Hi, Mrs. Conklin. Hi, Cassie," Meg answered. "Enjoying your walk?" Meg was embarrassed she could remember the gorgeous dog's first name but not her owner's. "Good to see you both. Lovely evening."

Cassie moved on, nose to the ground, pulling along her thin, frail owner. Mrs. Conklin waved goodbye and shrugged as if to say: *Wish I could stay and visit, but my dog is walking me.*

Meg watched their awkward dance until they crossed the street and vanished. Then she opened her journal and began to write.

I miss Moses, she wrote, and the questions sped in front of her eyes like Gary's game show credits.

Is Moses happy?

Is he healthy?

Does he know he's coming to visit me?

Has Gary taken care of him? Walked him? Loved him?

Meg wondered if her courage would show up when the boys did. She hoped that in the moment, with her family standing on her squat, square front lawn, she'd feel the strength to tell the truth.

I'll tell Moses I've missed him. She sketched a tiny heart as a period. *I'll compliment his coat, his weight, his smile, his teeth.*

I'll tell Gary he did well. He took care of him the same way I would have. He loved him just fine.

Or I won't, she wrote.

I'll ask Gary why he didn't shave to see me. Why he wore dirty shorts instead of slacks or at least a pair of jeans.

I'll give him one of my looks that says a million words without me having to speak. Then I'll look at Troy and let him interpret, mediate, negotiate.

Or I won't.

Maybe I'll hug Gary, let my arms hang on his sturdy shoulders. Let gravity pull my head into his chest. Let my cheek blush from the warmth.

I'll cry. I'll ask how he's been, and I'll care about the answer. I'll ask about the neighbors back home. I'll even ask about the team. Did they do well? Did he miss any games? Did Moses make any friends at the field?

Or I won't.

I'll ask why he didn't come sooner. Maybe I won't pretend. I'll ask why he waited for the team to lose. For Troy to force him.

I'll ask if he ever goes to the cemetery. Did he take flowers when I wrote and asked him to? Does he still think of Mallorie? Will he find peace saying her name again? Telling her story? Her ending? Has he cried? Has he tried to find Troy's father?

Or I won't.

Mrs. Conklin and Cassie reappeared from around the corner on the other side of the street. Meg noted that the woman on the leash was still hanging on for her life, being pulled and stretched and strained.

She closed the journal, tucked the pen under the cover and held it once again against her chest.

I miss Moses.

NINETEEN

Troy and Gary threw open the door of the Taco Bell, and while Troy raced toward the mound of wreckage, Gary ran to the bus. "Moses!" Gary yelled, his head swiveling in every direction. He moved in a circle around the bus and scanned the field where he'd last seen Moses sniffing and patrolling.

Bystanders gathered around the crash site, and within two minutes there were dozens more gawking than could have possibly witnessed the accident. "Moses?" Troy pushed his voice from his gut into the chaos around him. "Has anyone seen a black Lab?" Troy asked a group of teens standing near him. "Excuse me, did you see a dog? A black Lab?" He asked a man and woman watching safely behind their open car doors. Troy walked the perimeter of the intersection, a square prison cell holding two mangled vehicles. The compact car was nearly embedded into the hood of the pickup truck.

"Anything?" Gary called out from a dozen yards behind Troy. "He's not at the bus."

Even then, Troy knew he would remember that moment forever. The look of loss in his father's face. A spent man preparing for more pain. Smoke gathered, grieved, covered the curious crowd and then joined with the wind.

"Moses!" Troy yelled—screamed—and the name pierced through the noise so sharply it startled a stubby man standing to his right. His face was ashen, blood dripped from his receding hairline, his striped shirt was torn down the left side and the fabric seemed glued to a gash in the man's side. Troy looked at him and took a step closer. "Are you all right?"

The man reeked of body odor and alcohol. He didn't answer, didn't blink—shock was plastered across his splotchy face.

"I'm looking for my dog, Moses? Did you see anything?"

A woman began shouting and pointed at the speechless stranger. She strode toward him with purpose—her finger a weapon. "That's the other driver! He crawled out of the pickup. I saw it. He ran the light. I was right behind him." Her voice rose and crashed.

Then barking—steady and relentless, deep and courageous—came from the rubble.

"There's a dog!" another stranger called.

"Moses?" Troy pushed past other witnesses and felt the heat from the wreck slap his cheeks. "Moses?" Troy stepped over and around shattered glass, a fender and whatever junk the drunk man had been hauling in the back of his pickup. "Moses!" Troy neared him but then pulled back as the flames extended their dance. "Get out! Get! Get over here!"

But Moses stayed, refusing to look away from the crushed car, still barking, still pointing with his nose and eyes.

Troy pressed on, pulling his T-shirt collar up over his mouth and nose. "Moses!" The driver in the car came into sight. She was just a girl, so young, so small. Her cries were soft, desperate, barely more than begging whispers. Her eyes pled for help. The heat was suffocating, and when Troy got close enough, he gave Moses a kick and sent him back to safety. "I've got you," Troy said to the girl. "I've got you. You're okay. I've got you."

Troy unbuckled her and knew he had no choice but to move her quickly. He reached around her broken, bloody body and lifted her out. *She's just a child, maybe sixteen or seventeen,* Troy thought. Cradling her, he jogged away from the car and to the opposite side of the once-busy intersection. He set her safely on her back on a strip of grass by the sidewalk.

Then the explosion they'd feared swallowed the sounds, and the windows in the restaurants surrounding the intersection rattled in their frames. Plumes of fire and fat sparks shot up like ugly fireworks. The two broken vehicles were married in a ball of red, orange, white and gray fire.

Next came sirens announcing relief had arrived. Fire engines, police cars, two ambulances. EMTs wedged between Troy and several good Samaritans who'd circled the young woman. Moses and Gary stood close, both coughing and breathing heavily as the stubborn smoke refused to relent.

Reports and statements were taken on small pads and thick clipboards. The girl was given a ventilator to save her lungs. She had burns on her arms and face, and at least one leg was obviously broken. Troy smiled at her and squeezed her hand as she was loaded into an ambulance. She squeezed back, and her dark eyes blinked a thank-you before someone nudged him aside and slammed the door.

Two other EMTs insisted Troy be examined in the back of another ambulance.

"You're lucky," one said.

"She's lucky too," another said. "You saved her."

They're kind, Troy thought, *but also wrong.*

When the flashing lights were gone, when the drunken, disoriented driver had been taken away, when the brooms had cleared glass shards and tow trucks had driven off with what once looked like a pickup and a two-door Toyota, Troy noticed it was dark and finally allowed himself to exhale.

All three were back on the bus, still parked at the edge of the Taco Bell parking lot. Moses had slurped two full bowls of water, and Gary and Troy had used the restaurant's restroom to clean up. "I'm not exactly sure what happened," Gary said. "One minute we're eating. The next . . . I don't even know."

Troy nodded, but his father wouldn't have noticed. Gary was flat on his back on one of the four cots installed in the rear of the bus.

"Did Moses save that woman?" Gary asked the ceiling.

"No doubt," Troy said. "You're a hero, aren't you, Mo?" Moses turned and sighed. Other than having a large late dinner and more water than usual, there were no signs he'd been hurt by the smoke or heat. "Mom's not going to believe this one," Troy said, and he bent over and scratched Moses's belly.

"Hey, Son, should we get a hotel tonight? Sleep in a bed and get a shower that's not at a truck stop?"

"Totally up to you, Pop. But I'm fine here on the bus."

In the darkness on the floor, Moses slowly stood, looked at Troy and walked the length of the bus to the front door. Even in the darkness of night they saw his eyes staring back at them.

"A hotel it is," Troy said, and for the first time all evening, both men smiled.

TWENTY

Kaitie Funk—the well-meaning, orphan-loving friend from LWCOGB—was standing at Meg's front door just before eleven in the morning. "Isn't it a great afternoon?" Kaitie said, her hands extending up into the air as if the day were for sale and she was there to close the deal.

"I suppose," Meg said. "I mean it's still morning, but—"

"—I know!" she interrupted. "I'm always looking ahead."

"I see," Meg said. She didn't necessarily mind Kaitie's approach to life—she just didn't always understand it. "To what do I owe this . . . pleasure?"

"For starters, the pleasure is mine! I woke up today, and I had the most wonderful idea. Three words. The. Beee. Eeeach."

"I don't think that's three—"

Kaitie's hands were back in the air, like a conductor leading music only she could hear. "The beach! I woke up with this strong urge, even an impression, that I needed to serve someone in need today."

"At the beach?"

"Yes! At the beach. You and me. I bet you haven't been in a moon or more, and I brought my convertible. We don't even have to walk."

"I appreciate it. I do. But today probably isn't the best. My aide is coming a little later, and she's bringing some new prescriptions. I better be here." Meg regretted the lie before it even hit Kaitie's ears.

"What time?"

"Around three." Meg couldn't believe that given the chance to lie again and get Kaitie off her porch, she'd only made it worse.

"Perfect!" Kaitie squeaked and let herself into Meg's condo. "Let's grab a light jacket, just in case it gets a little breezy, and some sunglasses. We'll pick up lunch on the way and eat at the beach."

"I'm . . . not sure about all that walking."

"Oh, I think you're sure." Kaitie gave her a smile and a little squeeze on the arm.

Twenty minutes later they were parked in the lot under the giant beach ball at Pensacola Beach and walking slowly to the waterfront. Meg toted two white paper bags holding sandwiches and Snapples. Kaitie carried collapsible canvas beach chairs and a beach tote with sunscreen, bottles of water, towels, a novel she hadn't opened in a month and some stationery for letters, just in case the mood hit.

They set up near a lifeguard tower, and Kaitie introduced herself and Meg to Nathan Jones, a twenty-something-year-old man in the sky who looked like he was filming a Coppertone commercial without any actual cameras. Nathan's hair was longer than most lifeguards' the women had ever seen at any of the Gulf Breeze beaches, and the wind whipped it behind him.

"My heavens," Kaitie said, looking up at him on his white wooden perch and shielding the midday sun from her eyes. "And I do mean heavens. You're the god of Gulf Breeze, aren't you?"

"Okay, Goldie Hawn," Meg said. "Turn it down."

Kaitie flirted with the lifeguard until his radio squawked and Nathan excused himself to walk to another nearby lifeguard station.

"Mm-hmm-hmm," Kaitie said as she dropped into her chair.

"You know that kid is barely old enough to vote, right?" Meg said.

"Now, now, age is just a number."

"Sure." Meg laughed at herself. "And that number is fifty. As in, you're almost fifty years older than he is."

Kaitie ignored the ribbing and buried her bare feet in the warm sand. "This," she said, again waving her arms through the air, "is why I moved to Florida. What life could possibly be better than this?"

"I suppose," Meg said.

Kaitie removed her sunglasses and turned to face her friend. "I'm sorry, I know you miss your sister. You came here a lot, didn't you? Sandi sure was special."

"She was," Meg said. "One of a kind."

"Well, you're her twin." Kaitie grinned. "So maybe not *exactly* one of a kind."

As the beach filled with umbrellas, families and Frisbees, the women discussed tourists, food, health, husbands and their shared love-hate relationship with the Letter Writing Club of Gulf Breeze.

Meg discovered that Kaitie had also left her husband, though for dangerously different reasons. "When he got laid off," Kaitie said, "he didn't come right home."

"For how long?"

"Three months."

"Three months!" Meg's voice popped.

"Well, in fairness it was only eighty-four days." Kaitie smiled, and her white teeth radiated against her tanned face.

"I can't even imagine," Meg said.

"When he finally came home—I'm just so thankful our two kids were grown and gone—he came with some friends."

"What?"

"Yes, ma'am. He came home with a bottle and a big fist. And he wasn't afraid to use both."

"I'm so sorry." Meg said.

"Don't be. It's been a long time. Too long to dwell on it."

"Where is he now?" Meg asked.

Kaitie stuck her tongue out of the side of her mouth and rolled her green eyes back into her head.

"Dead?" Meg said. "Really?"

"Yes, ma'am."

"How? If you don't mind me asking."

"You really want to know?" Kaitie asked.

Meg nodded, curiosity coursing through her.

"He wouldn't come to the beach with me."

The women laughed until they ran out of breath.

"He's alive, somewhere," Kaitie finally said. "Talks to the kids. Says he's clean and sober and happy with a new life and wife, so . . . How about your husband? I don't know much—just what they say at LWCOGB."

"Oh gadflies, I hate that name so much."

The women laughed again, and Meg felt more at ease than she had in weeks. Maybe months.

"I'm still legally married, but you probably know that."

Kaitie winked. "That's beginner gossip. That's Meg Gorton 101."

"Sandi and I left Virginia a couple years ago. Three, I guess now. Summer 1989."

"Uh-huh," Kaitie said, and she closed her eyes and leaned back to bake her face.

"Our ending—I guess that's what it was. Or maybe a pause. I don't know. It was different than yours. Are you wondering if he hit me?" Meg asked Kaitie's surprisingly youthful profile. "Not once. Never raised a hand . . . Didn't yell, or at least not really at me . . . I mean we argued sometimes. Like all couples, I guess. Was he unfaithful? No . . . I don't think so . . . At least not with someone else. But he changed, I guess. And, oh, I don't know." She took a long breath and studied a family playing in the surf. "They say they'll always love us, don't they? They vow they will love us forever. Gary sure did. Our friends heard it. God heard it . . . But do you know how many times he said he loved me in the last decade before I left?" Meg looked back at Kaitie and was greeted with a soft snore.

"Me either," Meg told the sand.

With Kaitie asleep next to her—head back, mouth open, sunglasses askew—Meg lost track of time. She didn't know how long they'd been there or how many others had come and gone around them. She didn't recognize the children playing or the parents hovering nearby. She hardly even recognized this woman next to her, this version of Kaitie she'd never met before.

But she did recognize the voice yelling from behind.

"Meg! Meg Gorton! What in the world!"

Meg turned to see Macy speed walking toward her from between the dunes that separated the parking lot from the beach. "Macy?"

"Meg," she said, out of breath. "What are you doing? What are you doing here?"

Kaitie awoke and arched the stiffness out of her back. "Oh, hi, Macy."

"Don't 'Oh, hi, Macy,' me," she snapped. "What's going on?"

"Sweetheart," Meg said, and she reached out for Macy's hand, but Macy refused the gesture. "Kaitie invited me to the beach. That's all. I didn't think you were coming today."

"I knew it!" Kaitie giggled.

"Not now," Meg said. "I'm sorry, Macy. I should have left a note."

"That's funny," Kaitie said. "A note, you know, because of LWCOGB—"

"Please stop," Meg pled, sticking her hand into the air without looking in Kaitie's direction.

"No," Macy broke in. "You shouldn't have left a note. You should have left yourself. Do you know how dangerous this is?"

Meg looked out toward the water. "The ocean? The kids? The delicious lifeguards? We're just sitting, Macy. I don't understand."

"No, you're *not* just sitting. You're roasting, and you're on meds that specifically say to avoid the sun. You don't remember that?"

"I . . . I didn't. I'm sorry—"

"—And your face is bright red. And no hat? And you walked here?" Macy huffed. "Are you kidding me?"

"Actually, I drove," Kaitie said, raising her hand in apology. "We came in the convertible."

"I don't care if you came on a donkey. This was a mistake. Let's go."

Macy helped Meg to her feet, and Kaitie apologized again. "I really am sorry, Macy. This is my fault. I practically dragged her here. She put up a good fight."

"Not good enough." Macy shot the words over her shoulder.

The two women trudged slowly through the sand, arm in arm, and Kaitie stood amid the chairs and lunch trash. "No, no," she said. "I'll get this."

TWENTY-ONE

Day Three

All three men slept in. The queen beds were soft, the showers long, and if Troy and Gary had lingered any longer at the free continental breakfast, they might have been escorted out. When they returned to the room to grab their things and pick up Moses, Troy opened up a folded paper plate and fed the hungry Lab a pile of bacon and several sausages.

They let Moses wander the large field behind the Residence Inn, but they kept close, calling him back when he inched too far off. Neither man was in a rush to get back on the bus. When they finally pulled out of the lot, they drove less than a mile to a truck stop and spent an hour cleaning the bus, wiping the windows, and refilling their snack bins and cooler.

Moses was quiet, and the men expressed concern that the car crash had impacted him more than they'd realized. "Sure, he seems off," Gary said, topping off the bus's tank. "But I figure any dog would be, right? Think of it. Think of what he saw."

They drove just thirty minutes before stopping for a bathroom break. They were forty miles from Rock Hill and a reunion only two of the three were excited about. "I gotta go," Gary said. "Too much OJ."

While his father walked into the men's room, Troy pulled his phone from his pocket. From his wallet he plucked a Taco Bell receipt and typed in the number scribbled on it of a hospital in Spartanburg.

"I'm calling about a girl who came in last night. She was in a car crash . . . No, I don't know her name . . . Yes, yes. That one . . . No, that's fine, I understand . . . Could you give her or her family a message? Thank you . . . Could you tell her Troy called? Her friend from the accident? I . . . I saw it . . . Tried to help a little . . . Just tell her I checked on her? Just want to be sure she's going to be okay. I promised I would . . . You know . . ." Troy noticed Moses approaching in a slow trot. "Could you tell her Moses checked in too? Yes, yes . . . He's the dog . . . Yes . . . Oh, that's the best," Troy laughed. "I'll tell him. Thank you."

Troy ended the call and looked down at Moses. "Guess what, Mo? They're calling you 'hero dog' at the hospital back in Spartanburg. How 'bout that?"

Moses lifted and licked his paw.

"Stay humble, brother." Troy snickered.

When Gary returned to the bus, Troy took a turn in the restroom and Moses took his time lapping up another bowl of water in the shadow of the bus. When he was done, Gary threw him two ice cubes from the cooler. "You ready to do this, Moses? See Grace?"

Moses looked up, drool dripping from his jowls.

After a lengthy stare down, Gary shrugged. "How am I supposed to know?"

"Know what?" Troy asked.

"Nothing. Private discussion," Gary said. "Let's get to Rock Hill."

Moses was still deep in his first nap when they pulled off SC-5 and rolled down Albright Road into downtown Rock Hill. "Now, how do we find her?" Gary asked.

"How should I know? This was your idea, Nancy Drew."

"Can't you look her up on that thing? That cellular phone?"

"Sure, right, Pop. It's got a phone book and a map and everything in it. I can also watch movies on it if I get bored."

"Don't be smart, Son," Gary said, and he pulled up next to the York County Library. "Can we start here?"

Troy sighed. "Sure, you go. I'll stay with Moses."

"Uh-uh. Let's go," Gary said, and he pulled on the handle to open the bus door. "We had a deal."

"Nope, sure didn't," Troy answered. He met his father on the sidewalk and bent down to stretch and touch his toes several times.

"Last minute workout? Trying to look fit?" Gary slapped Troy in the abs when he stood back up.

"You're ridiculous," Troy said.

Gary laughed and walked into the library. Troy followed like a sulking pitcher entering a losing game. "What are we doing?" he whispered.

At the information desk, a friendly volunteer greeted them with big eyes and a handshake. "Hi! I'm Charlotte Huffine!" Both men thought she spoke much too loudly for a library. "Welcooome! How can I help you?" Her Southern accent dripped from her perfect smile and brown curls.

"A phone book," Gary said. "Let's start there."

"Which one?" Charlotte said, and her eyes lit up at the possibilities. "We have every single phone book in South Carolina!"

"Oh, wow. Okay. I figure we're in Rock Hill, right, Son?" He smiled at Troy. "Let's see that one first."

Charlotte pointed with both index fingers. "Smart! I like the way you think." She spun on her chair and rolled a few feet to a low bookcase jammed with yellow-and-white phone books. "Here you go. Let's see what we can find."

"So I think we're probably okay, if you don't mind," Gary said. "We'll just step aside so you can help someone else."

Charlotte leaned to her left and looked around them. "Seems to be—"

"—Thank you!" Gary said, and he clutched the phone book. Troy followed him to a rectangular table near the microfiche readers.

"Pop, this could be a wild-goose chase. You know that. All I can say for certain is she moved down here when we broke up. She's living with another family, I think. I don't even know their names. So it's pretty likely she's not even in there. Or even if she is listed, she could be in one of the other five hundred phone books Charlotte is hoarding over there."

"We'll never know unless we try," Gary said, and he opened the book and thumbed through the thin pages.

"And how long are we willing to try before moving on? Mom's waiting, you know."

"Grace . . . It's Dellinger, right? Grace Dellinger?"

"Yeah, Pop."

"Let's see . . . Dellert, Delles, Delley, Dellecarpini . . . Dellecarpini? We had a kid named Dellecarpini a few years ago with the Senators. Didn't we? Shortstop?"

"Pop, please. She's not there."

"Delligatti, Delling . . ." Gary stopped.

"See, nothing. Can we move on? Stop all this?"

Gary pointed at a tiny name on the white page. "Dellinger, Grace."

"Let me see." Troy slid the phone book toward his chest and studied the name. "Could be someone else," he said. "Really, I mean *Grace* is so common."

Gary snatched the phone book and returned to the information desk. "Charlotte, may I borrow a pen and some paper?"

"Some success, I see?" Charlotte rubbed her hands together. "I love a good mystery!"

Gary jotted down the address and noticed most names on the page had phone numbers. Hers did not. "Thank you, Charlotte. You made my day." The volunteer blushed and fiddled with a hairband that didn't need fiddling.

Once outside, Troy walked a few paces behind Gary and briefly considered tackling his father into one of the flower beds that lined the walkway. On the bus, Gary opened their atlas and was delighted to find Grace's street listed. "Looks like this is a major road. Easy to find," he mumbled to himself. "I figure it's less than five minutes away."

"Awesome," Troy said through a sudden bout of nausea.

Moses rested his head on Troy's left knee and looked up at him, his mouth and chest quiet and still.

"Agreed," Troy said.

TWENTY-TWO

"You can't park here."

"Why not?" Gary asked.

"Pop, she'll recognize the bus."

"So?"

"So she'll know we're here. Maybe she won't open the door. Or calls the police."

"Now you want her to open the door?" Gary asked.

"Seriously? We don't even know if it's really her."

Gary stood up from the driver's seat and took the three steps to the door. He looked through the glass, scanned left and right. Grace's address numbers were on a townhouse, at the end of a row of six. It was nicer than either of them had thought, although neither had any idea what they'd really expected. "You might be right," Gary said. "A big baseball bus parked on the street like this might draw some lookie-loos."

Troy looked down at Moses and just shook his head.

"I'll find a spot." Three blocks away he parked at the back of a health-club parking lot. "This works. Now we walk."

"How?"

"One foot in front—

"—No, how do we approach her . . . or whoever is living here?"

"We just knock. And wait."

"That's your plan, Pop?"

"What else is there?"

"What do we say?"

"We? *We* say very little. This is your pit stop."

Troy was certain he heard Moses laugh.

"Pop, I've spent three days thinking about this, and I still don't know what to say."

"Start simple." Gary put his hand on Troy's shoulder. "Try this. Hello. I like your townhouse."

Troy clenched his fist and grimaced. "If you weren't an old man . . ."

"Let's go," Gary said, opening the door and ushering them both down. Outside, Gary snapped a leash onto Moses's collar. "Sorry, pal. After last night . . . well, you get it."

They walked toward the townhouse, and Troy was relieved that the driveway was empty. They stopped across the street and slipped into a bus stop shelter.

"Ready?"

"Absolutely not," Troy said.

"Want me to come with you and Moses?"

"Absolutely."

They walked so slowly to avoid calling attention to themselves that they did just that. A neighbor at the opposite end of the row of townhouses was taking groceries out of her trunk when she spotted Gary, Troy and Moses approaching. "May I help you?"

"No, thank you," Gary said. "Just visiting a friend."

"You know Grace and Paul?"

Troy's stomach flipped.

"Yes, we do," Gary said, and they were then just steps from the front door.

"They're not home," the nosy neighbor said. "They get home after six, usually."

"Oh, all right then," Gary said. "Thank you."

"May I tell her someone visited?"

"We'll come back a bit later," Gary said. "But thank you."

"Nope," Troy said as they turned away from the woman and began the walk back to the bus. "We're not coming back."

"We sure are."

"And if I won't?" Troy said. "What's the point? She's married."

"You don't know that."

"Trust me, Pop. If she's living with a guy, they're married."

Moses stopped to sniff a motorcycle on the side of the road, and Gary tugged at the leash. "Keep up. Come on."

They said nothing until boarding the bus. Moses meandered to the back, and the men sat in familiar spots near the front. Gary pulled a soda from the cooler and tossed Troy a Gatorade.

"Hear me out," Gary said. "I figure her being married is good. Gives you . . . What does your mom call it?"

"Closure."

"Right. It's easier now, if anything. We say hello. She says goodbye to Moses. You get to tell your mother you had the closure thing."

For an hour they looked through the *Washington Post* they'd bought two days earlier at a travel plaza in southern Virginia. Gary scoured the baseball box scores, and Troy caught up on the Bush versus Clinton campaigns. "There's no way that guy beats the president," Troy said. "Right, Pop?" But Gary was lost in the numbers.

"It's time," Gary said fifteen minutes later. They walked the three blocks back to the townhouse and once again stood across the street looking at an empty driveway. "It's after six thirty," Gary said. "Should we trash the neighbor's car?"

Before Troy could react, a silver, plain sedan pulled into the driveway. "Get in here." Troy pulled his father's arm, and Gary yanked reflexively on the leash. All three stumbled into the bus stop shelter, and Troy knelt down behind an ad for Clint Eastwood's summer movie, *Unforgiven*. "Down," Troy commanded, and both his dog and father obeyed.

Troy peeked over the poster and watched Paul and Grace get out of the sedan. He scoffed when Paul didn't open her car door. Paul entered a code, and the garage door opened, revealing another car and boxes stacked to the ceiling. He navigated a narrow walkway between the vehicle and a wall of cardboard. "Pack rat," Troy said.

Grace walked to a bank of well-protected mailboxes in the corner of the lot. They sat beneath a roof that matched the townhouses'. As Grace flipped through a stack of mail, another neighbor appeared at his front door. "Good evening, Grace," the man said.

"Hi!" Grace said. "How's the back?"

With those four words, Moses broke loose from Gary's lazy grip, bolted away from the bus stop and sprinted across the street like he hadn't in years. A delivery truck honked and swerved, but Moses ran unafraid, his leash bouncing behind.

"Moses?" Grace said. He stopped at her feet, assaulting her hands with licks and love. "Is that you? Moses?"

Gary stood and stepped out into view.

Grace checked Moses's tag.

Troy finally rose from his weak knees and hated that his fingertips tingled. It was a sensation he'd felt only during the bottom of the ninth when he was on the pitcher's mound trying to close out a win, and every single time he'd ever looked at Grace Dellinger.

Moses licked Grace's face, and her laugh lit something in Troy that he knew would be tough to douse. "Why did we do this?" he said to Gary, and his father knew it wasn't really a question.

Grace was still bent down petting Moses when she finally spotted Gary and Troy. The men waved awkwardly in unison, like two men forced to ride a parade float. They crossed the street, and while Gary made the final steps toward her, Troy stepped into the past.

Troy thought he saw Gary hug her. Troy thought he heard Grace ask Gary something and then hug him again. Troy thought he noticed Moses staring at him, willing him to move.

Her face was pure Grace. She still looked like the Shenandoah Valley. Soft but colorful. Bold but humble. There was something different about her hair. *Maybe an inch shorter?* Troy thought.

In seconds, the motor in his mind took him to their eighth-grade dance. Then to their first kiss by the swings at W. O. Riley Park. Then to painting posters for her sophomore-class presidential campaign. Then to junior prom. Her dress was blue and matched her eyes. He blinked and landed at their senior prom. Her dress was red and white that year, and Troy had gone to four florists between Harrisonburg and Winchester with a piece of red fabric until he found a corsage that matched. She cried when she saw it and heard the story. The tears cost them fifteen minutes while her mother helped fix her makeup. Troy hadn't minded then, and even in the memory five years later, he still didn't mind.

"Troy?" Gary said. "Are you going to say something?"

He shook free from the past and saw her again. "Hello," he stammered. "I like your townhouse."

TWENTY-THREE

Macy opened the plastic pill container and poured out the daily contents onto Meg's place mat. The women hadn't said much since returning from the beach, and the early dinner was an indicator that her aide would be leaving soon.

"Macy, I really am sorry. I am. I just wasn't thinking."

Macy placed a chef salad in front of Meg and sat across from her in her usual seat. "I know. It's all right." Macy placed her hands flat on the table and stretched out her fingers.

"No, dear, it's not all right. I do need to be more careful, you're right. I think I just got swept away today." Meg pecked at her salad.

"I'm sorry too. For overreacting. For embarrassing you."

"Well, you didn't do either. You're just doing your job. And you're the best. You really are. I know how much this means to you." Meg stabbed a piece of ham, then freed it against the edge of the large bowl.

Macy slid her hands across the table until her fingertips reached the edge of the place mat. Meg placed her fingers atop Macy's.

"Meg Gorton, this isn't a job to me. How many times do we have this same discussion?"

"I know. You love the work, and I'm not a client. I'm sorry."

Macy tapped on Meg's fingers like piano keys and sat back in her chair. "You know your sister was persistent, right?"

"That's one way of putting it." Meg let a smile grow that was so unique, even Macy knew it was reserved for memories of Sandi. "She is the woman who got me down here, after all," Meg said.

"Exactly," Macy said. "And did you know . . ." Her words tumbled off.

"Know what?"

Macy breathed, held the air in and set it free. "Did you know that when she was trying to get you to agree to having an aide brought in, it was me she was talking to?"

Meg rested her fork on her bowl. "What do you mean?"

"When you first started to get sick, lost your energy, I was the one she called. But you, you were so stubborn, weren't you?"

"Guilty."

"And I promised her, Meg. Even before you found out she had cancer. I promised her that no matter what, when you were ready for help, it would be me. Whether she was still with us or not."

"That's sweet. I had no idea. Did you tell your company that?"

"Uh . . . sort of?" Macy grinned. "What matters is that this is personal for me. You're . . . family."

Meg felt a tug and the lift of tears. "That means so much. It does. But that's a lot of pressure, isn't it? Do you get this close, make these promises to your other . . . friends you work with?"

Macy put an index finger across her lips. "Shhh. You want to know a secret?"

Meg nodded.

"You're the only one I have."

TWENTY-FOUR

Grace eased into Troy's chest. She was barely five feet tall, and the hair on the top of her head brushed against Troy's chin. She wore a lime-green shirt, white shorts, and pink tennis shoes. Troy admired the look and remembered her unique gift for always looking like she'd dressed inside a box of crayons. He wrapped one arm around her in a nice-to-see-you-at-the-high-school-reunion kind of hug. Grace lifted her head and gave him a look he knew well, and he wrapped the other arm around her petite frame. Her hair, blonde as ever, smelled like . . . *spring rain and grapes,* he thought.

"It's so good to see you," Grace said, pulling away from him at the same slow speed she'd fallen in. She tugged on the sleeves of his shirt. "What are you doing here?"

"That's quite the story, isn't it, Son?" Gary stood a few feet behind him. He choked up on Moses's leash with one hand and scratched the top of the Lab's head with the other. "Why don't you start," he said. "We'll tag team."

Grace crossed her arms and closed one eye. Troy instinctively looked for her tattoo scar on the bottom of her left arm. She'd crashed her bike in the seventh grade, and the road-rash scar looked like a red mermaid. At least it had to the former couple.

"The story of why you're in Rock Hill is so big you have to tag team? Call me intrigued."

Intrigued, Troy thought. And the memory of her habits and his responses crushed him. "Okay, Pop. Let's not oversell it."

Grace looked past him, toward Gary and Moses and smiled at something. "You start, Troy. I'll be the judge of that."

Troy poked his thumbs in the pockets of his blue jeans and began with the letter from Meg and her health.

"Oh!" Grace pulled her hands together and buried them under her chin. "I'm sick to hear that."

"Then there's Moses. That old man. She wants to see him again, and you know that dog as well as anyone. He acts like he wants to see her too. Right, Mo?" Troy turned toward him, but Gary and Moses were already a block away. "Ridiculous," he whispered in their direction.

Grace reached over and pulled on his sleeve again. "You want to come in?"

"No," he stammered. "For sure, no. We just wanted to say hello. Let you love on Moses for a minute. He missed you, obviously."

"You know that I had no doubt—no doubt—that was him when he started bolting across the street. And what's it been? A couple years? Maybe three?"

"Something like that," Troy said, though he could have offered a much more precise time frame.

With Grace's back facing the townhouse, Troy had a perfect view of the front door, and his pulse hiccupped when it opened. Paul appeared, and from the top step of their brick entryway, he looked nine feet tall. He wore a blue button-down shirt, and either it was a size too small or Paul really liked ab-and-chest day at the gym. It was tucked into a pressed pair of slacks, and the sleeves were rolled up. His arms looked like the sturdy, thick poles that support carnival rides. He'd had on a skinny black tie when he got out of the sedan, but it was gone now, and the top buttons of his shirt were unbuttoned—one more than seemed necessary.

"Grace," Paul called. "Everything okay?"

"I shouldn't have come. I'm sorry," Troy said.

"What? Why? No." She spun to face Paul. "We're fine. This is Troy. Troy Gorton."

She looked back at him, and something filled her eyes. Troy didn't know what to call it, but it looked something like . . . *history*, he thought.

"Troy's an old friend. One of my oldest, in fact."

"Nice to meet you, Troy," Paul said, adding what was either a military salute or a clunky wave.

"You too," Troy offered, and he mimicked whatever motion he'd just witnessed.

Grace was still looking at Troy. Her hands were down now, fingers interlocked below her waist. Her hips swayed so slightly only Troy would have ever noticed. "And . . . he also happens to be my first kiss."

Troy suddenly wanted to run back to the bus stop shelter and either hide in it or under it.

"Cool?" Paul said, amused. "Hey, Grace, you want pasta? Troy, you want to join us?"

"Yes, please," Grace said, looking right through Troy's stunned expression.

"No! Thank you." Troy answered with more punch than he'd intended. "I gotta get going. Catch up to Pop and Moses. We're probably going to get a few more miles on the bus before stopping for the night."

"Why not stay? Have breakfast in the morning? All of us? Then start fresh on the road. We've got this amazing diner that just opened. Pilgrim's. I'll give you the address."

Troy's mouth was still forming words when she ran off, pulled a pen from Paul's pocket and jogged back to her spot. "Here, gimme," she said, and she held one of Troy's hands in her own. She turned it over and pretended to find the perfect spot. "I forgot about all those calluses."

Troy's hand went light. As she always had, she spoke every word she wrote. But he didn't hear them through the electricity running through his bones.

"Can you read that?" she asked, tracing the name of the restaurant and street name on his massive palm.

For the first time Troy noticed Grace's simple, unassuming wedding band. It was just what he would have expected. "Got it," he said, and he pulled his hand away to pretend to examine the note more closely.

"You'll find it. It's near the interstate. You might pass it anyway on your way out of town."

Troy looked back up. "You sure? About this?"

"Of course. It's just breakfast, right?" She closed one eye again and cocked her head slightly to the right.

The look sent Troy right back to middle school and their every-morning locker meetings. "Yes, just breakfast," he said.

Grace stepped in for another too-long hug, and Troy struggled to make eye contact when she finally let go. "I'm so glad you stopped. So glad. Pilgrim's then. Eight o'clock? See you tomorrow?"

"See you tomorrow," Troy repeated. But he knew that was a lie. In his mind's eye, he'd see her all night long.

TWENTY-FIVE

Day Four

Moses couldn't believe his luck. Pilgrim's, the diner Grace recommended, had what they called "Pilgrim's Pet Patio"—a space behind the building where patrons could eat with their furry friends. Moses wasn't even crusty about his leash being hooked to the leg of Gary's chair. *Trade-offs*, he thought.

He listened as Gary, Troy and Grace ordered their breakfast and settled into small talk. Gary told the rest of the story about Meg's letter.

"No second thoughts?" Grace asked.

"I'm way past that. I'm at eighth and ninth thoughts," Gary said. He meant it as a joke, but everyone sensed his statement was laced with truth. "I mean, not really. We need to do this. I need to do this. I figure it's what we both need, you know?"

"I do," Grace said, then she pressed with the confidence of an old friend to better understand why Meg left in the first place. Gary recalled the story of the night she left in colorful, pitch-by-pitch detail. To his own surprise, he shared details that seemed new even to him. The guilt. The sadness. The what-ifs. The quiet that had moved in after Meg left. Much of it was new to Troy, and Gary predicted he would have plenty of follow-up questions when they were back on the bus.

Grace asked Troy about baseball just as their plates hit the table. "So what happened in Texas?"

There's that Texas *word, again,* Moses thought. And he inched closer across the ground.

"Baseball happened," Troy said. "I wrecked my shoulder, and they cut me."

"While still under contract?" Grace asked, and she dropped a piece of bacon next to Moses's head.

Bless you, Moses thought.

"Long story, but they didn't need me. Could be a long rehab."

"Gosh, I'm sorry. That last game I saw . . . you almost had that perfect game. No hits, no walks. You went . . . eight scoreless innings?"

"Eight and a third," Troy said.

"Ahhh. Two outs away. You brought so much heat that game. I remember. You were really painting the corners," she said.

Gary took a sip of his cranberry juice. "A beautiful girl who knows baseball," he said. "I missed this."

Me too, Moses thought, putting his chin on Grace's knee.

The discussion weaved through and around Virginia's weather, Meg's health and friendship with her aide in Gulf Breeze, Troy's cellular phone, Moses's mood swings and the crash they'd witnessed two nights earlier.

Moses heard Grace set down her silverware and watched her napkin disappear from her lap.

"I just can't," she said. "I can't picture it. I'm so glad she's okay. And you!" Grace looked down at Moses. "You really are something, aren't you?"

Troy and Gary looked down at Moses too.

"When I contacted the hospital to check on the girl, the nurse or whomever it was said the accident was all the talk. They couldn't believe the other driver didn't have a scratch or bruise. Or that the girl he crashed into was going to be fine. She actually told me they'd heard about Mo from the EMTs. They're calling him—"

"Ya'll ready for a check?" the perky server said, appearing from nowhere with a leather folder and pen.

"I think so," Troy spoke for the group.

"Son," Gary said, "don't you want to know anything about Grace? What she's up to?"

Grace crossed her arms and closed one eye. "Hmm. Not much to share, I'm afraid."

"Why the move to Rock Hill?" Gary said, even though he'd already heard the story.

"When things . . . changed in Texas and I got the nannying job . . . I was looking to maybe get back east. I loved the family a lot. They were so good to me. I guess it was a great opportunity when they asked me to move with them. They had some company, a computer thing I didn't really understand, and they sold it to a bank in Charlotte. We were here less than a year, and then they decided they wanted more. They had like a bazillion dollars and no reason to stay, so they left."

"For where?" Gary asked.

"Paris," Grace said.

"France?" Gary asked.

"That's the one. But they're in Italy now. Or Prague. I don't know. They wrote me a nice check—like a really, really nice check—and left." Grace poured more water into her glass, took a drink and continued. "I miss them. The kids mostly. Three darling girls."

Moses's mind turned the page. He imagined himself with Grace and the three girls at the park, on a walk, at a game, on the bus, at the Shenandoah River.

"So what about Paul?" Gary said. "How did you meet?"

"Pop, that's not our business."

"What do you mean?" Grace said, and she took another drink of water.

"I mean your husband, Paul. Where did you two meet?"

Water spewed from Grace's mouth onto her plate, the spray reaching as far as Troy's forehead.

Moses had no idea what to make of this. He'd seen people spit but never Grace. The look on her face was something between amusement and surprise.

"Husband?" Grace asked.

Gary, Troy and Moses all exchanged looks.

"Paul's my cousin."

Moses stood, stepped over his leash attached to the chair and rested his chin on the table inches from Grace's arm.

"You married your cousin?" Gary said.

"Pop! Stop! Let her finish."

"Paul's family. He grew up in Oregon with his family, and we didn't see him much as kids. He moved to Rock Hill a few months ago for some training. Knew I was here and called me. It just worked out."

Troy stared at Gary as if he were guilty of something.

It was obvious to everyone at the table—and possibly the diner—that Troy was trying to recover.

"Cool. Cool. So what does he do?"

"It's some FBI thing. He had to do some kind of field training or something in Charlotte. Then he'll get a job back in LA. At least that's his plan."

"Well I'll be," Gary said. "So what about the ring?"

"Pop—"

"What? You weren't going to ask," Gary said.

"Oh gosh," Grace said, and she held up her left hand. "I'm sorry. I've been wearing this so long I don't even think about it. When they left for Europe, I took a job at this health club. A week into it, and I had . . . this sounds terrible . . . but . . ."

"Every guy in South Carolina hitting on you?" Gary said.

Troy looked at Moses and shook his head.

"No, no. Not every guy . . . There's one in Columbia who wasn't interested."

Troy grinned, Gary laughed and Moses wagged his tail.

"So you wear the ring to slow them down," Gary said. "Makes a lot of sense."

Grace looked at her hand again. "It's awful that I have to do it, but it works. Got the idea from a couple other girls there. I mean it doesn't keep all the guys from flirting, but it helps."

"I figure it does," Gary said. "So are you seeing anyone?"

"I'm not," Grace said. "I mean except for Paul."

Moses caught the sly wink she shot Troy.

"I'm focusing on me, I guess. And I know that's very cliché. But everything happened so fast. I'm in Rock Hill. The family leaves. I buy this townhouse with my modest windfall. Paul and I reconnect, and he gets settled here. I'm just barely finding my way."

Moses watched both men studying her face, hanging on her stories, watching her lick her fingertip and pick up toast crumbs from her bread plate.

"Do you like your job, then?" Gary asked.

"It's a job," Grace said. "It's something of a trendy club—a lot of wealthy members. It pays me pretty well, and I work out there for free."

"I just gotta ask this," Gary said.

Troy looked nervous. He wiped his mouth again, even though he'd been done eating for at least twenty minutes.

"Why don't you come with us?"

Moses didn't get it all, but he surely recognized the word *come*. He wagged his tail harder, as if the more commotion he made, the better the idea was.

"Back to the bus?" Grace asked.

"Yes, and then to Gulf Breeze."

"I..."

Moses saw that Troy was holding his breath, his eyes laser-focused on Grace.

"Why not?" Gary asked. "You said yourself you're in transition, figuring things out. Come with us. See Meg. See some beautiful sights. Have an adventure. We'd love to have you. We can get the gang back together again." He looked at Troy. "Right?"

"Pop, she's probably got commitments, besides work, you know?"

Without lifting his chin from the tabletop, Moses spun his head a few degrees to face Grace.

"Troy's right," she said, and Moses noticed that the air on Pilgrim's Pet Patio suddenly smelled like fear. "I have work. I have some community things I do, volunteering, that kinda thing. And I'm training for a half-marathon."

"So we can't help with work. I mean you'll have to just quit, right? But we can give you service opportunities all day." Gary laughed. "You can clean up Moses's messes."

Moses loved it when Gary talked about him.

"You can run every morning, keep training, and maybe you can help with Troy's shoulder rehab."

Grace folded her napkin and placed it on her plate. "Guys, I really wish I could." She looked over at Moses, leaned down and kissed the top of his nose. "I just can't. If only I could just take off and road trip..." Her voice fell lower than a whisper. "But I can't."

Out in the parking lot, Moses watched the goodbyes and hugs and waited for his own. When she put her face next to his a final time, she simply said, "I love you, Moses. I always have. You're the glue for these guys—remember that."

Moses licked her face, and she didn't seem to mind. So before she stood back up, he licked it again.

Grace waved as the men boarded the bus. When it rolled down the street, Moses was watching from the very back through a window at the bottom of the emergency door. He couldn't understand why Grace hadn't come, and he wondered if he'd ever see or smell her again.

After her beautiful figure blurred into nothing as their bus got farther away, Moses turned and walked to Troy. His eyes were quiet. Just like Grace. Just like Gary and Meg. Humans were odd like this. They distanced themselves from the ones they needed most. But at least the bus was headed toward Meg. That was a start. Moses put a paw on Troy's knee. *I'm here for you*, Moses thought. *At least for a little while longer.*

TWENTY-SIX

Where are they? Meg thought.

Troy had promised to call on that portable phone she once thought was a terrible idea. Now she thought it was genius. *But why hasn't he updated me? They left four days ago.*

Meg sat alone at the kitchen table and ate leftovers for lunch. *I wish it was a Macy day.* Some days the loneliness was harder than on others. Staring out the window at the row of cookie-cutter condos, with happy neighbors coming and going, today tasted cold, thick and gray, like stew left overnight on the stove.

Meg sighed at the message shouting at her from the erasable memo board stuck to the refrigerator with magnets. *Tomorrow! LWCOGB! Don't forget!* Macy had left the reminder on her way out the day before.

Not today, she thought, even though she'd promised Macy she wouldn't spend the day watching out the window.

"Meg," she'd said, "I'm not suggesting a trip to the beach . . . Too soon?" She'd laughed at her own joke and then apologized again for her march down the sand in front of Kaitie. "No, no more all-day outdoor excursions, please. But going to your letter-writing club would be good for you." Then she'd scribbled the note in orange-colored marker on the board.

"Fine," Meg had said. "I'll go."

But what if they call while I'm gone? Meg thought. *What if they drove through the night and they pull up here while I'm down at the community center?* She imagined Sandi in her recliner behind her in the living room. "Would you go, Sandi?" Meg asked aloud. *Of course you would.* Then Meg pictured Nicavary, Jada and Julia—the geriatric triplets—applauding another absence, and the decision was made.

The gang was gathered in their usual seats around the table in Activity Room 2. She'd just missed Veda's weekly greeting, and the club president made a point of glancing at the clock and smirk-smiling at Meg when she sat. "Thanks for joining us," she said.

"Relax, Veda," Kaitie said. "This isn't the House of Commons."

Veda blushed and continued with the agenda.

Kaitie, sitting to Meg's right, winked at her and whispered, "Lifeguard hunting later? Maybe that tasty Nathan kid has a friend?"

Meg rolled her eyes and began setting out her supplies for the day.

"So, I have to confess," Veda said, "I'm really excited about today's project."

The group members heard this faux confession every week, and every week reacted with oohs and ahs and what-could-it-bes. "We're writing letters to our heroes in the military today. I have a list of soldiers and their addresses in Iraq. I'm told they haven't gotten letters in months." Veda shook her head and seemed disgusted at the thought.

"She's told? Really? By whom? General Schwarzkopf?" Kaitie leaned in and whispered.

"She has people," Meg said with a sly grin.

"And how about a surprise!" Veda said. "It's card grab-bag time!"

The club oozed with more oohs and ahs and a few what-will-I-gets tossed in.

Veda held a quilted bag and walked around the circumference of the table. Each letter writer reached in and grabbed at random a handmade card from Veda's private stash. Then they quickly turned it face down in front of them until it was time to reveal the cards to the entire group.

One by one they flipped their cards over and admired Veda's work. Meg had to admit that Veda was very creative, and she'd enjoyed her grab-bag finds in the past. The cards that day were wildly different. One featured three cats playing cards; another had one of Veda's favorite Bible verses in gorgeous calligraphy; Kaitie's had a flamingo wearing a straw sunhat. When it was Meg's turn, Kaitie slid closer again and whispered, "Please, please, please be a self-portrait of Veda."

Meg flipped the card over. The single, striking image was beautifully drawn in colored pencil. No background. No clouds or sun. No critters in the corners. It was an antique biplane with a woman in the pilot's seat. Goggles on her face. Long hair flowing behind her. A blindingly bright future ahead.

As Kaitie, Caleb, Kaleigh and the rest of her fellow club members sunk into silence and began thinking of men and women in foreign lands, Meg's thoughts went to a field in New Market.

There were few days in Meg's life she remembered from dawn to dusk. The day her father died. The day she married Gary. The day Mallorie, her only biological child, was born at Shenandoah Memorial Hospital in Woodstock.

And August 7, 1972. The day Mallorie flew alone.

Their twenty-year-old daughter had been taking flying lessons since her seventeenth birthday. Mallorie was " . . . different . . . than other girls," her dad had always said. Other girls her age sang in the school choir, learned an instrument, took childcare and home-economics classes. But

Mallorie had plans and a bucket list before anyone knew what a bucket list was.

A dream board in her bedroom told the story. Mallorie would earn her pilot's license. She would fly her parents across the country. She would get married and fly her and her husband to their honeymoon. She would build a better plane with a better engine. She would fly larger and larger planes until one day she flew to space. One drawing on her dream board had her in the stars wearing a spacesuit and waving down at her family.

When Gary and Meg gave her an introductory lesson as a birthday gift, they thought Mallorie's thirst might be quenched and she'd rebuild her dream board. Instead, when she stepped out of the plane flown by an instructor from Harrisonburg, she hardly touched the ground.

Struggling to breathe, to talk, to articulate anything at all, Mallorie looked at her parents in the nearby parking lot and yelled, "That! That! That is what I'm going to do forever!"

The expensive lessons came slowly, and her father was constantly explaining that the cost of flying wasn't just the lessons. It was gas to and from New Market, time in the plane, the required airport-club dues. "It adds up, Mal," Gary told her when the pace of lessons didn't match up with Mallorie's dream board.

In 1971, during Mallorie's senior year at Central High School, she met a baseball player named Robert Basham, one of at least a dozen Roberts in the school and three just on the baseball team. During his freshman year he'd started going by Robbie, and soon no one in the building called him anything else.

Robbie won over her dad's heart with his hand-eye coordination at the plate and reflexes at third base. The relationship moved from flirting to pre-engaged before their senior prom. Robbie didn't understand Mallorie's fascination with flying, and she didn't understand his desire to remain grounded.

Still, Mallorie's parents knew the love was real. Whenever Gary mused aloud that the relationship was too serious too soon, Mallorie simply laughed and pointed at her dad's wedding band.

Mallorie and Robbie were married September 1, 1971, and although Mallorie was in the sky as often as possible, she didn't have a license to fly solo, and Robbie was less supportive than he had been when she was just a teenage girlfriend and his pals thought it was cool that his girl knew how to fly when most of them had never even been on a plane.

On Christmas morning 1971, Mallorie and Robbie announced they were expecting. During the early weeks of the pregnancy, Mallorie hit her goal and amassed enough hours to qualify for a solo license. But before she could fly alone, the flights stopped.

"There's a time and a season," Meg said.

"Be patient," her father said.

"You don't need to be up there anymore," her husband said. "You're having our baby."

Revising the dream board that she now kept only in her head, Mallorie continued reading flight manuals, studying her own flight logs and hanging out at the airport whenever she could. For almost three years she'd been one of the few women at the small country airport. Then suddenly she was waddling around, talking to other pilots, learning about engines and helping with record keeping in the office.

On Tuesday, August 1, 1972, Mallorie gave birth to a long, healthy, beautiful baby boy. They named him Troy.

Six weeks later, Mallorie was approved for her first solo flight in the only plane she'd ever been in. Meg, nervous and uneasy, watched baby Troy at home, and Robbie was too busy with work for something he would not agree with either before or after.

When Gary and Mallorie checked in, they learned the plane had unexpectedly been booked by a wealthy family from Washington, DC, who was new to the club.

Mallorie took it well, Gary would later say. The family of three had come to take the plane to Charlottesville, and Mallorie was still standing in the office when they pulled in. She watched the husband, wife and a little girl walk from their car. Others there that day said they were well dressed and smiling. Mallorie chatted with the woman and her child while the father signed paperwork and handed over a check for their flight time.

Soon they were led to the plane, and Mallorie watched from the parking lot as they loaded up. But instead of a speedy departure, after five minutes the two doors on the small plane opened and the family poured out. The daughter, crying, appeared to be covered in something. The mother scooped her up and carried her back to the building and rushed her into the only restroom. The father, clearly frustrated, closed the doors and followed them across the field.

The girl had thrown up, and the trip would need to be rescheduled. "I knew she ate too much junk on the way," her father reportedly complained to anyone listening as they said goodbye.

As quickly as they'd come, they'd left. "Maybe I shouldn't go," Mallorie had said.

"Why not?" Gary asked her. "It's your day."

Within an hour, Mallorie was up in the sky. The foul smell of cleaner and vomit did not bother her a bit. From the freshly cut grass below, Gary watched his daughter soar and blaze across the sky. He watched her tip her wing on one of her high passes above him.

Then he watched smoke clap and smack from the engine. A flame followed. The plane twisted and dove awkwardly, like dance steps it had never practiced. But then it steadied, recovered, and Gary watched as Mallorie seemed to line up for an emergency landing. Then, just a few hundred yards from the runway, another plane came into view. Gary didn't recognize it, didn't know the type or engine, but it appeared in a flash and was much too low.

The collision was unlike anyone at New Market Airport had ever seen. Violent. Colorful. Loud. Hateful. Complete.

TWENTY-SEVEN

An hour after saying goodbye to Grace in the diner parking lot, Gary was behind the wheel approaching Blacksburg, South Carolina, and the I-85 interchange. He looked in the rearview mirror and saw Troy on one of the beds in the back.

And they thought I was crazy, Gary thought. He'd customized the school bus he'd bought from Shenandoah County at a steep discount as a thank-you for his years of service as head of maintenance for the school district. He'd painted it red, white and blue to match the team's colors and paid a local artist to add the team's name on the side. He also had several rows of seats removed and replaced with surprisingly comfortable cots with safety rails. Even with Troy on a cot and Moses on the floor in his usual spot, the bus felt empty and cavernous. *A ballpark with no fans,* Gary thought.

Just nine hours from Gulf Breeze—maybe more if he lightened up on the gas pedal—Gary was game planning the reunion he'd been forced into. He imagined Meg in a chair in some cutesy condo under a blanket. Her color pale, her eyes droopy, her wrinkles deeper than lies.

Or maybe she'd be dressed up. Perhaps in a dress she knew he'd liked. Maybe she'd lean in to kiss him instead of the other way around. She might take his hand without even needing a reason.

No.

The three years since they'd separated had been too long. Maybe she felt free, at last. Maybe she'd confess to being happier than ever. Maybe loneliness had been only his houseguest, not hers.

An ambulance raced past the bus and, because of its height and speed, shook the windows and rattled the long side-view mirror mounted to Gary's left. The trigger was as automatic as breakfast in the morning and mosquitoes over the Shenandoah. He fought it, pushed the images to the side of his mind and into his memory trash bins. But they returned—over and over—whenever lights and sirens appeared.

Gary watched the ambulance disappear in the traffic ahead, but his eyes saw New Market and the flames, carnage and grief. He replayed the hours that had followed as if they'd happened yesterday, not two decades ago.

The call to Meg. The drive home. The fight with Robbie in the same yard where Meg said goodbye. The drive back to New Market and the crash site. The numbness ignited in his head by shock and that spread like a virus to his mouth, heart, limbs. By the time they buried what was left of their Mallorie a week later, he had tingling in his fingers that never went away.

It's back, he thought. The pit with no name. The dense ball of regret and guilt that the memories mushed and molded in his gut. He'd tried to remove it, but the years only made it heavier. It was a barbed anchor. One that kept him a prisoner in Virginia. Meg had suggested they leave so many times, but he never gave the idea life. Not even a breath. Leaving the valley meant leaving Mallorie, and leaving Mallorie meant facing that guilty, mangled morning in New Market.

Gary looked in the mirror again and noticed Troy now on his stomach. Asleep. Dreaming. Injured. Gary wondered what was hurting Troy more on this foolish trip to Gulf Breeze: his ego or his shoulder. *I pray he pitches again,* Gary thought. But even to him, the idea felt like a lie.

Gary peeked again in the mirror and thought he saw Mallorie sitting near her son at the back on the bus. She would have been thirty-nine now. *My baby girl,* he thought. *Would she have been flying jumbo jets by now? Would she have been to space?* He knew the answers didn't matter. *Heaven's good enough,* he thought.

He drove on, eyes locked ahead. He wanted to look again in the rearview mirror, but he knew what he'd see.

Meg. Not at the back of the bus near Troy, but right behind Gary. Just feet away.

Her lips are narrow and tight. Her eyes are confused. She'll ask—again—the same question. The one that haunts and taunts them. "Why haven't you cried yet?"

Lights appear again from behind, but they aren't trying to pass the bus. "What the heck?" Gary said. The South Carolina State Police cruiser hit its siren, and Gary signaled to the right. "You've got to be kidding." He looked at the speedometer and knew even if he wanted to, he wasn't going faster than sixty.

"Troy! Troy!" he yelled. "We got company."

The trooper pulled up behind the bus on the shoulder of the highway less than a mile from their exit onto southbound I-85. His flashing lights danced on the ceiling of the bus as Moses also awoke from his back-of-the-bus slumber. The trooper stepped out of the cruiser and walked safely around the rear of his vehicle to the passenger's side.

"Were you speeding, Pop?" Troy asked, wiping afternoon cobwebs from his eyes.

"Only if the signs are wrong. This thing doesn't know how to speed."

The trooper reached in his cruiser and pulled out a CB handset on a long, curly cord. "Gentlemen," he said, and Moses jogged to the front of the bus to join the others. "My name is Trooper Lund. Do not exit the bus. Please remain until backup arrives."

Gary opened the bus door and moved down to the lowest step. "What's the issue?"

"Sir!" Trooper Lund spoke with authority. "Please stay in the vehicle!"

Gary stepped back up, closed the folding bus door and made eye contact first with Troy and then with Moses. *More like . . . stay in Woodstock.*

TWENTY-EIGHT

Moses could hardly breathe. *This. Is. Awesome,* he thought, though he wasn't entirely sure what the phrase meant. He also didn't know exactly what was happening outside the bus, but it involved lights, sirens and the kind of energy that put a little spring in the step of even the oldest of old-timer Labradors.

He watched Gary and Troy move from window to window looking for a better view of Trooper Lund. Moses could sense a mixture of worry and anger. He barked.

"You probably need a potty break, don't you, Mo?" Troy said.

"Not now he doesn't," Gary said. "Who knows what happens if we open the door and step out."

Moses knew the words *potty* and *out*. It was a great idea, but no one moved toward the door.

"Pop, come on. You have to have some idea what's up." Troy stepped away from one of the windows and put his hands on his hips.

"Troy, I figure I'm as stumped as you are."

"Is the bus legal?" Troy asked.

"Legal? Like is it stolen? From a mob? It's my bus."

"Pop, I just mean something's up. This isn't funny. And this isn't a normal traffic stop."

Moses detected for the first time a hitch in Troy's voice. *Fear?* Moses thought, but he chased the insane idea away with a lick of his left leg.

"Son, let's be patient. I'm sure it's nothing. Maybe another baseball bus robbed a bank this morning."

"Funny," Troy said, and he dropped into a chair and rested his head on the back of the seat.

Moses watched him breathe in and hold it so long he almost leapt onto the seat next to him.

"I'm sorry, Pop," Troy said.

Gary sat across from him, his feet in the aisle. "For what?"

"For this. For this trip."

"I'm a grown seventy-year-old man, Troy. I make my own choices."

Moses heard the words perfectly but wondered if Gary actually believed them.

"We shouldn't be here," Troy said.

"Son, relax. It's nothing—"

"—I don't mean this—on the side of the highway. I mean we shouldn't be on this bus in forsaken South Carolina driving to see Mom."

Moses watched. Waited. The noise from the highway was covered up by a blanket of doubt and tension.

"If I hadn't come home, if I hadn't talked you into this . . . I never would have seen Grace."

"I'll give you the first two," Gary said, "but that last one was all me. I did that. I'm the one who should be apologizing. And you came home because you're hurt. That's what we do, Son. Home's where we go."

Moses wiggled his nose. The sound of Grace's name reminded him of love, which reminded him of bacon, which made him realize he was hungry again and needed a tree. Moses barked twice. The first was light, just a white smoke signal that something else was coming. The second was booming and reminded the men of young Moses.

"I know, Mo. Won't be much longer," Troy said.

But Moses didn't let him finish; he was trotting to the back of the bus. He barked again, and this time he didn't waste breath with a warning. The aggressive woofs echoed over and around the green seats.

"We heard you," Gary said. "Stand down."

Moses barked again and stared through the emergency door at the back of the bus. *What's it going to take to get you to come back here and see what I'm seeing,* Moses thought.

"What's up?" Gary said, and he rose to check on him. "Whatcha see?"

Gary stood just behind Moses and looked at the police cruiser. Another car with lights in the grill had arrived and was parked at an angle behind the first. "What is happening?" Gary asked.

Exactly, Moses thought. He looked up at Gary's thin, aging face. Moses realized for the first time that Gary hadn't shaved since they'd left Woodstock. Moses looked back outside as Trooper Lund, who'd stopped them, got out and swiftly moved to the safe side of his car. He stood with his back to the bus, his hat on perfectly, his hands on his hips and at the ready.

What's he looking at? Moses thought.

Gary and Moses both shifted as far to the right as possible for a better view of the second vehicle. "It's like an FBI car or something," Gary said. "I figure it's unmarked."

"Like I said. We shouldn't be here," Troy said again from the opposite end of the bus.

Moses, his body still facing the action outside, spun his head in Troy's direction and barked again. Then again. And again.

Troy's head was still leaning back, and his long arms were stretched across the top of the seat to his left and right.

Moses whined and turned to face what had become so obvious. Then it seemed to Moses that Gary finally saw it too.

"Uh, Troy. We got company. Again."

TWENTY-NINE

A letter-writing club shouldn't be that exhausting, Meg thought. She'd walked home alone from the community center, fallen into her recliner and hadn't moved hardly anything but her eyelids in two hours.

The sun suggested it was late afternoon, and Meg held the cordless phone in her lap. She'd pressed the green talk button every ten minutes or so, just to be sure she had a dial tone. *Why hasn't Troy called? Is he okay? Is Moses okay?*

She stretched her legs and pointed her toes as far as she could across the recliner's footrest. She was sore, but overall she felt better than usual. Macy had tried to convince her it was because she had something positive to look forward to. "Your mind is on something else for a while," Macy had said.

Meg's eyes gave up and fell closed, like blinds at the end of the day. But instead of a deep sleep, Meg's mind stepped into something between dreaming and memories. A colorful place she visited all too often.

She saw the doctor's office; stubby coffee tables with outdated magazines; fake plants in the corners; patients, confused and sick, scattered like unpopped popcorn kernels at the bottom of the bowl. A nurse invites Meg and Sandi back to an exam room, and Meg dons a gown while Sandi reads a CPR poster on the wall.

A doctor is in the room now. But Meg doesn't remember him walking in. He's saying something about a new test, a new study, a white paper or some other kind of paper, a university, German researchers? The words are mostly a meaningless meatloaf of information Meg won't remember.

He's asking me something, Meg thinks. She squints her eyes, begging the memory to find a better frequency. *What's he asking?*

The doctor's hands are buried in the pockets of a white coat that seems too big for him. He's not twelve, Meg knows this, but he looks it. *Why is he here? He should be playing outside. Pushing Matchbox cars across the ground. Swinging with his best friend.*

"Meg," he says, and his voice is clearer now. "We're still trying. This chronic fatigue you're experiencing is new to us. In fact, medically speaking, it's new to many of us." His voice begins to squawk, a static line burning it in half.

"Recoverable. Patience. Persistence. Rest." The adolescent doctor's words are no longer connected; they're just stones skipping across the river at home in Virginia.

Eventually they sink.

Meg's memories are home again. She's in her recliner. Sandi's in hers. It's dark outside, and neither has the energy to stand and turn on a lamp. They're sharing secrets. Meg's been in Florida a year already, but the sisters still have much to catch up on.

Meg's eyes flashed open, and the half-dream was gone. She looked at Sandi's recliner to be sure. Empty.

She looked at the mantel, the photo, the black and burnt-orange urn that kept Sandi close. "I miss you," Meg said. Then tears came. First just light sprinkles, so few she could count them, name them, wipe them with a finger dab. But then like a spring Shenandoah shower, the drops multiplied, gathered and grew into a storm. "I'm lost, Sandi. I'm sick. I'm lonely. I'm tired." Meg sobbed, pain bursting from her belly to her head. "Why, Sis? Why am I still here?" She kicked down the footrest and struggled to catch her breath. She bent over, head between her knees, facing the ground like a flooded flower that couldn't take another drop.

Her head pounded, and in time the tears slowed, but the pain flowed on.

When she felt strong enough to stand, she walked to the bathroom and looked in the mirror. Her light mascara ran south on her splotchy cheeks. Her hair was messy and clumped in the back. Her eyes were puffy, red and sore.

I'm so old, Meg thought, inventorying her wrinkles and lines. Then she gave the words breath and said them to the old woman staring back. "Maybe inviting him here, doing it now, after these three long years, was a mistake."

THIRTY

Gary watched a man and woman get out of their vehicle, mostly obscured by Trooper Lund's police car. The three met in the grass away from the road, and Gary could see only a profile of Trooper Lund and the upper backs of the two new officers.

Troy arrived at the back of the bus, and as he put his face close to the window on the emergency door, Trooper Lund turned briefly, and Troy thought he saw him smiling.

"I'm going out there," Troy said.

"Just wait, Son. They'll come."

"No, I'm going," Troy said, and he began moving toward the front of the bus. "Moses! Come! And bring your bark."

"Troy, just wait," Gary said, alternating looks between the angry militia about to disembark the bus and the three guests outside.

Troy opened the door, quickly snapped Moses's leash to his collar and stepped down to the roadside. "Excuse me?" he yelled. "What's going on? Hello?"

Moses barked and pulled at the leash, daring Troy to follow or be pulled over.

"Officers?" he said to their backs. "Why are we being stopped? We have rights."

Trooper Lund stepped to his left, and the two who'd arrived as backups turned to face Troy.

"Grace?" Troy said, and Moses's bark got even louder.

Even in the fuzzy seconds processing the scene, Troy noticed Grace was wearing a different outfit since their breakfast at the diner. Paul, her companion in the car, put his hand on her back and appeared to give her a gentle push.

Grace stepped forward until she reached Moses, and she bent down long enough for a lick on her face and a whisper in his ear. Then she closed the gap between herself and Troy. "License and registration, please," she said, without bothering to suppress her electric smile.

"What is . . . what are . . . ? What is you . . . I mean, what are we doing here? I mean, what are *you* doing here?"

"I volunteer with the South Carolina State Police—you didn't know?"

"What?"

"Troy, I'm here because I need a ride."

"A ride? To where?"

"To Florida."

"Why?"

"Because I was invited," Grace said, and she looked at Gary now standing on the bottom step of the bus and grinning like a rich gambler.

"Who are they?" Troy nodded in the direction of the other men.

"Well you already know my *cousin*." She emphasized the word. "Paul. And honestly I have no clue who the other guy is. But his breath smells like beef jerky."

When Troy didn't react or ask a follow-up, Grace continued. "I had a change . . . of heart . . . I want to go. And Paul didn't want you getting too far ahead. So he called in a favor. To . . . slow you down."

Moses looked at Troy and then back to Grace. He sniffed but was pretty sure she hadn't brought any bacon with her.

"Troy, I need this. A break. A trip. An adventure. And I'd love to see Meg. She's been like a . . . mother."

"So . . . you're coming? With us?" Troy said.

Moses barked.

"You're pretty slow for a guy with a ninety-plus fastball." She closed one eye, crossed her arms and gave the look that had melted him for years. "Yes, Troy. I'm coming. If I'm still welcome."

"You are!" Gary yelled, and Grace smiled back at him.

"How about it, Troy? Still room for one more on the bus?"

THIRTY-ONE

Macy sat alone at a wobbly picnic table to the side of her favorite taco truck. There were a thousand things she could do on her day off, but none brought her comfort quite like Welty's Wonderful Tacos. The truck was a Pensacola favorite, and on a nice day it was within walking distance of Macy's apartment.

She looked at the plate of four carne asada tacos and smiled at them, as if she were seeing her favorite neighbors on a Saturday morning. Macy hadn't been to Welty's in two weeks. *Eternity.*

Macy wished that eating alone hadn't become so comfortable. She'd promised herself that, at least in public, she'd never eat solo. Never afraid to open her mouth and make a friend, she'd met hundreds of people through the years at cafes, diners and ice cream parlors and on airplanes. Macy had once struck up a conversation with a widow at the library that led to the woman staying in her spare bedroom for a long weekend. That weekend became a second, then a third, and two-and-a-half years later the woman finally moved out.

Though she hadn't been a professional caretaker for long—Meg was currently her only client—she'd spent several years caring for her ailing mother in San Diego. It was there, watching her mother slowly die, that she first fell in love. *With tacos,* she thought, and she took another bite. Onions, cilantro and a pint-sized puddle of hot sauce escaped from the back.

She had been raised mostly on the East Coast. Her parents had divorced when she was in middle school, and she and her mother started a new life in Southern California with a massive stash of money they'd gotten from the divorce. Her mother was wealthy, gorgeous, single and depressed. By the time Macy graduated from UCLA at twenty-two, her mother was slowly stepping into her own grave, taking all of her addictions with her.

Macy had stayed another two years in San Diego, learned to spend money she didn't need to, then returned to the East after her mother's death. Macy learned to grieve through music. She wrote songs, sang in a couple of bar bands, volunteered and even spent some time in Washington, DC, working on Capitol Hill.

Her father was somewhere in Europe with his third wife. Macy imagined him reading foreign newspapers in four-star hotel lobbies while the new love of his life shopped local boutiques on cobblestone streets. Macy loved her dad, but time had proven that distance was healthy for their relationship.

Macy added lime to her next taco and savored it. She wondered what Meg was doing at the condo and if she'd kept her promise to attend her letter-writing club. *She's such a mess,* Macy thought. *A beautiful, caring, complex mess.*

At the table next to her, Macy watched a young married couple share a gargantuan burrito that could feed a family of five. The man took his fork and dabbed sour cream on his wife's nose. She grimaced, wiped it off but missed a spot just above her nostril.

You going to get that? Macy thought. The husband hid a smile but said nothing, and they continued eating from opposite ends. When Macy finished her lunch, she walked past them on the way to the trash can and took a clean napkin from the dispenser on the couple's table. "Here you go," Macy said. "You got a little something . . . right . . . there."

The woman thanked her and threw a tomato chunk at her husband. They laughed, kissed, laughed more, and he apologized by filling her Styrofoam cup with more horchata.

Back in her car, Macy sat behind the wheel and watched the couple's long lunch continue. She wondered where they'd met, why she'd fallen in love, how he'd proposed. *Do they have a child at home?* she wondered. *Do they have goals and dreams? Are they changing the world together?*

When the couple finally threw away their trash and wandered away, they walked hand in hand. Macy left too—home to her apartment, home to her memories, home to a collection of what-could-have-beens.

THIRTY-TWO

Grace spent her first half hour on the bus sitting up front and catching up with Gary about sports, the old neighborhood and the latest Shenandoah County gossip.

"Do you miss it?" Gary asked, his eyes darting back and forth from the highway ahead and the young woman to his right.

"The gossip? Not really," she teased. "But I miss Virginia sometimes, sure."

While Troy and Moses studied the AAA road atlas in the back of the bus, Gary asked Grace about their time in Texas. "In twenty minutes," he said, "I've learned more about Troy's two seasons there than he ever bothered to tell me."

Grace looked back at Troy's profile—his hunched pose over the map, his baseball cap on backward, hair poking out the sides and hiding his ears. "The truth?" Grace asked Gary, even though her eyes were still focused on the past.

"Always."

"I bet I know his stats from those two seasons better than he does."

Gary nodded and made a noise Grace couldn't quite interpret.

"How's he doing?" Grace asked, again looking backward.

"Moses?"

"Well, yes, but I mean Troy," she said. "How's he doing—I mean *really* doing?"

Gary snuck a peek at his son in the wide rearview mirror overhead. "He seems all right. Distracted, I figure . . ."

He paused, and Grace watched a stadium-sized smile expand across his face. "You stop that now," she said. "This is just a break for all of us. Nothing more to it."

Gary made another noise that Grace couldn't entirely understand.

Some things never change, she thought, and she leaned in closer. "What about you?"

"I'm good."

"You can't fool me, Gary Gorton. You've got to be a wreck."

"Why do you say that?"

"Let's see. We're . . . Where are we right now?"

"Powersville," Gary said. "Three hours still to Atlanta."

"And we're on a bus. A baseball bus. With your son's ex-girlfriend, the family dog and Troy."

"In that order of importance, you might add."

"Granted," she said. "And this crew is driving to the panhandle to see your wife that you haven't spoken to in . . . how long?"

"A long time."

"Yes, a long time," Grace agreed. "You know, Gary—"

"—Call me Pop."

"Really?" she asked.

"Sweetheart, when you end it with a guy, you don't have to end it with the guy's dad."

I'd forgotten, thought Grace, *how sweet this man can be.* "So . . . Pop

... on the way to catch up to you guys, I was thinking..." She paused, recalibrated. "I was wondering why you're really going to Florida."

Gary stole a longer than normal—probably longer than he should have—glance away from the road and right at Grace. "So Meg can see Moses, say goodbye. Like she asked."

Grace closed an eye, squinted with the other and crossed her arms. "Are we sure?"

"We?" Gary asked. "I can only answer for me."

"I just don't know, Pop. Seems there has to be more."

They sat quietly as a mile passed. Grace watched Troy making and reviewing notes in a notepad. "Hey, Pop," she said. "You know what motivation is?"

Gary grinned. "Is this a trick question, kiddo?"

"I'm serious—do you know what it means? What it really means?"

"It's why we do what we do, I figure."

"Perfect. It's why we do what we do. Everything we do has a motive behind it. A minute ago Troy was looking at a map. Why? To see where we're going, I'm guessing."

"Okay," Gary said.

"Troy went to Texas to play baseball. He loves it. He's motivated to play. And I followed him. We loved each other." Her voice trailed off, and another mile passed. "He was my motivation."

"I figure your point—"

"—Just hang on," Grace interrupted, insisting he stop with a raised hand, like a crossing guard. "This thing you're doing—"

"—*We're* doing," he corrected.

"Sure. This thing we're doing. This trip to Florida. Everyone has a motive. It's just what people do."

"And dogs?" Gary asked.

"Yes," she smiled. "And dogs. It's how we work. Moses's motivation is

143

to be where you are. To be happy. To eat bacon. His motives aren't complicated."

"Sometimes," Gary laughed, "it almost seems there's more in his noggin than that."

"Maybe," she said. "Just maybe . . . And Troy? What's his motivation for pushing you into this, into responding to Meg's letter?" When Gary didn't answer right away, she pressed on. "I think it's a break. A chance to clear his head and reconnect with you and Meg. Get away from baseball . . ."

"And you?" Gary asked, swiping another glance in the mirror.

Grace sighed and crossed her legs. She picked lint from her yellow pants. "I guess it's not too much different. A break. Chance to see Meg. Hang out with you guys. Love on Moses as much as I can. An adventure can be . . . enlightening."

They sat in the quiet again, and Grace watched Troy pour water into a dish for Moses.

"So that leaves you. What's your motivation?"

"I'm not sure I have one," Gary said.

"Of course you do. Have you even heard a word I've said?" Grace didn't mean for the words to land with a slap, but they did. "How about this," she said, and she stood in the aisle next to him. Grace put her left hand on his shoulder and steadied herself with her right. "Let's say you're in a movie or, better yet, a book. And you have to tell us why you're making this trip or no one will believe you would actually go."

"Am I handsome in this book?" Gary asked.

"Dashing," Grace said.

"I figure I'm going because I have time—I'm retired, you know—and I own a bus . . ." When Grace didn't save him from an awkward pause, he continued. "And I want Troy to be happy . . . and Moses too. And I guess Meg deserves this, you know, if she's sick."

"I think you deserve this too," Grace said. "You know, to be happy." Another mile passed and then another, and Grace leaned in to kiss him on the cheek. "I know there's more," she said. "But you're still my hero. And I'd read that novel any day."

His eyes watched her walk away in the rearview mirror, but his mind went to the Washington Monument on New Year's Eve 1950.

THIRTY-THREE

Just a few miles before the South Carolina–Georgia border, Moses made it clear it was time for a break. Gary exited toward the town of Fair Play and pulled into a gas station parking lot. Moses stepped onto the pavement and stretched out his legs, arching his back and pointing his rear end to heaven.

"That hit the spot, Mo?" Troy said, crouching near him and rubbing behind his ears. "Maybe we overestimated how hard this would be for a retired old Lab."

Troy and Gary went inside to use the restroom, and Grace walked Moses on his leash around a square patch of weeds at the corner of the parking lot. Moses moved slowly, taking deliberate steps, sniffing the ground and looking up often to be sure Grace was still on the other end of the leash.

"You still doing okay?" she asked.

Moses licked her hand. The rattling of the bus and the lack of a comfortable bed made him feel like peanut brittle. But the truth Moses couldn't completely convey was that, with the exception of his tired bones, he felt better than he had in months.

Gathered with the others outside and by the bus, Gary wondered aloud if they should find a motel for Grace and Moses and stop for the night.

"Probably a good idea," Troy said.

"I'm totally fine on the bus with you guys," Grace said. "That was my plan. I brought a sleeping bag, and you've got four, I think . . . cots in there? I'm happy to crash with the team."

Moses licked Grace's hand again.

"But I mean . . . If it's better for Moses, you know, to sleep on a bed with some cool AC blowing, I suppose I could sacrifice . . . You know, for him."

"So generous of you," Gary said with a grin. "Let's see what we can find."

A few miles off the interstate, they pulled into a local motel, and Gary paid for a first-floor room with one king-sized bed. They parked the bus at the back of the motel near the room and ate an early dinner at a burger joint within walking distance. After the sun set, they sat in camp chairs outside the open door and finished off large milkshakes they'd carried back.

"So, Gary." Grace stopped herself. "Sorry . . . Pop."

Gary smiled, nodded, and they tapped cups.

"I know Troy was all over that map earlier," she continued. "What's the route? What's the schedule? We can't be too far."

"What did we decide?" Gary asked. "Stay on 85 or move more south? Off the interstate?"

"I think we avoid Atlanta—just so much traffic. Head south through Macon and then west again toward Columbus. Slower speeds, and on this beast that's probably better."

Troy used his spoon to scrape the settled cookies and cream from the bottom of his cup. As he savored the last bites, he wondered if Grace had noticed he'd changed into his Central High School 1989 graduation T-shirt.

Grace and Gary chatted again about the car crash they'd witnessed, and Troy flashed back to the flaming wreckage. *If I live to be one hundred,* he thought, *I'll never know how anyone survived that.*

When he stood to throw away his trash, he offered to take the others' cups and excused himself. He entered the bus and a moment later returned with his cellular phone. "When we're done, you mind if I charge this up in your room overnight?" Troy asked.

"Of course, please," Grace said.

Troy sat, and Grace admitted that she'd also considered buying a similar phone, but the expense seemed tough to justify. "To each his own, you know," she said. "But those things seem like a gimmick."

"How so?" Troy asked.

"I just think it's an expensive toy," she said.

"Cheers to that!" Gary said, raising a fist into the air as if celebrating an inside-the-park home run.

"It's not a toy," Troy countered. "It's a way to stay in touch with people. Don't have to use payphones or borrow a phone if you're not home."

"I doubt they catch on, personally," Gary said. "I don't see it. I figure it's another fad. Just wait."

"Well, old man, we're not in the Stone Age anymore. This is how I call Mom and keep tabs on her."

"And vice versa," Grace poked.

"I guess," Troy conceded.

"Maybe that's my problem with it," Gary said. "What if you don't want to stay connected all the time to people? Or to some new gadget?"

Troy looked at Grace and apologized with his eyes. *I'm sorry for my caveman father.*

"Could you survive without it?" Gary asked.

"Sure I could, of course." *No, really, I am so sorry for him,* Troy thought. "Where are we going with this, Pop?"

Gary inched forward in his chair. "In the Stone Age, before those things only a professional ballplayer can afford—"

"—Minor league," Troy interrupted.

"Before you had that thing, didn't we all manage to still stay in touch? Communicate?"

"Again," Troy said, "where are we going?"

"Geez, Troy, when we made trips when you were in high school, to tournaments or summer baseball camps, whatever, we didn't have a phone. When your mom couldn't come, we said goodbye and we left. When we got there, I figure we called to say everything was okay, right?"

"I get it," Troy said, and he couldn't help but notice the smile on Grace's face. The parking lot lights were now on, and even under their harsh glow her skin looked . . . *perfect,* he thought.

"Stay with me, Son," Gary said, pulling him back in. "What if you didn't have a phone to make calls? What if portable—"

"—Cellular."

"Whatever. What if cellular portable phones didn't exist? Or the fad was over. And we were still sitting here outside this bus making our way south to Gulf Breeze? What would we do?"

Troy shrugged at Grace, begging for relief.

"No, sir," she said. "You're closing this one out."

"I guess we'd drive and call from a payphone somewhere, use a calling card or something."

"Exactly—we'd make do without that phone, which looks like a black brick, by the way."

"I want to throw something at you right now," Troy said. "You know that, right?"

Grace laughed—a long, from-the-toes giggle that grew until it consumed her face with joy.

"Let me see that," Gary said.

"The phone?"

"No, your bad attitude. Yes, the phone."

Troy handed it over, and Gary examined it, poked it, spun it, pressed numbers at random. "When Mallorie was little, ten or eleven, we went to Nags Head. I ever tell you this story?"

"Of course, yes. To see the Wright brothers spot."

"Kill Devil Hill, their memorial. She was so excited . . . Meg, though, she couldn't come. It was last minute, but our neighbor right around the corner on Church Street, Darla, broke her hip and had nobody. Nobody at all to help. So Meg stayed, even though it killed her to miss the trip—rarely saw her so disappointed to miss something. But, well, you know Meg . . . Anyway, I remember when we left Woodstock, we said goodbye in the street in front of Darla's place. And you know when we talked to her again?"

"Darla?" Troy said.

"No! Wait! I know! Call on me!" Grace raised her hand high—the student who knows every answer.

"Our front yard, Troy. After the trip. And that was just fine. Mallorie hugged and loved her and told all the stories of our adventures."

"I get it, Pop." Troy said. "Lay off the calls. Lay off the travel reports. Live in the moment. Fine. I'll leave the phone in my bag more."

Gary held the phone up, pulled out the antenna and pointed at Grace with it.

"I'm not sure I believe him. Do you?"

Grace soaked up the moment with that same intoxicating smile, an eye closed, mischief tattooed on her face. "You know, Pop. I don't. I really don't."

"You're both ridiculous," Troy said. "Just give me the phone."

"How about a deal?" Gary said. "If I see the phone out too much, I get to toss it in the ocean when we get to Gulf Breeze."

"You're not tossing my phone in the sea," Troy said.

"Oh, but I will. I figure you've forgotten how crazy your old man can be."

"Well, I sure haven't," Grace said, and Moses barked from under the table.

"Son, I think deep down you believe me. And I think you'll keep our deal."

"Really?" Troy said.

"Really. Because I just gave you . . ." Gary looked at Grace. "*Mo-ti-va-tion.*"

Grace's jaw dropped. "I am so proud of you right now." Then she tapped her heart. "So proud."

"What do you say, Son?"

"And if I do use it just sparingly—keep it stashed away—what do I get in return?"

Gary grinned and handed the phone back. "A ride home."

THIRTY-FOUR

I wish I could sleep, Meg thought. It was 8:15 a.m., the sun was beating her windows, and she'd tossed, turned, flipped and ached all night. *Getting old is for . . . old people.*

She felt light-headed and nauseous when she trudged to the bathroom. She looked at her reflection and grimaced. *I miss being young.*

She was hungry, but by the time she reached the end of the hallway, she was out of breath. She fell into her recliner, and suddenly her mind was in the community center down the street.

"Thank you for coming," the woman had said at the start of the free seminar.

Meg's memories mushed together, and it was hard to remember what the woman had said next. *Something about credentials,* Meg thought. *Something about our ages, risks, family history . . . diet?*

"Signs." Meg heard that word pop out, crisp and clear. "Women, yes, women." Those words too.

What's happening? Meg thought.

"It's pressure." The woman definitely said something about pressure.

"Your arms," she said. "One or both . . . pain . . . jaw, neck, even the back. Squeezing, right here." Meg could envision the woman now, clearly standing in the community center by a portable screen. An overhead projector just in front of her. The woman was wearing a white jacket and pointing at her chest.

What does this mean? Meg thought.

The nameless woman in the white jacket continued. "And that's when you know . . ." she'd said that day, more than a year earlier.

Know what? Meg pressed to remember.

". . . that you're having a heart attack."

THIRTY-FIVE

Gary lay on his back on his cot in the back of the bus. He glanced at his cheap digital watch and pressed the light button on the side. 10:15 p.m. *This was a mistake*, he thought. But he didn't know where to start. The trip. Sleeping on a cot at his age. Bringing Moses. Forcing Troy to agree to the Rock Hill detour. Inviting Grace to join them. The extra-large milkshake.

He stared at the ceiling of the bus. Grace was inside the stale motel room he'd gotten her and probably had long been asleep.

Moses was no doubt asleep next to her, snoring, content, his frail frame enjoying the soft mattress.

Insisting he couldn't sleep, Troy had gone for a long walk to get out and burn some calories. "I just need to do something besides ride on the bus or sit in a chair. I'll be back."

Gary imagined how differently his night might have unfolded at home. A frozen dinner with Moses. Maybe a walk around the block. *Wheel of Fortune, Jeopardy, M*A*S*H* reruns.

Everything about his new world scared him. He rolled to his side and

154

faced the side of the bus, his nose inches from the cool metal. He pulled the sheet up and tucked his hands under his chin. He pictured—again— the moment they would pull up in front of Meg's condo. The neighborhood was probably a perfectly planned community with matching front doors and manicured lawns. Happy residents drove golf carts to and from shuffleboard, game nights and homeowners' association meetings. The accents were surely some cocktail of California money and Boston attitude. *I bet there's not a Southern accent in the whole place,* he thought.

He thought of Sandi—the twin sister who had never been far from his thirty-nine-year marriage to Meg. They'd initially gotten along, even liked each other. He and Meg went on double dates with Sandi and her husband and talked about raising their kids together in the valley. But Sandi and her husband weren't together long. Her second marriage was more successful—at least if measured by the number of anniversaries— but hadn't led to children. Sandi did well enough in the second divorce to buy the place in Florida. The place that eventually lured Meg away from Woodstock.

Gary imagined the day Sandi had died. Had Meg been alone? Did Sandi die in their condo? Will Meg tell the story? Will I ask? Will she want to come home with me? Will I ask her to?

Gary tried to remember the last time he and the woman he was still married to had been happy. *Or even content,* he thought. But he wasn't confident that he knew what content felt like. Not since Mallorie had died.

He checked his watch again. 10:47 p.m.

Gary's instincts were to worry, like any father would, about the grandson he'd raised as his own. He remembered the sleepless nights he and Meg would wait up for Troy when he was in high school. Gary worried he'd do something stupid and lose his eligibility to play ball. Meg prayed her son would just come home—period.

She had this look when Troy was late—a blend of concern and faith that he'd been raised well. He imagined Meg's eyes as she sat at the kitchen table. When she was nervous, she'd eat saltines with peanut butter and sip water from her favorite glass. But no matter how nervous or busy the rest of her face and body became, Meg's eyes were kind, loving, peaceful, still, hopeful.

Gary wished Grace were awake and sitting across from him. Her smile, her laugh, her stories were a reminder of when Meg's eyes were happier. His brain flipped through the snapshots like a flipbook.

Sunday dinners for four at their kitchen table. Troy and Grace couldn't stop looking at each other.

Fishing the Shenandoah. Taking canoes out when the river was high and fast. The road trip to Baltimore to see the Orioles play.

Weekend trips to their friends' place just outside of Charlottesville. Catherine and her mother, Jenni Sue, owned a gorgeous farm in Albemarle County, and Meg always said that visits there reset her soul. Gary still didn't know what that meant, but he knew that Meg's eyes had had that same look the moment they drove up their beautiful long driveway. Kind, loving, peaceful, still, hopeful.

I miss those eyes, Gary thought.

Troy returned to the bus just after eleven. "You awake, Pop?"

He was but said nothing. And soon enough he was asleep with his memories.

THIRTY-SIX

Macy sprinted into the emergency room at Gulf Breeze Hospital just after midnight. "Meg!" she called out. "Where's Meg Gorton? I'm here for Meg Gorton."

An employee met Macy in the center of the lobby. "May I help you?"

"Are you a doctor?" Her voice was tightly strung, like a guitar string ready to snap and slice anyone holding onto it. "I'm looking for Meg Gorton, seventy-something, came in a few minutes ago. Where is she?"

"I'm Nancy. Are you family?" the employee asked as she placed her hand on Macy's arm.

"No, not exactly, but I'm all the family she has here. Where is she?" Macy's eyes scanned the lobby and waiting areas, the vending machines in the corner, the other employees working behind a glass window marked "REGISTRATION."

"I WANT TO SEE HER."

"Just sit for one moment, okay? Tell me your name. Let me help."

"Macy. Macy Chrisman. I'm her home health aide."

"Okay. Just stay here one moment. I'll go back and see what I can find out, okay?"

"Fine, fine," Macy said.

"And it's Macy?" Nancy looked for confirmation, and Macy nodded back. "You said she has no immediate family close? No one in Gulf Breeze?"

"No—I said no already. Just me."

"A husband or children? Siblings?"

Macy's voice rose again, both in pitch and volume. "I said I'm it."

Nancy patted Macy's arm again and swiped her badge at a black box on the wall and skipped through the automatic doors as they opened. Macy briefly considered slipping through before they closed, but her heart was pounding, and she felt like she was running on a ten-second delay. "I said I'm it," she heard herself whisper.

At the five-minute mark, Macy knocked on the glass window and asked for an update.

At the eight-minute mark, she stopped Nancy passing through the lobby.

At the twelve-minute mark, the automatic doors opened and a man with a bandage on his head was wheeled out by an attendant with a woman standing next to them, holding the patient's hand and mumbling encouraging phrases. "You're so lucky. You're just fine. You're going to be better by Monday. What a blessing. God sure loves you."

When they cleared the zone in front of the doors, Macy hopped up and dashed across the glossy floor, shoving her hand into the closing doors, triggering them to reopen.

At the fourteen-minute mark, Macy walked back through the automatic doors with a short, middle-aged and slightly overweight security guard.

For the next half hour, she sat quietly while the guard tried to stay awake. Another woman and a girl Macy assumed was her daughter were quickly taken back for help with what was likely a broken arm.

A twenty-something young mom came in with a grumpy, red-faced toddler who'd been running a fever all day. They sat across from Macy and the guard, and Macy watched the mother comfort and soothe her little girl. *Poor thing,* Macy thought. Her imagination wandered, and she wondered what and who waited at home for her waiting-room neighbors.

As the minutes marched by, like tired soldiers, Macy juggled her fascination for the mother and daughter with her anxiety and panic for Meg. "I just want answers," she said, and the woman looked up.

"I'm sorry?" she said.

"No, I was just . . . thinking aloud . . . I apologize. I'm here with . . . for a friend . . . and they haven't told me anything yet."

"Oh. That's hard," the stranger said. "I'm sorry. Is the person family?"

Macy smiled. "Yes, but not really. I'm her caretaker."

"I see," the woman said, and she resumed stroking her daughter's long, straight brown hair.

Macy heard a thin snore and realized her security pal had finally lost the battle.

"I don't even know . . . Well, I guess I know nothing . . . She was brought here in an ambulance tonight. Not even sure why."

"Oh. That's hard," the woman repeated.

"She's done so much for me," Macy said. "Given me so much." The words were quieter now, shorter, softer—like handwritten notes on pastel postcards. "I don't know what I'll do . . ." Macy couldn't even say the *if.*

Soon the mother and her daughter were called back behind the automatic door. The woman carried her toddler in her arms like a baby. Just before the doors closed, the woman turned and smiled a subtle goodbye.

Meg has done so much for me, Macy thought. *Given me so, so much . . .*

Her thoughts stumbled on tears that threatened to rise and pour but did not. *All she's done is give. All I've done is keep secrets.*

At the forty-five-minute mark, the automatic doors opened and a new face appeared and made eye contact. "Are you Macy Chrisman?"

THIRTY-SEVEN

Day Five

Troy woke up first and walked to a convenience store he'd seen the night before. As the rest were rising for the day, Troy returned with a plastic bag of fresh fruit and three bagels that were hard but edible. Moses ate his usual dog food and might have been moodier about not having any greasy bacon or sausage as an appetizer, but his family noticed the same pep in his step he'd had since Grace's decision to join the party.

The adults showered—Moses declined—and they sat outside near the bus eating their light breakfast and planning for the day. "So we're still going through Macon," Troy said. "Right, Pop?" Troy had the map on his lap and half a bagel in his hand.

"Yes, Macon," Gary said. "Probably four hours, maybe more. She's not running well over about fifty."

As the guys continued game planning the day, Grace put Moses on his leash and walked him to the grass for his morning routine.

"You think she's still glad she came?" Gary asked.

"I dunno. I hope so," Troy said.

"I figure she's having a good time. Seems like the old days, doesn't it?" Gary asked. "Like the gang's back together?"

"Whatever you say, old man," Troy offered, and he rolled up the atlas and whacked his dad's leg.

Across the lot, the men noticed a panhandler and a scruffy mutt standing on the gravel strip between the road and the motel's welcome sign. "Wonder where he's heading," Gary said.

"Can't . . . quite . . . read the sign from here," Troy said, craning his neck.

They watched a trucker stop and the man and his dog approach the passenger window, but after a moment the semi drove on and the hitch-hikers returned to their spot. A brand-new Honda stopped, and a hand reached out with what looked from a distance like several bills. The man bowed slightly, and the car moved on.

Troy and Gary watched Grace and Moses meandering slowly around the property. Moses barked at a monster vulture that had landed near them and pecked at something in the grass. The vulture was unphased until Moses pulled hard on the leash and got within two or three feet before Grace steadied him. He watched the muscular bird flap and fly away, but only to the other side of the two-lane highway. Moses resumed sniffing everything and anything and often looked up to make sure Grace was still there. "He sure loves that girl," Gary said.

Yes, Troy thought. *Yes, he does.* "Let's pack up." As Troy folded the chairs and loaded them on the bus, Gary checked out of the room and grabbed Grace's packed duffel bag from the foot of her bed. When they looked again to spot Grace and Moses, she was talking to the hitchhiker and Moses was sniffing the other mutt.

"What's she doing?" Gary said. "Son, run over there."

"She's fine, Pop. They're just talking. She's being friendly."

"Exactly," Gary said. "I'll go—" But before he'd taken a step, all four were walking toward the bus. "Uh-oh. We might have more company."

"You really need to stop with that, Pop."

When they arrived at the bus, Grace was quick with introductions. "Guys, this is Mark." She turned to her new friend. "Mark Richards, right?"

The man smiled and nodded. He was short, his beard unruly and red. He wore jeans, a denim shirt and a baseball hat with a patch that said Red Rock Leather Company. He carried a canvas military bag, his cardboard sign and a leash.

"And this is . . . Beverage?" She gestured down to Mark's dog.

He nodded again.

"Nice to meet you," Gary said. "And I'd love to hear the story behind that name."

"Well," Grace said, and she looked at Moses. "You wanna tell them, or should I?"

When Moses didn't bite, Grace continued. "Fine, wimp . . . So, Pop, you'll have plenty of time for that story. Because Mark and . . . Beverage are coming with us for a while."

"I'm sorry, what?" Gary said.

"Mark and . . . Beverage," she said. "I apologize—that name is really tripping me up . . . These two fine folks are traveling south, so says their sign, and we just happen to be heading south."

"How far south?" Troy asked.

Mark spoke softly—a whisper aspiring to be more. "As far as we can get," he said.

"I don't know, Grace," Troy said. "Do we have room?"

Gary, Mark, Grace, Moses and even Beverage all looked at the bus in near unison, then back at Troy.

"Right, the bus," he said. "What if the dogs don't get along?"

Grace crouched down and scratched both under their chins. "They'll be fine, right? Beverage looks like a perfect lady, and we know Mo will behave himself. They've already sniffed all the appropriate parts and gotten the awkward hellos out of the way. They're good."

Troy looked at Beverage and tried to imagine how many breeds could be found in her family tree. She was mid-sized, slightly smaller than Moses. Her coloring was brown and gray, but there was enough dirt and mud caked on her that she could have been all white.

"What kind of dog is Beverage?" Troy asked, and he bent down to rub the mutt's ears.

"I . . . I don't know, for sure," Mark said quietly. "I found her years ago. She needed a friend."

"Maybe you both did," Grace added.

Gary also leaned down and took Beverage's small head in his hands, as if he were a veterinarian in training. "I figure there's some Lab in there, like Moses. Maybe some retriever. Gosh, maybe even some poodle. What do you say? That sound about right?"

"Okay, Doctor Doolittle," Troy said, and he stood up. "Pop, it's your bus and your trip. Up to you."

Gary looked at Grace, and the South Carolina sun sat perfectly behind her head. The light burst out from around her hair and face, and her bright eyes were the answer to the question he didn't need to ask. "All right, Mark and Beverage, welcome to the official team bus of the Shenandoah Senators. Can't promise how far we'll get you, but we can drive you out of Powdersville, at least."

Mark nodded, put his hands together and again bowed politely. "Thank you, thank you."

"All aboard," Gary said, and he moved to stand at the door to the bus.

Mark and Beverage stepped up first. Moses was unleashed and followed closely behind. When Grace passed Troy, she placed her hand flat on his stomach, and he flexed his abs instinctively. "It'll be fine," she said, and she gave him the exaggerated wink he loved. "Everyone needs a lift sometimes."

Troy nodded and looked at his dad. They stood on either side of the door—guardians at the gate. Gary gestured up the steps and said, "After you, all-star."

Troy had plenty to say but nothing came.

"I agree," Gary said with a shrug. "What could go wrong?"

THIRTY-EIGHT

Macy had the dream again. She was curled up on a sea foam–green half-couch near Meg's room at Gulf Breeze Hospital. Macy considered herself young and fairly healthy, but her back was aching and her hips shouted some profanity for sleeping so awkwardly.

She turned over on the couch and wiped spittle from the right corner of her mouth. It was early, but the morning was already saying hello through the open blinds. Macy lifted her head to see if Meg was still sleeping and found her friend's eyes wide open and staring right back at her from the edge of her pillow.

"Good morning," Meg said. "Come here often?"

Macy rattled her thoughts loose and sat up. She stretched her arms up and twisted left and right. "You scared me to death, Meg Gorton. You know that?"

"You?" Meg smiled, and her dry lips cracked. "I woke up at three in the morning, and you were snoring on my couch."

Macy stood and stepped to Meg's bedside. "What do we know? Anything new? Doctor told me last night you had a heart attack."

"Sounds about right. I don't remember much of it. I was home, in my recliner, and I suppose the symptoms started, and . . . here I am."

"And here you are," Macy said. "Thank heaven."

The women talked about Meg's rough night, her health history—some of which was new to Macy, despite being her home health aide—and the impatient patient's desire to go home. Meg said, "I just can't be here when the guys get to town. They can't see me here. Like this. They just can't. They can't." Her voice scratched and skipped like a record.

"We'll figure it out," Macy said. "That's not for you to worry about." Macy took Meg's hand and held it with both of hers.

"They just can't," Meg said, again.

Macy and Meg watched *The Today Show* as Meg forced down oatmeal and raisins. Just after eight, Dr. Samuel Ward entered with a grin and a clipboard. "Meg, you're awake," the doctor said.

"You look surprised," she said.

"Not at all. Good morning." He smiled. "How'd you sleep?"

Meg wiped oatmeal from her lips. "I've had better nights."

"Forgive me," he said. "You must be Macy, her aide." Dr. Ward moved around her bed and shook Macy's hand.

"I am, yes."

Dr. Ward checked Meg's monitors, made notes on her chart and flicked an IV bag with his finger. "You're lucky, Mrs. Gorton. Many seniors living alone don't fare as well."

The word *senior* scraped at Meg's smile. "How so?"

"Well, you were wise to act. To call for help. To not wait."

Macy retook and squeezed Meg's hand. "So she's all right then?"

"She's fine," Dr. Ward said, looking down and making another note. "It was a mild attack. Just get a little more exercise. Maybe try to reduce any stress. All that will help."

Macy giggled. "Stress. What stress? Right, Meg?"

Meg grinned.

"We see this sometimes. Stress and anxiety—they have a way of making things seem worse than they are. Plus your chronic fatigue is an aggravating factor."

"What do you mean?" Macy asked.

"I mean that the symptoms were mild. It was wise to call for help, naturally. And as I said, you're lucky because many ignore the signs and never get a chance to have these discussions . . . if I may be so bold. But your heart is fairly healthy, and it's not uncommon for life's pressures—family, work, money—to trigger something like this." Dr. Ward pulled the clipboard to his chest and crossed his arms around it. "The overnight nurse mentioned you have some stressful times ahead, or already happening? A family reunion or something?"

"Or something . . ." Meg said.

"All right then, my suggestion is to take it easy. Breathe. Take breaks. Don't let yourself get worn down. Get plenty of sleep. What do they say? Don't sweat the small stuff."

Meg looked at Macy again, and her eyes seemed to suggest that the good doctor couldn't begin to imagine what might lie ahead.

"How long do you think she'll need to stay?" Macy asked.

Dr. Ward flipped back several pages and appeared to check and recheck some test results. "I'd love to tell you we could release you tomorrow, but realistically we'd like to keep you admitted two more days, maybe three." He looked at Meg and preempted her response. "Just to monitor you, that's all. Give you a . . . think of it as forced rest compliance. At least I know if you're here, you're not running yourself—and your heart—into the ground."

"Thank you, doctor," Macy said, and after a few more questions and scribbles, he said goodbye and promised to return a few hours later.

"He seems nice," Meg said. "And smart."

"And cute," Macy added. "Speaking of . . . have you heard from the bus?"

Meg shook her head. "Nothing. I've called and called that stupid phone Troy carries."

"You want to give me the number, and I can try too? Update him if he answers?"

"Why not. Yes, thank you."

"How about visitors? You up for any?"

"I don't know, Macy. If I don't want my family seeing me like this, all old and laid up, I don't think I'd want my friends here either."

"Don't be ridiculous. They'd love to see you. Maybe your neighbor? Jessie?"

"I'll think about it," Meg said.

After another half hour of channel surfing, Macy kissed Meg on the cheek and asked for a break to go home and shower, and she offered to pick up some items from Meg's condo. As Macy blew a kiss from the doorway, Meg pretended to catch it and took a deep breath. "Thank you," she said.

"For what?"

"For always saving me."

Macy blew another kiss and allowed the heavy door to shut behind her. She pushed the elevator button, and when she was alone inside the shiny steel box, she whispered, "Not always."

THIRTY-NINE

By mid-afternoon, the bus to Gulf Breeze was cruising along south of Athens and skirting the Oconee National Forest. Troy was up front near his dad, and the rest had gathered near the cooler and snacks in the rear. Grace sat sideways, her bare legs on the sticky vinyl seat, one row ahead of Mark. She quizzed him on his nomad life, and Moses and Beverage lay next to each other against the emergency door chewing on rawhides.

"Thirteen years?" Grace was slack-jawed. "You've been homeless for thirteen years?"

Mark spoke louder, but only because Grace had told him it was hard to hear him over the clanks and cranks of the bus. "I prefer not to think of myself as . . . homeless," he said. "I have a house. Just not a home."

Grace, curious and with nothing but time, pressed. "I'm so fascinated, Mark. What does that mean? A house but not a home?"

Mark took a sip from a cold water bottle—his third since boarding the bus that morning. "My wife and I had a home in Rochester. Rochester, New York. I'm from the Finger Lakes area. My wife is from Palmyra."

"Is she . . . still living?" Grace asked, as Troy arrived and sat in the seat across from her.

"She's not," Mark said, looking down and fiddling with the clear cap of his bottle.

"I'm sorry. I shouldn't have asked," Grace offered.

Troy looked, listened, watched the dogs trade rawhide but said nothing as the conversation unfolded.

"No need to apologize," Mark said. "She was sick our entire marriage. I always knew she'd leave me before we were done."

"Done?" Grace asked.

"With the journey. She was my love." Mark pointed to his chest, and his voice fell into a canyon. "She was my heart."

The miles passed, and Mark, in simple but colorful strokes, painted the picture of his life. He'd graduated from NYU and taught humanities at a community college. He met his wife there, a career counselor just three days younger. On their second date, she confided that she was a cancer survivor four times over, and she knew it wasn't a matter of if but of which follow-up appointment would be the one that moved her from four to five.

They were married between semesters, and doctors found another tumor during their first year of marriage. "Nothing surprised us," Mark said. "It was the . . . perfection of our relationship. No secrets. No surprises."

"She must have been so special. So, so special that you chose to endure knowing all that."

Mark smiled—a slight curl and a spark. "You don't endure love, Grace. You breathe it."

Troy remained quiet as Mark's life continued, revealing itself milestone by milestone.

"We couldn't have children, not with all the treatments. But we still built a family. We had a home, our own traditions, the college, our friends, our students. When she finally passed, her last breaths took a week."

Grace wanted to probe, to pry, but it was obvious she wouldn't need to.

"No one ever asks me about her," Mark said, and for the first time Troy and Grace noticed his eyes were wet. "I think about her every single day, but I haven't talked about her in . . . a long time. A very long time."

Mark breathed, drank, bent down and rubbed Beverage's belly. Then he looked out the window as the trees of the Oconee National Forest passed by in a gorgeous green blur. "I had never known a woman like her."

Grace reached across the seat and placed her hand on his. "I don't think you told us her name?"

Mark grinned again and wiped a thick tear from the corner of his eye with his thumb. "I know." He took a long, pensive pause. "If you don't mind, I'll keep that to myself. I don't mean to be rude, I don't. But I don't have much left anymore but her memory and her name. I keep her name here." He pointed again at his heart. "She's mine. All mine. Her name?" His voice popped. "It's my most prized possession."

Grace shook her head. "That is the most beautiful thing I think I've ever heard."

This time, Mark wiped tears from both eyes. "So this? This life— it's my choice. I couldn't live there in that house without her. I tried. I even got a dog." He nodded at Beverage. "Friends were good to me—they were. But I realized one day that I didn't have a home without her. I took Beverage on a walk one day, and the clouds started dumping on us—just a deluge. We were standing at an intersection a couple of miles from home, and I was crying. More than that really. Even Beverage knew something was really wrong. This man stopped and offered us a ride home . . . The next day we walked maybe ten miles? Do you remember, Beverage? We walked for three or four hours and then hitched a ride home." Mark finished and finally looked back at Grace.

"And here you are," she said.

"Here I am . . . I don't ask for money—don't need it. Just rides."

Troy slid forward on his seat and into the discussion. "So the sign you carry?"

"It's different every day, or most days. Right now I'm traveling to Orlando, and so anything south helps."

"Why Orlando?" Troy asked.

"Disney." Mark smiled. "It's on the list."

"List?" Grace said.

"Before my wife died, during her last few months, she made a list of places she had never visited." Mark pulled a pocket-sized, dark-blue and faded Moleskine notebook from his bag and held it in the palm of his hands like a newborn.

Grace nodded and let her throat choke and kill a soft cry.

"So I'm going to Disney. Not to ride rides or any of that. Just to be there, in the park, near the families."

Grace touched the back of his hand again. "She'd be so proud."

"Maybe, but that's not why I travel to the places on her list."

"No?" Grace said.

"I go because . . . these places? These spots on the list right here? If I want to be with her, to feel her, I've got to go where I know she's waiting for me."

Why fight it? Grace thought, and she let the cry go. She choked and coughed, and Troy handed her a clean napkin from the snack bag and a bottle of water. "That love—your love." She looked at Mark. "That's what I want. A man who would walk the country to all the places he thinks he'd find me."

As that line rose and fell, a loud thud cracked from the front windshield. "Come on!" Gary yelled, and he muttered an expletive that only Moses and Beverage heard.

"Pop, what happened?" Troy said, and he stood and walked to the front of the bus.

Gary pulled off the road, and in seconds, Grace, Mark and the dogs were all up front staring through the large windshield. It was shattered—a spider web of cracks covered every inch and was decorated with black feathers and bits of red and brown.

"What was it?" Grace asked.

Gary turned off the bus but kept his eyes straight ahead. "A humongous vulture," he said. "A vulture the size of a dog. Sorry, boys," he added.

They each stepped off the bus and moved to see the carnage from the front. "I can't believe this," Grace said.

"Now what?" Troy asked.

Gary looked at him. "Where's your phone?"

FORTY

Macy turned the key and stepped into Meg's cozy condo. She'd been in the home countless times since first arriving as Meg's aide. But never alone. She moved quietly through the house, stepping lightly as if trying not to wake the empty house or stir its secrets.

She carried a scribbled list on a small, square piece of hospital stationery, torn from a complimentary notepad on Meg's bedside. Change of clothes. Personal items. Check mail. Check fridge. Check answering machine.

Macy gathered the items and placed them in a bag from Meg's closet and checked off the other to-dos. Then she pulled one of the fat photo albums from the shelf in the living room and sat in Sandi's recliner. *Meg wouldn't mind,* she thought. *After all, she's already shared one of the other albums.*

She opened the leather-bound cover and read the cover page. In beautiful cursive lettering, a talent acquired and refined from her membership in LWCOGB, Meg had written the words:

Gary and Meg Gorton Family Memories
1953–1960

Macy traced the flat, black letters with her index finger and turned the page.

Under laminate sheets, Meg had arranged photos in collages. They began with both color and black-and-white baby photos of Mallorie. Two side-by-side pages were dedicated to birthday photos, and through a one-dimensional faded lens, Macy watched Mallorie and her parents celebrate her first seven birthdays. Though taken from different angles, each photo seemed to be taken at the same kitchen table. And while Macy had never been inside the Gortons' home in Virginia, the photos and Meg's stories made it all feel familiar.

Macy flipped through the pages, lingering on each longer than she would have if she'd had company. She smiled at a photo of Gary, Meg and Mallorie tubing in a river.

Mallorie wore a too-big life jacket that bunched up near her neck and hid her ears. Her straight black bangs were wet and matted against her forehead.

There were scenes of camping trips. The family eating matching clouds of pink cotton candy at what looked like a county fair. Mallorie's first day of kindergarten. Mallorie riding a large gray stone turtle in a mulch bed in front of a house. Mallorie standing in front of the Washington Monument. Mallorie posing with a tour guide in a cavern. All three at a baseball game.

Macy swapped albums and flipped through the next seven years of Gorton family history. More fishing trips, Christmas mornings, toothless smiles, birthday cakes, choir concerts and class photos. The final page of the second album featured Mallorie and Gary at what seemed to be a daddy-daughter dance. Mallorie was thirteen or fourteen, and she wore a purple dress with puffy sleeves and white high heels that looked like they could topple her at any moment.

Macy replaced the album on the shelf and saw the next one in the row. "I should go. This isn't right." She looked at Sandi's urn on the mantel. "Right?"

Silence.

Macy pulled the next album and returned to the recliner. The photos took her well into Mallorie's teens, and by the middle of the album, Robbie was popping up in pics of family trips and at school activities.

Four full pages were dedicated to Mallorie's sweet-sixteen birthday party at a roller rink. The photos were marked with the date 1969, and Meg grinned at the hair styles and outfits. In one photo, the teenage couple stood in their roller skates under a disco ball. Robbie had an arm around the much shorter Mallorie, and she rested her head on his chest. Their faces radiated joy, and Macy thought they weren't just looking at the camera, they were looking through it.

To the next birthday, Macy thought. *Then prom, graduation, wedding, children, vacations and albums full of their own children's lives.*

Macy closed the album and returned it to the shelf. She stepped back carefully, slowly, still looking at the row of family albums, like a mourner in a cemetery saying a long goodbye.

So many memories, she thought. *And so many memories unmade.*

FORTY-ONE

Almost two hours after a vulture destroyed their windshield, a specialty tow truck finally arrived and loaded up the Shenandoah Senators' team bus on the side of US-129. The driver, Carter, said he would deliver it to Ruby's Repairs on the outskirts of Macon. "They're great," Carter said in a low, marbly Southern accent. He handed them a glossy business card with a photo of a little beautiful blonde girl with pigtails smiling in greasy overalls and clutching a heavy wrench with both hands. "That there is Ruby. She's their kid, but she don't do the repairs," Carter said with a crooked-toothed smile. "Don't ya'll worry. This is their thing. Semis. Buses. Campers. They'll fix ya'll up and getcha to wherever your headin'."

With room for only one passenger in the tow truck, Carter insisted Gary join him so he could be there when the bus was unloaded at Ruby's. Using his CB, Carter called his tow company's dispatch and requested a cab into Macon for the rest of the group.

"Yeah, Yvonne, we got three adults—a couple, a homeless guy, I think—out here on 129, southside, needin' to get into Macon. And their two dogs, I reckon . . . I got the bus loaded up, and the driver's comin' to Ruby's with me."

"Sir, excuse me," Mark said, stepping toward the tow truck's open driver's window. "Me and my dog don't need a ride. But thank you."

"What? Why?" Grace joined him near the driver's window.

"I'll find my way," Mark said, too softly for the circumstances on the side of a highway. "It's all right."

"Scratch that, Yvonne," Carter said. "Jus' two adults. A couple and their mutt."

"Wait, wait," Grace said. "Let us get you into Macon. We'll grab some dinner at least before you leave . . . Carter, get two cabs here, please."

"Sorry, Yvonne, two of 'em—"

"Sir, thank you, but not necessary," Mark said. "I appreciate you—all of you—but I'll just put my sign and thumb back up and make my way south. You don't need to worry about me and Beverage."

Carter squeezed the button again on the side of the CB and gave the curly cord a yank. "Sorry, Yvonne, jus' one cab. Room for the couple, the dog and their bags—"

"—No, no, Carter, put that down." Grace pointed at the CB handset. "And we're not a couple."

Troy laughed. "Just play ball with her!" Troy half yelled to be heard as cars continued to whiz by. "She gets what she wants."

"Not always," Grace whispered to Mark. "Listen, please let us get you and Beverage off the road and into Macon. Have a nice meal, enjoy some air-conditioning, and then we can say goodbye."

Carter looked at Grace, then Mark, then the CB, then back to Grace.

Grace smiled again at Mark and reached inside the cab to take the CB from Carter's muscular, callused, tanned hands. "Yvonne, this is Grace. Please get us a cab big enough for three adults and two well-behaved dogs. A minivan maybe? Or two smaller cars."

Yvonne agreed, but only after confirming with Carter twice, and the tow truck eventually pulled onto the highway and faded away in the distance.

"Huh," Troy said, when the bus was out of sight and all that remained on the side of the road was the weary traveling party. "That went well."

FORTY-TWO

"You know what they say," Macy offered as she led her long parade of LWCOGB visitors through the hospital hallways. "You can ask for permission or forgiveness. I prefer the latter."

"Just don't get us arrested," Kaitie said.

"As if *that's* ever stopped you," Veda said.

"Ladies, shush, please," Skye said in her usual wife-of-a-pastor's voice. "We're in a hospital."

Macy, still at the head of the gaggle, rolled her eyes. She'd borrowed the community center's large fifteen-passenger van for the short drive to the hospital, and second thoughts were already at high tide.

Macy didn't know the club particularly well—she wasn't a member, as some of them often reminded her—but Meg had shared sacks of stories about Veda, Skye, Caleb, Lili and the rest of them. They'd been colorful and sometimes unbelievable. But now, all the stories Macy had heard were moving from fiction to nonfiction in real time.

They turned a corner and started down the final long straightway. A few doors before Meg's, Macy turned to address the group. "All right.

Shhh. We're here." Some chatter continued at the back of the crowd, and club president Veda asked them to quiet down.

When they didn't, Kaitie whistled with her index finger and pinkie in her mouth.

Veda crossed her arms, and the hallway fell silent.

"Thank you, Kaitie," Macy said. "We're here. Now, as I said yesterday, she doesn't know we're coming. You know she doesn't like to trouble people, put them out—you know. But she needs her people right now."

Veda grinned with pride. "She's right. We're her people. We're all she's got."

Skye raised her hand half into the air as though she were a student not sure she really wanted to be called on. "Macy? Are we sure it's okay that we're here?" When no one responded, she said it again, louder.

"Skye!" Kaitie barked. "Show some respect. We're in a hospital."

Macy made a T with her hands, calling a time-out. "You're making a scene. Let's just quietly go in, give her some TLC, leave whatever you might have brought and let her be . . . Okay? She doesn't need to be coddled or patronized. Just loved."

The group grinned and nodded, and Macy led them the final fifteen feet to Meg's room. She poked her head around the doorjamb to be sure Meg was awake and alone, but before she could turn back to the group, they were pushing past her.

"Oh, Meg!" Veda said, one hand over her chest like an actress on *Guiding Light.*

"Bless your heart," Skye added.

"Our sweet Meg, how are you?" Caleb said.

Choking on tears, Kaleigh took Meg's hand in hers. "I am so, so sorry. So sorry."

"Meg!" Kaitie said in a whisper-shout that was more shout than whisper.

Macy closed the door when the final LWCOGB member had entered. *What was I thinking?* she thought. She began prepping an apology to Meg for later.

"Meg, my girl," Kaitie said as she wedged her way between the bodies to her bedside. "We're here to give you your last rites."

"Kaitie!" Skye snapped, and she flashed her fingers up over her mouth as if protecting her lips from the blasphemy. "Inappropriate."

"Relax, Tammy Faye. She knows I'm kidding."

Meg shook her head on her pillow and smiled up at her friend. "Do I?"

Kaitie nodded and patted her hand. "You do."

Macy made her way close enough to make eye contact. "Surprise?" she said, her voice creating a question from the obvious.

"Yes, yes. I'm surprised," Meg said, scanning the faces staring down at her. "How did you get past the nurses?"

Kaitie held a finger to her lips. "Don't ask. Don't tell."

Meg's eyes found Macy's again, and she mouthed a subtle "Thank you."

Macy winked, and the members of the Letter Writing Club of Gulf Breeze took snappy turns updating Meg on club gossip and the latest neighborhood news. Meg hadn't even missed a single meeting yet, but her visitors acted as if she'd just awakened from a coma that had kept her in the dark through the 80s.

Meg presented an update on her health. "Barely a heart attack," she said. "But they're keeping me a couple days and watching me. I don't have a lot of energy yet. That's what they tell me, at least."

"Well, do you?" Kaitie said.

"Enough," Meg answered.

"Then tell them you're good to go. Want me to? Or should I just tell them to go to—"

"Kaitie!" Skye coughed out her name. "Please."

Macy took control again. "This was terrific," she said, "but I've got to get the van back. It's reserved for something else tonight." Each visitor handed Meg a card or handmade something. Some gently shook her hand; others hugged her tightly.

"We love you, Meg," Veda said with surprising sincerity, and most nodded and agreed.

As they began the goodbyes, Kaitie asked the question on everyone's minds. "Wait, wait, before we go, someone needs to ask, right?"

Macy shook her head but knew the question was coming anyway.

"Any news?" Kaitie asked.

"News?" Meg answered.

"From the bus?" Kaitie said.

The room quieted, and everyone collapsed again around the bed.

"What bus?" Meg asked. "Did I buy a bus while in the coma?"

Kaitie smiled. "Don't make me kidnap you and take you back to the beach, Meg Gorton." She looked across the room at Macy. "Sor-ry," Kaitie said, tapping both syllables on the head but not meaning either one.

"Oh, so you mean the baseball bus then?" Meg asked, and she fluffed up her flattened, unwashed hair.

"Yes, the one with a couple cute guys and a dog headed this way."

Meg surveyed the faces of the club members. It was obvious every single one knew the score. "I suppose I didn't realize this was—"

"—Common knowledge?" Kaitie said. "It is surely that. Everyone's told everyone."

Kaitie looked to her left, spotted Skye and put her hand up to shield her mouth but made sure to speak loudly. "Skye even told God about it. I hear He's super pumped."

"Kaitie!" Skye said, but Macy had already arrived at Kaitie's spot by the bed and nudged her backward.

"Meg, this isn't *Matlock*," Macy said. "You don't have to answer a single question. We're saying goodbye."

As quickly as they'd ambushed her, Meg's visitors disappeared, and only Macy remained. She gave Meg a light hug and held on a moment. "It seemed like a good idea at first," Macy said.

"Innocent, innocent Macy," Meg said with a bright smile Macy could hear in her voice. "All your ideas start out that way."

Macy stood and fussed with Meg's hair. "Maybe so, but you'll never forget you're loved by me and this group of weirdos, right?"

"Right," Meg agreed.

"I should go. Kaitie and Skye are probably brawling in the lobby by now. Anything else you need?"

"Just the address. Any luck?"

"My goodness, I'm sorry. Yes." Macy pulled a slip of paper from her back pocket and handed it to Meg. "Too much excitement for one day. Sorry about that. This looks right, but you won't know until you try, right?"

"Right," Meg said, and she studied the pink piece of paper carefully.

Macy blew her a kiss and backed up until she felt the door handle behind her. "You sure about this?"

Meg nodded. "Not really."

Macy paused, blinked, felt a wave of love that left goose pimples on her arm and said simply, "That's my girl."

FORTY-THREE

"You want the good news or the bad news first?" the mechanic said, finally looking up from his monitor. He'd been pecking and tapping away at a keyboard for ten minutes.

"I figure it's up to you," Gary answered.

"Well, here at Ruby's we always eat the frog first, as my mama used to say."

"Fine. Give me the bad."

"You see, we don't stock bus windshields. It's going to be two days, maybe three, before I can get one in."

"Really? You've got to be kidding?" Gary said, sounding more surprised than he meant to. Even though he didn't have extensive experience with bus repairs, a career in maintenance at the school district back home in Virginia had exposed him to all kinds of issues. "Was hoping maybe you'd have one and we could get back on the road today."

"My friend, here's your good news. Once we get it here, we can have it in and get you on the road in a hurry."

Gary sighed, looked down and placed his hands on the counter. "I figure we have no choice."

"Well, sir, I could take out the shattered one, and you could try driving without one, but you wouldn't make it far."

"No thanks," he said. "Been pulled over once already on this trip." Gary groaned at the price, pulled his wallet out of his back pocket and handed over a credit card. "What was your name again?"

"Cash," he said as he swiped the credit card. "Nice to meet you," he added, and they shook hands.

As Gary signed the slip, a woman appeared from a room marked "OFFICE" and kissed Cash on the top of his head as she passed by. "Don't worry," Cash said. "My wife knows."

"Ha. So funny. Sell the shop. Open a comedy club," the woman said, and it seemed to Gary that Cash's jokes and his wife's answers were a familiar routine. As she rifled through hanging folders in a beige filing cabinet, she looked back over her shoulder, smiled at Gary and introduced herself. "I'm Foz. At least that's what they call me. And the comedian is my husband."

"Got it," Gary said, giving a clumsy thumbs up. "I figured."

"You're the guy with the baseball bus?" she asked, still apparently on the hunt for something.

"Unfortunately, yes," Gary said.

"We hear you. Those vultures are big ol' boys. Not the first time we've replaced a windshield."

They swapped small talk for a few minutes, and Cash called the same cab company in Macon to get Gary back to the gang hanging out at a Holiday Inn off the freeway.

"Shouldn't be too long," Cash said. "Fifteen minutes, maybe less."

"Thanks. You'll call me? At the hotel?"

"Yep. You want some stuff to do while you wait around Macon?"

Cash jotted down a few popular local joints and sites and then took a phone call. When he hung up, Gary was still standing at the window across the shop's lobby, watching the parking lot. "Hey, man, you said you got pulled over? Here in Georgia? You all okay?"

Gary slowly spun around. "Depends on what 'okay' means in Macon, I figure." He meant it to be funny, but it was obvious from Cash's face that he hadn't read it that way. "We're all good. Just been . . . an adventure."

"There you are," Foz said, and she yanked a canary-colored invoice from the filing cabinet and shoved it shut. "An adventure? I guess so. You're driving a baseball bus from someplace in Virginia with some hitchhikers and a couple dogs."

Gary's eyes narrowed, and his eyebrows became one. "People talk," she said. "Sorry about that."

"No, you're not," Cash teased.

She smiled, and Gary noticed she had two gold teeth. "You're right. I'm not."

Gary leaned against the wall and gave the ten-minute version of his trip to Gulf Breeze. The plot flowed more comfortably than he'd expected. The letter, Meg's condo, Troy's career. At some point during his story, a blonde teenage girl walked through the shop's office eating a bag of Doritos. She stopped, Foz put her arm around her, and she swiped a chip. "This is Ruby," Foz said.

Gary pulled the business card from his pocket and held it up. "Spittin' image," he said. "But you've grown."

"All right now, people," Cash said. "That cab won't be much longer." He was still seated at the counter, but he leaned back comfortably in his rolling office chair, clearly enjoying the show. "Make popcorn. We want the rest."

Gary laughed and rushed through the remaining highlights. Breakfast in Rock Hill, being pulled over by the South Carolina State Police, meeting Mark and Beverage. Then—of course—the vulture. "Oh, wait, and I threatened to toss my son's portable phone thing into the ocean when we get to Florida."

The audience guffawed. "I want one of those so bad!" Ruby said, and her mom smacked her rear end.

"Please, child, like you'll ever need a phone you can take outside. Keep dreamin'."

Eventually Ruby poured the final chip shards into her mouth and excused herself.

"Sounds to me like you got decisions to make," Foz said when her daughter left.

"Decisions?"

"Duh, yes," she said. "You going to love your wife again or not?"

The question felt like a hailstorm. "I'm sorry?"

"This isn't that complicated," she said. "She doesn't care about the dog—"

"—Hold up, Foz," her husband interrupted. "Of course she does. That's why she wrote him."

"Were you even listening?" Foz said, and she pulled on her own ears for effect. "She wants her family back, her whole family . . . Gary, may I ask you something else?"

He smiled and shrugged. His answer wouldn't matter one bit.

"The day after she left. Meg?"

"Uh huh."

"How did you feel?"

Gary looked at Cash, then back at Foz. "Honestly?"

"Obviously," she said.

"Like I was missing something."

"Something?" she asked.

"Like an arm, a leg, a piece of me. I felt kind of . . . broken."

"Oh! That's beautiful!" Foz said. "Did you ever tell her that? I mean, you have to, right?"

Gary shrugged again.

"Well now you can," Foz said sweetly. Then she slugged her husband hard in the arm. "You ever felt like that, babe? Like me being gone was a missing limb?"

Cash laughed, and while the couple teased one another, Gary looked out the window and saw his cab waiting under the shop's awning. He tried to say goodbye, but his new friends were deep in discussion about love, marriage and reunions. So he simply gave an index finger wave and walked out.

As he was driven to meet his motley crew of travelers, his mind raced back and forth between memories and anxiety. He leaned his head against the headrest and closed his eyes and saw Mallorie in everything and everyone. In Troy, in Grace, in Ruby.

He even saw Mallorie in Meg's condo. And even though he'd never seen Meg's home, he thought it could be only one thing. *Suffocating.*

FORTY-FOUR

I'm tired, Meg thought. *Tired of being here, tired of nurses, tired of walking the sterile square loop on my floor. Tired of tests. Tired of beeps and lights and questions. Tired of waiting for good news—or even better news than yesterday. I'd like that. I'm just tired of being tired.*

The volume was down on the television hanging from the ceiling in the corner of her room. Meg looked at the empty bed in her shared room. She'd been told the hospital was crowded and they couldn't guarantee she would have the room to herself, but so far she'd been lucky. *Or have I?*

She watched the quiet television again. The evening anchors were obviously talking about the fall election. President George H. W. Bush and his challenger, Bill Clinton—a no-name, long-shot governor from Arkansas—were both trailing independent billionaire Ross Perot in a new poll. Nothing was more depressing to Meg than politics, and she didn't miss her estranged husband's musings on the topic. She pictured him on the couch at home talking to the television, narrating debates and teaching Moses everything the poor dog never wanted to know about American presidential politics, the electoral college and approval ratings.

With the television still muted, Meg turned the channel and watched a talking head she didn't recognize interviewing New York real estate developer Donald Trump. Next to Trump, the station flashed the same poll and a photo of Perot. *Even Trump is being interviewed about politics now? What does he know? Gary would eat this up.*

She flipped through a few more programs, mostly news and soap operas, then turned the television off. If she couldn't sleep in a few hours, she'd turn it back on and watch the news out of Pensacola. *A taste of normal,* she thought.

Meg hadn't had a visitor not wearing a white coat or blue scrubs since Macy had left with the rambunctious letter writers. She wondered if Jessie across the street or anyone else in the neighborhood would come. If nothing else, she knew Macy would be back in the morning.

She looked at the letter she'd written, then twice sealed and addressed. One of the nurses had "borrowed" an overnight envelope from a friend in the hospital's accounting department, and Meg had slipped her small stationery-sized envelope inside it and readdressed the red-and-blue label. She checked the time on the clock below the television and hoped the nurse would return in time to get the letter in the day's mail.

She had no idea if the address was still right—or ever had been—but she couldn't fight the urge another day. It had been building since her move to Florida with Sandi and had only grown since her passing. Now with Gary, Troy and Moses on their way, she'd waited long enough.

The moment, the arrival, the meeting, the mending—Meg would manage it all her way. Then she'd let the Gulf breeze do what Macy had always predicted it could.

And then I'll say goodbye, Meg thought, and she drifted off to sleep.

FORTY-FIVE

As he did for most of the expenses on their trip, Gary insisted on picking up the tab for the hotel in Macon. The others all objected, as he knew they would, and he told them either he covered the costs or they'd walk the rest of the way to Florida. "Look, Son," Gary said as they settled into their shared room. "Meg and I didn't agree on everything during our marriage. But my gosh, she was frugal, and I actually learned to appreciate that about her. That lady didn't spend a penny without interviewing it first to be sure it knew where it was going. But it served us well, and I can cover this. We're okay."

Troy objected again, but only for the record. He knew Gary would never change or relent—on this or anything else. "I'll buy breakfast tomorrow then, all right?" Troy said.

"At the free breakfast downstairs? You got it."

Across the hall, Mark and Beverage chatted about their spacious room with two comfortable queen beds, a huge television and a view of downtown Macon. "What do you think, Beverage? Nice to be indoors for a night?"

The dog didn't hear a thing. She was sprawled across the bed on her side, already deep into an evening nap.

"That's my girl," Mark said. "Enjoy." He sat on the bed across from her and emptied his bag. He pulled out a photo of his wife and stared at it until tears pooled and the image blurred.

Three doors down the hallway, Grace stood in the bathroom and washed the day off her face. Moses had once again chosen to bunk with her, and she smiled at the sound of his snoring from his bed. Downstairs at the front desk, Grace had also insisted on paying for her own room while they waited for the bus to be repaired. She'd given up quickly and decided that when she was back in Rock Hill, she'd send Gary a certified check for her portion of the trip and give him no choice but to take the money and be grateful. She'd also extracted a concession that she could pay for the group's dinner that evening in the hotel restaurant.

Troy, Grace and Mark had all wondered aloud if they needed a place quite so nice while they waited for the bus to be roadworthy again, and all balked at the steep pet deposit Gary had paid to let the dogs join them. But when the gang walked to the elevators and saw the hotel's restaurant, gym, indoor/outdoor pool and large library with overstuffed couches and even bigger windows, they stopped questioning Gary's generosity.

An hour later the men arrived first in the restaurant and were seated at a table just to the right of the hostess stand. Mark wore clean jeans and a cream-colored button-down shirt he'd ironed in his room. Gary and Troy wore matching blue golf shorts—an accident, they insisted— and polos. When Grace arrived ten minutes late, Mark stood and pulled her chair out while Gary and Troy gawked. She was wearing a sun-bright yellow sundress, no makeup, and her blonde hair was pulled back and draped over her right shoulder.

"Thank you, Mark," she said as she sat. "Such a gentleman," she added, and she nodded her head at the two Gorton men across the table.

"I was just about to stand," Gary said.

"Me too!" Troy said, and he looked to everyone like an embarrassed sixteen-year-old.

"Uh-huh," she said, and she dove into her menu. "I'm famished."

They each ordered and sipped ice water and strawberry lemonade. As they picked at side salads, Mark reluctantly answered questions about the spots he'd visited on his deceased wife's behalf.

"And have you sensed her?" Grace said, trapped in his stories and cadence like a willing prisoner. "Like she's been there?"

Mark took a drink and nodded. "Almost every time. Yes. I feel her near me."

"Like she's coaching you . . ." Grace said.

"I don't know," Mark answered. "Perhaps more like she's rooting for me."

Grace looked at Troy and Gary. "Imagine that, gentlemen. A love so strong, so real, that even from heaven you feel them cheering for you."

Their dinners arrived, and each appreciated their finest meal in days. Gary and Troy retold stories from the road and laughed and teased one another. Gary was almost emotional as he shared with Mark the story of the wreck near Spartanburg. "I'm sorry," Mark said so softly the words barely carried across the table and cloud of restaurant noise.

"Thank you," Gary said. "But I figure there's no need to be sad, right, Troy? No need for sadness about the near misses. We're all okay."

"I understand," Mark said. "Still sorry. Sorry you had to witness something like that. Those things can be hard to forget."

The other three let his observation land and get swept away by silence and the arrival of dessert. "I'm in actual heaven," Grace said, plunging her fork into an oversized piece of cheesecake.

But before she could take her first bite, a man approached the table and apologized with his hands as if surrendering. "I am so sorry to interrupt your dinner, but you're Troy Gorton, right?"

Troy wiped his mouth with his napkin and said, "That depends. Am I in trouble?"

"No, no, I'm Frank Yurkovich. I'm a baseball scout for the Dodgers."

"Then yes," Gary said, his voice piercing through the awkward moment. "This is my son, Troy Gorton. The kid with the best fastball and sneakiest slider you've ever seen."

Frank extended his hand. "I know. I've seen it. I watched you pitch a few times in Texas last year. I was there the night you got two outs from a perfect game."

"Hey!" Grace squealed. "I was there too. Almost perfect."

Troy smiled politely, thanked him for saying hello and turned to face the others.

"Stand up." Gary leaned in and whispered too loudly.

"No, it's fine." Frank said. "I don't want to interrupt. You doing okay? I heard your rotator cuff needs surgery."

Troy, still seated, nodded and forced a closed-mouth smile.

"Tough break, man, but you'll be back. Your stuff is so good. Just a matter of time before you're pitching for someone like the Dodgers."

"That's what I tell him," Gary said, reaching over and slapping Troy on the back several times. "World Series talent here. Couldn't be prouder."

"I bet. Hey, would you mind if we took a photo? My wife is right over there. We're staying here tonight. I think she has a camera in her purse."

Troy reached out to shake Frank's hand again. "No thanks, but have a great night. Enjoy your dinner. We just want to finish up here and get some rest."

Frank finally shook his hand, and Grace leaned across the table.

"Come on, Troy. Take a photo. We don't care. Maybe you'll be a Dodger someday."

Mark shifted uncomfortably, snatched his napkin off his lap, refolded it and put it back down again without looking up.

Gary slapped his son's back again, with a little more force than fatherly pride might call for. "Yeah, kid, take a photo. Maybe you'll look back and—"

"—I said no thanks, but nice to meet you, Frank. Maybe another time. My best to your wife."

Frank nodded at the others, apologized again for the interruption and walked away.

"My best to your wife?" Gary said. "For real? What was that?" He took the napkin and tossed it on his plate.

"Nothing, Pop. Just trying to enjoy some dinner, eat some cheesecake, with you all. That all right?"

"Troy," Grace said, and her head was turned at a disappointed-schoolteacher angle. "He's right. That wasn't you. Why not just take the photo? I watched you take photos and sign autographs back in Texas all the time after games."

Troy took a long drink of water until all that was left were a few puny ice cubes. "I guess we're not in Texas, are we? And this isn't a game."

They sat in silence. Mark studied his hands. Grace pulled at her ponytail and looked across the restaurant. Gary examined and reexamined the check and tucked a credit card into the leather folder. Troy held his glass and spun the melting cubes in the bottom with a straw.

"Yes, Troy," Grace said. "You're right. This isn't Texas, and it sure isn't a game."

FORTY-SIX

Day Six

Finally, Troy thought. Moses and Gary had finally left their hotel room for their morning walk, and Troy turned on his phone. He entered the number for Meg's condo and was surprised to hear her answering machine. He smiled at the familiar greeting in Macy's joyful voice. "Hi, you've reached Meg's condo. She can't answer the phone right now because the music's too loud to hear the phone. Plus the blender is running, and the hot tub jets are just so noisy. When the crowd goes home, she'll call you back. But only if you leave your name, number and one interesting thing about yourself. Beep." Troy kept smiling because there were two beeps—one from Macy and then the digital beep of the machine.

"Mom, it's Troy. Are you there? Pick up."

Nothing.

"Take your time. I know you're . . . what . . . probably in your recliner. Small steps," he teased.

Nothing.

"Are you there?" Troy looked at his watch—8:20 a.m. "Maybe you're walking? You up for that?" Troy moved the corded phone from one ear to the other. "Maybe you're still asleep. I'll try again. Love you."

Troy showered and dressed and was surprised that Gary and Moses weren't back. *Must have gotten breakfast without me.* He called Meg's condo again, got the greeting and left another message. "It's almost nine. I'll try again. If I don't get you this morning, I just wanted you to know we're in Macon. Bus has had some trouble, and we're stuck a day or two. Love you."

After hanging up, Troy retrieved his notebook from his duffel bag, checked his to-do list and returned the two phone calls he'd missed as he continued closing loops in Texas after his abrupt departure. Then he called Meg's condo again but did not leave a message. He flipped through his notebook and found Macy's number. Shortly after she'd been hired, she'd given it to him in case of an emergency. Troy entered the number, and after four rings, he finally had someone to talk to.

"Hello?"

"Hi. Someone finally answered their phone. Thank you. This is Troy . . . Troy Gorton."

"Yes, Troy, I know who you are."

"This is Macy?"

"It is. I'm glad you called. I've left you a couple messages in Texas. I even tried the number for the portable thingamajig Meg gave me."

"Yeah, so, there's a story about that. It's been in my bag a lot more than usual . . . Anyway, I'm sorry. And I'm worried because she's not answering."

"I know. That's why I've been trying to track you down."

Troy stood. "What's wrong? Where is she? Macy, what's up?"

"She's fine, Troy. She's fine. But she's not home—"

"—Where is she?"

"Just. Easy. She's fine. She's in the hospital. But she's fine."

Troy felt flushed and sat back down on the edge of his bed. "Hospital? Why? Hospital? Macy?" He threw the words at the air like splotches of paint.

"Troy, she's fine—"

"—You keep saying that."

"Because she is. Listen, she had something like a heart attack day before yesterday—"

"—Day before yesterday!?"

"Like I said, Troy, I've tried to find you. But I'm glad we're talking now—"

"—What do you mean by 'like a heart attack'? What is that? What does that mean?"

"It means it was very mild. The hospital brought her in, and they're watching her, but Troy, really, truly, she's okay. I've visited her several times. Going back in a few minutes, in fact, after I run by her place."

Troy pulled the phone away from his ear, tucked his wet hair behind his ears on each side, breathed and caught his reflection in the mirror on the wall at the foot of the bed.

"Hello?" Macy said.

"Sorry," he said. "The news just scared me, I guess. What else can you tell me?"

Macy shared all she knew from the moment Meg arrived in the emergency room, including Macy's hot-headed attempts to sneak past security and the visit by Meg's letter-writing club. "We just don't know exactly when she'll be home. They're 'observing' her, whatever that means, right?"

"So she's totally out of the weeds? Or woods? Or whatever?"

"Well, Troy, I don't think that's true for any of us, ever—certainly not for your mom. But they're keeping great tabs on her. And so am I."

"Thanks, really. Thank you for that. I'm sorry. I just don't . . ."

"Stop. It's all right. You're allowed."

Troy picked up his notebook off the nightstand. "Can I call her room?"

"Of course," Macy said, and she gave him the direct number. "Now how about you? Where are you? How's the trip?"

Troy stood again and stretched. "Long version or short?"

"You choose," she said, and Troy could tell she was smiling.

He dove into the details of the trip since last updating Meg. The detour, the phone, their new friend Mark, the vulture, the hotel, the tension and the dogs. "I suppose to Mom all that matters is that Moses gets there."

"Well that's not true," Macy said. "She's excited to see you all."

"I guess we'll see."

"How's your dad?"

"He's . . . my dad, I guess. He seems to enjoy the detours and disasters more than anything else. But . . . he's trying. Seems to be anyway."

"And Grace?"

"Wow. You know a lot about our family," he said with an inadvertent high chuckle.

"Ha, you have no idea," Macy said. "I mean seriously, Troy. Meg doesn't have a lot of people she really trusts, but she trusts me."

"Good. I'm glad," Troy answered.

"I'm going to run," Macy said after a long pause. "Call Meg, but don't stress her out, okay? No need to overshare. Best she stays calm and cool. You know."

"I know. I will."

"And Troy?"

"Yeah?"

"Don't tell anyone. Just come. Okay? That's what she wants."

Troy sighed, but it was the least surprising thing he'd heard since leaving Woodstock. "I won't."

"Drive safe."

"We will. Thanks, Macy. For everything."

Troy hung up the phone and walked to the window of their sixth-floor room. Next to a sand volleyball pit to the south of the parking lot, he spotted Gary, Grace and Moses sitting at a picnic table. Then he picked up his notebook and added one more item to his growing to-do list.

Tell Grace the truth.

FORTY-SEVEN

Gary and Grace had invited Mark to eat with them in the hotel restaurant again while Troy slept in, but he declined. "Thank you," he said in his now familiar near whisper. "But I'm okay this morning. I have a few snacks in my bag, and I'm going to take Beverage on a long walk."

An hour later Gary and Grace sat at the picnic table outside as Moses napped in the shade off his leash, deep in sleep. They recapped the night before, Troy's odd behavior and their new friend Mark's sweet mission to honor his wife.

"I want a marriage like that," Grace said, picking at wood slivers on the picnic table.

"Good luck," Gary said. "Those are one in a million."

"You really think so?"

Gary laughed. "No, I figure it's more like one in ten." He let the number hang in between them. "Ten million."

"Now, Pop. You know that's not true."

"I figure I've known a lot of people, lots of couples—never known a marriage like what Mark and his wife had. Whose name we don't even know."

Grace nodded and drummed her thumbs on the table. "I think it's sweet, the way he cherishes her. Reveres her."

"Still," Gary said, looking down for a moment at Moses on the ground. "It's more than rare. I figure you might live your whole life and not meet anyone like that. Finishing her list? Trying to still be close to her? Most men aren't that dedicated even when their wives are alive."

Grace grinned, closed an eye and cocked her head to the side. "But most men get second chances. The good ones, anyway."

They sat quietly a while and listened to traffic pick up on the busy road that faced the hotel.

"Can I ask you something, Pop?"

"I figure there's only one answer, Grace."

She winked. "You're smarter in your old age."

"The smartest thing I ever did was marry Meg. I went downhill after that."

"About her," Grace said. "Why do you think she left?"

Gary counted the lines on the backs of his hands.

"Pop?"

Gary shrugged, but at himself more than her. "I don't really know . . . Tired of me, I figure."

Grace leaned across and laid her hand on his. "Wrong. Not tired of you. Not at all."

"How do you figure?" Gary finally looked up and met her eyes with his.

Grace smiled. "Pop, she didn't get tired of you. She just missed who you used to be."

Gary bristled. "And who's that?"

"A man who loved her more than anything. A man who would give up anything and anyone for her . . ." Grace looked back toward the hotel and saw Troy step outside through the automatic doors and walk toward them. "A man who . . ." Grace's voice broke. "Who would take his sweetheart's list after she died—that beautiful notebook—and put it in his pocket . . ." Tears trickled down her left cheek. "And then dedicate himself to visiting those places . . . And why? . . . Because he knows that's where she'll be. Her soul, her spirit, her heart, her memory . . . her love."

As Troy approached, Grace looked toward the road and discretely dried her cheeks, and with her fingertips dabbed unfallen tears from her eyes.

"Am I interrupting something?" Troy asked on arrival.

Gary shook his head. "No, please."

After an awkward moment of silence that felt like a too-long winter, Gary stood and tugged on Moses's leash. "Let's go back to the room and get you some water."

When Gary and Moses were gone, Troy moved to Grace's side of the picnic table. "Can we talk?"

FORTY-EIGHT

An hour after talking to Troy, Macy knocked on Meg's door. "You up?" she said, and she pushed the door open before waiting for a reply.

"I am—literally—up," Meg said with a tired smile. She was standing at the edge of her bed in her hospital gown.

"Are you supposed to be?"

"Nurse told me a few minutes ago I need to walk this morning, before the doctor comes by. I was just about to buzz her."

"Meg Gorton, I think you're supposed to hit the button before you actually get out of bed."

"Technicalities," Meg said, and she pulled at her gown to be sure she was covered. "Want to be my escort?"

"Thought you'd never ask."

They stepped into the hallway and began walking the well-worn route around her floor. "I have good news," Macy said as they passed the nurses' station and Meg got a thumbs-up and a smile from the two who looked up.

"I could use some of that," Meg said.

"Troy called."

Meg stopped and put a hand on the wall. "They're here?" Her voice was breathy and thin—barely a breeze.

"No, no, not yet. He'd been trying your place and leaving messages and getting worried, obviously. So he called me. I'm glad I was there."

"A blessing," Meg said. "Where are they?"

"Now that's a story," Macy teased. "Your heart up for it?" Macy looped an arm inside Meg's, and they rounded their first corner.

A young orderly delivering breakfast to another room passed them and said, "Morning, Mrs. Gorton."

Both women smiled and continued their slow march down the shiny, sanitized hallways. "Spill it," Meg said.

"They've had some . . . detours." Macy detailed her call and skipped ahead to the newer developments from the gang on the bus.

"Gary is going to chuck his phone in the ocean?" Meg said, laughing until she coughed.

"Easy now . . . And yes. He just might. If Troy keeps spending time toying around with it."

Meg shook her head. "All these gadgets people are inventing. They come and go . . . But . . . at least that explains why I wasn't hearing from him. I've been worried," she quietly finished, and it seemed to Macy her friend was really just talking to herself.

"Well, my dear, you'll hear from him today. He promised."

When Macy was done with the recap, Meg stopped again and put her hand on the wall under a framed color photo of some handsome hospital administrator. "So how many days? They can't be long. Macon, you said? That's how far?"

"Troy says it's six hours, depending on the bus and their breaks." Macy paused and watched Meg's mouth and eyes process it all. "They're close."

Meg looked up, nodded, and they resumed their stroll.

"I'm praying, Macy. Praying so hard."

"For what?"

She took a deep, full breath. "To get home."

Macy, arm still looped in Meg's, pulled her close. "I hope you mean home to your condo and not, you know, home . . ." With her other hand she pointed up to heaven.

"You're funny," Meg paused and made eye contact. "Not. That's what the young kids are saying. I know. It's silly."

They took a few more steps and turned left again. A man pulling an IV tipped his imaginary cap.

"I'm only half-kidding, Meg. You know that, right?"

"Oh, I know. I just want to be home, in the condo, living. Not here being . . . monitored . . . observed. The other trip home . . . will happen when it happens. I want the bus to pull up to the condo, not a hospital. And I want to meet them outside. I want him to jump up on me—"

"Your husband?" Macy stopped and feigned surprise.

"You're on a roll today," Meg said. "Please. You know what I mean. I want him to wag his tail and lick my hands and face."

"Gary? Gross."

Meg laughed so hard a nurse poked her head out of a room to be sure everything was all right.

"We're fine," Macy said. "Seriously, Meg. You need to clarify these things."

They walked on, waved at some children trying not to race each other down the hallway, and watched as two teens pressed an elevator button as if playing a video game.

When they rounded the final corner onto their hallway, Macy noticed Meg's eyes were wet. "You okay?" Macy asked, leaning in and nudging her slightly with her shoulder.

Silence.

"Meg? Talk to me." They moved in unison—an accidental marching band—and in a dozen more steps arrived at Meg's door. "Meg?"

Finally Meg looked up and met Macy's stare. The tears in Meg's eyes were stuck in place, as if she'd threatened them not to give in to gravity. "How does this end?" Meg said.

"Oh, Meg, I don't know. In your front yard, I hope, with the people— and pooch—that you still love gathered around you."

Meg nodded so subtly—like she had a sweet secret. "I hope you're right."

Macy pulled her friend into a hug and didn't fight her own tears. There was more to say, but both women knew the moment didn't call for words. Instead they walked into the room, Macy helped Meg back into bed, and they sat quietly, considering what had been and what was to come.

After a quick visit from the doctor, the phone rang, and Meg melted at the sound of Troy's voice. "I am . . . so glad to hear from you."

Macy listened to one side of the call and quietly imagined the other.

"I know," Meg said. "Macy told me the story. I wouldn't test that father of yours . . . Oh really? I thought you were sleeping on the bus? . . . Must be much more comfortable then . . . What about a car? Or some- thing else? Can you just come and pick up the bus later?"

In her head, Macy heard Troy telling his mother what she already knew. For Gary it was the bus or nothing.

"I know . . . Just seems . . . pigheaded . . . I know. I'm sorry. I know."

Macy mouthed "Thank you" when someone came to retrieve Meg's breakfast tray and left a form for lunch.

"Have you talked to him yet?" Meg said. "Troy, what are you waiting for? What else do you have to do while you wait?"

Macy smiled as she predicted Troy's response. *Let's see . . . there's*

Grace, a hitchhiker, two dogs, his own troubled dad, bus trouble, motels, hotels, the unknown, the tension.

"Now, Troy," Meg said.

Macy crossed her arms, closed an eye and hugged the moment.

"Now, Troy," Meg said again.

A few minutes later the call ended with another "I love you. See you soon," and Meg settled into her pillow and rolled onto her side. "Oh, Macy. How does this end?"

FORTY-NINE

Troy and Grace sat side-by-side at the picnic table with their backs to the hotel. They watched traffic, counted cars and followed the flaps and heard the tweets of birds in the trees. For a long time they heard everything but the sound of one another's voices.

Troy wore a Shenandoah Senators cap and moved it from his knee to his head several times. At last, only after Grace thought she'd tortured him long enough, she bumped her leg into his. "So you know you called this meeting, right?"

Troy put the cap back on his knee and tucked his long hair behind his ears. "I know."

Another minute passed. More chirps and beeps, a siren in the distance that seemed to get closer but never appeared. "So?" Grace said, arms crossed, one eye closed, head tilted, hair hung and teased around her neck.

"About last night," Troy said.

She straightened up, leaned her arm on the table and turned toward him. "That's a good place to start."

"Right . . . I know . . . It was . . ." He put the hat back on his head and spun it backward.

"One of the rudest, most disrespectful things I've ever seen from you?"

Troy's eyes flew open, but his mouth did not.

"And embarrassing to the rest of us?" Grace added. "And a reminder of . . ."

"Of?" He asked.

"Of how . . . different . . . you can be."

Troy pulled the cap off again and picked at the embroidered Senators patch. "I was going to say that it was . . . handled poorly," he said with a thin grin.

"Then you're welcome. I said it for you."

More silence. More quiet memories.

"Grace, I'm sorry. It was strange. Strange timing?" He was asking, but he didn't know why.

"You're in the public eye, Troy. It's always going to be strange."

"I don't think being a minor league ballplayer qualifies as being 'in the public eye.'"

"Huh," Grace said, and she looked back to the bustling road that fronted the hotel. "You were in public, and a fan—"

"—Scout."

"Fan."

"Grace, he's just a scout."

"Troy, I don't care if he's a Girl Scout with a JanSport backpack full of Thin Mints. He was so obviously a fan too."

"Nice, and by the way, I could handle a couple boxes about now."

Grace smiled, but it was slight, simple—a spoiler for what Troy hoped would follow. "I bet you could," she said.

A stout man in holey sweatpants and a blue tank top approached.

"A few dollars?" The words spilled out of his mouth like alcohol. "A few dollars? Please? For a meal?"

"Not this time," Troy said, and the drunken man nearly tripped on his own feet as he turned to walk away. The man cursed and looked back over his shoulder once before plopping on the curb at the edge of the lot. He sat against a tree and spoke to his hands.

"Not even a few bucks for that man? You're either not the same Troy or you're . . . distracted."

"Maybe a little of both," Troy said, embarrassment in his eyes.

"I doubt that. But go on, " Grace pressed. "What was that all about last night at dinner?"

"I get it. I was rude. I was caught off guard. It had been a weird, long day—"

"—Week. You mean week," Grace said.

"And maybe more. Nothing's been right since Texas."

"So why'd you leave?" she asked, and she pivoted again in his direction.

The wind stopped, and stale, humid air fell on them both. Troy set his cap on the table behind him. "I hate baseball," Troy finally said.

Grace waited, watched.

Troy turned his head and faced her—their faces a foot apart. "I hate baseball. I do."

"Troy—"

"—Hold up. I don't really *hate* baseball, like hate hate."

Grace's brow wrinkled and shrunk. "I'm lost."

"I love baseball. I do. I've always loved baseball."

"Hmm," Grace said, and she briefly glanced away and then back to meet his eyes. "Nope, still lost."

"Grace, I haven't loved baseball for so long."

"How long?"

He exhaled—the breath like an innocent man finally exonerated. "A long time, Grace."

"So why? Why keep playing?"

Troy reached over his head and grabbed the cap. He held it in front of his chest and spun it slowly, like a piece of evidence. "Do you know what it's like to play for someone else?"

"I suppose lots of people do that. Play for a crowd. A coach. Whatever."

"No, I mean really play *for* someone else. Every pitch, every out, every inning, every ridiculous game. Played for them."

"You mean your dad?" Grace said.

"Yeah, and his dad. And probably his dad. And who knows how many other Gortons throughout history. Game was probably invented by a Gorton."

"Pretty sure it was Doc Adams—"

"—Really, Grace? Seriously?"

Another beat passed. "So this . . ." She gestured to the space around them with both hands, palms facing the sky. "This is what?"

"This is for Mom. This isn't about baseball."

"Right, but Troy, you came home because you're hurt. Your life has been . . . baseball."

Troy let loose a smile so wide it freed his face. "Exactly! But why?"

"Because you love it? Or hate it? Or . . . I'm not even sure," she was gesturing to the air again, making a case she didn't understand herself.

"Grace, I've played baseball my entire life."

"And you're good, Troy. Don't let your shoulder tell you you're not."

"Grace, you're not hearing me. I played for a few years as a kid because I actually enjoyed it. Dad loved watching me, and it connected us, because you know he was just, like, so friggin' old. I mean so much older than my friends' dads. You know how bizarre it was to be in high school and have parents in the stands who aren't really your parents?"

"Wait, wait, wait. Yes, they are. We've had this conversation a hundred times since what, middle school?"

"Sure, I know. They're my mom and dad, always have been, at least since my mother died and my father took off. But when you're a kid, your friends don't care about anything other than why my pushy grandpa thinks he knows more about baseball and our team than the coaches."

"Well, in fairness, Troy, he probably did."

Troy laughed and looked up. "Fair . . . But you get it, right? I was that kid with the obnoxious grandpa who was also my dad who was also sometimes my coach. So I played and kept playing more and more, and it's what we had together. I heard all the stories about his dad and the war and our family legacy and . . ."

"And you've always been *the one*," Grace said.

"But I'm not. I know I'm not. I'm no better than any of them . . And you know what I wanted? Like all I ever really wanted?" He faced her again. "Just to play well enough that my birth father would care enough." Troy's voice trailed off, and he looked straight ahead to the road. "I didn't care about being *the one* to make it. I just wanted to be the one he came home for."

Grace slid close, their hips touching, and studied the road too.

"I used to think that if I pitched a no-hitter, my birth father would come back. So I did—five of them in high school. And he never came. Then I went for a perfect game . . ."

"Like the one you almost had in Texas," Grace said.

"Yes, like the one I almost had in Texas. But he didn't come. Didn't write. Didn't anything. I spent an entire fall and winter in a batting cage my first year after graduation. I thought maybe if my game were more complete. If I could swing the bat. Like really hit. Hitters are more flashy, right? And I got good."

"You got *great* at the plate," Grace corrected.

"And nothing. All I did was get Pop's hopes up that I could be *the one*. It's been nothing but cleats and new gloves and pressure since Little League."

Grace put her right arm around his broad frame. "What about your shoulder? How is it?"

Troy grinned but did not face her. "It's fine. Perfect. I'm probably healthier than I've ever been."

Across the lot, Grace and Troy watched the homeless man stand and stagger toward the highway. When he got to the guardrail, he sat and sipped on what looked at a distance like a flask. Then he looked up at heaven and began screaming something they couldn't quite understand. "So, you're not hurt?"

Troy shook his head.

"Not hurt at all?"

"Nope."

"Would you like to be?" Grace said, and she punched his bicep.

"Easy. I said I'm sorry."

"Not for this," she said. "Really, Troy. You've been keeping this up for Pop? And for your birth father who ran out on you when your mom was killed?"

"And for you . . ." Troy confessed.

"Absolutely not. Not for me."

"Why not? You loved me playing too. Right?"

"Hold on now. I loved you. You. Troy Gorton. Baseball wasn't you. That was just something you did. I grew to appreciate it because I loved you. Not the other way around."

They sat in peace, reflecting and replaying scenes from their lives.

Some a decade old, some so fresh the words hadn't been blown away yet. Behind them, Gary walked from the hotel's main entrance and approached the picnic table.

"Troy, you have to tell your dad. You have to stop pretending to be something you're not."

"I don't think it's that easy, Grace. This is who I am. If I'm not a baseball player, what's left?"

"Yes! Ask that. See who else is in there. You said you still love it—parts of it—so start there."

Gary was now behind them, ten feet from their table. Moses was inside the room, stretched on the bed, cool and well fed.

"Just tell him. Everything. All of it. About the shoulder. The pressure."

Troy exhaled again, and the hat went back on his head. "Just like that?"

Gary's face, faith and heart fell to the earth. He took ten steps backward, his feet light on the pavement. Then he stopped, saw Mark and Beverage returning from their walk, stood straight and took a single, small step forward. "Hey, can I join you?"

FIFTY

Moses hadn't slept long. He loved the bed and the air-conditioning—
he wouldn't deny that. But he didn't like being alone. He took a drink
from his dish, carefully left out on a folded bath towel in the corner of the
hotel room. Drool hung from his mouth, and he left a trail of drips and
drops between his dish and the window that overlooked the parking lot.
It stretched almost the entire length of the exterior wall, and Moses had
left nose prints and slobber from one side to the other.

He saw Troy, Grace and Gary sitting at a picnic table, and even
though he knew the afternoon heat was knocking at the door, he still
wished he were with them. At their feet, under the table, hearing every
word, understanding more than they knew and waiting for Beverage.

Moses sat and breathed, fogging the glass in a round, cloud pattern.
The air-conditioning was cool enough that his breath cleared quickly.
Even Moses recognized it was like watching a snow globe that every few
seconds was shaken and then settled.

What am I missing? Baseball? The bus? Meg? Mostly he wondered if
life would soon return to the good days when young Moses had owned

his front yard in Woodstock and they resembled the other families he saw in the neighborhood or at the games.

At the front of the parking lot, Moses saw the scraggly man in the tank top sitting on a guardrail. Moses stopped breathing and enjoyed a longer, clearer view through the window. His lungs were still, but his mind was racing. His tail went walk-the-plank straight.

Mark and Beverage also came into view, and Moses could tell Beverage was enjoying every last second and step of their walk. Beverage sniffed, pulled on the leash and nudged litter with her nose. As they approached the middle of Moses's view, it seemed Beverage had spotted the tank-top man on the guardrail. She watched him, judged him, and Moses saw the man stand and move closer. Mark and Beverage walked on a narrow patch of median, and Moses watched the space between the two men shrink until he didn't have to move his eyes back and forth to see them both.

Moses looked left to the picnic table and saw his people talking. Troy and Grace were sitting close on their side of the table, and Moses blinked in approval.

He looked back up an inch or two, and as another breath cloud cleared, he saw the distance between Mark and the new man was almost nothing. Moses barked. *What's happening?* He barked again, but no one looked.

He couldn't hear her, but it was clear from her pose and face that Beverage was now barking too. She pulled at the leash and was flashing her teeth in anger.

The tank-top man raised his hands up to the sky and seemed to be angry with the clouds. He pounded his fists in the air and moved toward Mark.

Mark backed up, pulled on the leash, put his other hand up in the air—not in anger, but kindness.

Then the tank-top man lunged forward.

Moses barked again and ran to the hotel-room door. He put a paw up on the door—he didn't know why—but nothing happened. He raced back to the window and saw Grace running toward the hotel and Troy and Gary racing toward the road.

Mark was on his back looking at heaven.

The tank-top man pulled something from Mark's pocket and shoved it into his. Then he stumbled away, something shiny and sharp in one hand.

Beverage was standing next to Mark's head, licking his face, sticking her snout in Mark's bushy reddish beard.

Troy and Gary knelt at Mark's side. Troy's hands were wet and thick with something.

Moses barked again. Then again, again and again.

Across the busy intersection, the tank-top man sat against a fire hydrant and seemed to be singing at the sky. Three cars had stopped in the road next to Mark. Two more had pulled into the hotel parking lot.

Moses had never felt so helpless.

Cars and trucks and people arrived. Red and blue lights flashed across their hoods and faces. Gary and Troy stood close to one another. Grace returned. She moved in between them, her hands on her face. Their arms pulled her into a huddle.

The tank-top man was knocked to his side, turned over. A knee placed on his back. His arms pulled behind him. His hands tied. His singing hadn't stopped.

More people came, and Moses's throat, teeth and tongue hurt from barks and growls and anger that went unheard.

Soon the tank-top man was bent into the back of a police car.

People with matching jackets lifted Mark on a board, and he

disappeared inside one of the big trucks with flashing lights. Then more noises, lights and commotion, and the vehicle Mark was in left as fast as it came.

Moses watched the caravan of chaos disappear down the highway.

Then he did the only thing that seemed appropriate for a dog watching helplessly from a distance—he howled toward heaven.

FIFTY-ONE

Beverage planted her paws like talons in the pavement and guarded the darkening pool of blood on the ground. She growled, snarled and threatened to punish anyone who approached.

"Someone get that dog out of here!" a deputy yelled. Gary and the others stood nearby, processing, watching, wondering what had gone wrong. "Someone call animal control!" the deputy barked.

"Wait, wait," Gary said, stepping back into the circle. "This is Mark's dog. Don't call animal control. We'll take her."

The deputy looked at the other first responders still on scene. "Guys? We got next of kin yet? In case the victim doesn't make it?"

"You won't find anyone," Gary said. "He was alone."

"Homeless?" the deputy asked.

"Yes, technically, but not exactly. He's . . . traveling with us."

A much younger deputy reached in quickly to grab Beverage's collar, but the dog snapped and nipped his hand. "For cryin'!" He kicked Beverage away, and Gary rushed forward and put his hands on the deputy's chest.

"Whoa, whoa, come on. Easy there. Stop."

"Sir, back away. Back away, now. Hands off, now."

Gary stepped back, hands up in surrender, then bent down and calmed the dog.

"This mutt is gone," the young deputy said, and he shouted over his shoulder. "Call it in. This thing bit me."

Gary motioned for Troy to come closer and stay with Beverage. "Deputies, officers, whichever—look, the dog is losing her mind." Gary approached again with his hands extended. "Her owner was just stabbed in front of her, all right? We'll take her. Don't call animal control. *Please.*"

"We have no choice. She bit someone, a deputy even."

"Please," Gary said, and he nodded at Troy to begin backing away with Beverage, his big hand looped into the dog's collar. "He's fine. Your guy over there? Didn't even break the skin. I figure he provoked her anyway. Please? We'll walk away . . . *Please.*" Gary's voice dipped and pleaded.

Beverage's bark returned with energy and force, and she pulled hard on the collar, willing herself to where Mark's body had been.

"Shut the dog up!" the nipped deputy yelled. "Shut! Her! Up!"

Gary moved closer and pleaded with his eyes again for Troy to retreat. "Gentlemen, please."

"Back up," the more senior deputy said. "Back. Up."

But Gary persisted, and Troy successfully pulled Beverage back to the picnic table, where Grace grieved and watched in disbelief. Troy sat and lifted the big dog onto his lap. They stroked her back, and Grace began humming something only she knew.

"Please. We know this man. We know the dog. We know them. Let us take her with us. We'll be out of town tomorrow. We're just passing through. We're guests here at the hotel."

"Take another step, and you'll be a guest someplace else," the younger deputy said, his face red and his eyes wide.

Later, when Gary would retell the story, he'd say he didn't know why he took another step. But he did.

It took less than five seconds for Gary to find himself on the ground, his hands behind him, cold cuffs on his wrists. "Come on. Is this—"

"—Time to stop talking," the deputy said. As Troy, Grace and Beverage watched from thirty yards away, Gary was read his rights, charged with failure to obey, pulled to his feet and tossed into one of the waiting vehicles.

From his spot in the hotel room, high above the ground, snout pressed to the window, Moses watched the scene unfold. *Where's he going?* Moses wondered. *Why's he leaving me?*

For the next hour, Troy and Grace gave witness statements on Mark's attack and swapped contact information with police. Gary gave his statement from the back of the cruiser.

The army of vehicles thinned. Someone in a jacket entered the hotel and later walked out with Mark's duffel bag in one hand and a white bag in the other. Someone else, this one with a camera, took pictures of the ground, the traffic, the fire hydrant, something in the grass near the spot they tackled the tank-top man.

Another new vehicle arrived, and someone with thick sleeves on his arms approached Troy, Grace and Beverage. The person attached a strange collar to the dog and pulled her away. Troy looked like he was shouting, the veins in his neck popping, and Grace's face was again covered with her hands.

Beverage was forced into a metal cage attached to the back of the new vehicle, and unlike the others, it quickly left the hotel parking lot.

Moses watched it roll out of sight, and he noticed his people were watching too.

Please stay, Moses thought.

FIFTY-TWO

Later that afternoon in Gulf Breeze, Macy organized a cleaning and decorating party at Meg's condo. Kaitie and Veda were the only members of the LWCOGB available, and they stood in the kitchen. "Okay, team. Thanks for coming. There's not all that much to do, but she'll appreciate this."

"You're sure?" Veda asked.

"Well, even if she doesn't, there's only so much she can say. Doctor told her to take it easy and keep the stress down."

"Uh-oh," Kaitie said. "Should I cancel the cake and dancers?"

Veda groaned, and Macy giggled. "Maybe give it a week or two," Macy said.

"Got it," Kaitie said, and she pulled an invisible pencil from behind her ear and made a note on an invisible pad.

"Meg keeps a clean house, as you know, but I thought a deep clean and a little extra TLC would make her smile when she comes home. Let's get it done."

For two hours the three women dusted, vacuumed, wiped down

surfaces and pulled weeds out front. When they were done, they sat at the table and cut out construction-paper hearts and added encouraging magic-marker messages on them. Then they covered the front door with dozens of the hearts until all that was visible was the gold-colored knob.

Before leaving, they sat in the living room, and with Sandi's urn watching them from the mantel, they talked about the club and the topic most on everyone's mind—the bus to Gulf Breeze. "I think it'll all work out," Kaitie said, sitting in Meg's recliner and kicking out the footrest.

"It?" Macy asked from her spot in Sandi's recliner.

"All of . . . this," Kaitie said. "I think it works. Meg's husband pulls up—"

"And son," Veda added.

"And son's high school sweetheart," Macy added, pointing up as if scoring a point.

"Yes—son, girlfriend—"

"—Don't forget the dog," Veda said, sitting forward on the couch, legs close together and fingers crossed on her lap.

"And Moses, of course."

"Aaaaand the hitchhiker," Macy added. "And the hitchhiker's dog."

"Good grief, yes. All of them. The bus arrives, they pour out, and they all live happily ever after."

"Well I don't know about all that," Veda said, adjusting an earring that didn't need adjusting.

"So what say you then?" Kaitie asked.

"Me? Oh, I don't know . . . I choose to believe it will all work out, but nothing is ever as easy as we think."

"How insightful," Kaitie said, and even Sandi's ashes knew she was being sarcastic.

Veda slid back into the crease of the sofa. "Maybe I'm wrong. Just seems it's more likely than not that it gets harder before it gets easier. I love a happy ending as much as anyone, but those stories don't happen very often anymore, do they . . ."

Looking up at the ceiling, still reclined, Kaitie called out to Macy. "What do you think?"

"Happy endings? I'm a sucker for them. I saw the movie *Splash* five times in theaters."

Kaitie disappeared behind her eyes a moment. "Oh yes. Tom Hanks. Just give me a minute, girls . . ." After another pause she blinked open her eyes. "Right. So yes, that's great. Happy, sappy endings and all. But how do you think this one plays out? Will this work? This weird family reunion?"

Macy let air escape through her lips like a chatty horse. "Oh, who knows? I hope so?"

"You can do better than that. Even President Veda here beat *that* prediction."

Macy grinned. "Ladies, I have no earthly idea. I want it to work. I've pushed and prodded Meg along since Sandi died. I've cried and laughed and everything in between . . ."

They sat, let the ceiling fan ruffle their hair, looked at photos on the wall and silently imagined their own versions of what was to come. Then Kaitie chipped at the moment. "You ever think how much easier life would be if we never grew up?"

Neither Macy nor Veda spoke up.

"Seriously, sisters. If we were all kids again, solving problems on the playground, loving everyone. No judgment, no baggage. If we went back in time and could live again, I'd have so much more fun. I'd never have another argument or criticize someone for doing things differently than I would. I'd go to the beach every day."

Veda offered something between a snort and a chuckle. "Don't you go to the beach every day already?"

"Yes, precisely. But not always. This is the new me," she said with a laugh.

Another season of silence passed. "I suppose you're not completely wrong," Veda said, and Kaitie pulled her footrest down and sat up.

"Come again?"

"I remember being little. I remember life was easier. Make people happy. Love your parents. Be whoever you want to be before you grow up and realize you can't."

As Veda and Kaitie explored the topic, Macy's mind began to drift. *They're right,* she thought. *How I'd love to be a little girl all over again.*

FIFTY-THREE

Ninety minutes after Mark and Beverage had been taken away, the others gathered in Grace's hotel room and shared shock, awe and pizza. "You're lucky, Pop," Troy said.

"How do you figure?" Gary said, shoving a folded piece of pepperoni and sausage pizza into his mouth. Grease dripped from the back and landed on his shirt, but he didn't notice and wouldn't have cared even if he had.

"Come on, Pop. They wanted to take you, charge you with who knows what, make a point, you know. Send a message."

"A point about what? Those guys had no business taking Mark's dog. They're staring at a possible what—murder? And worrying about a mutt . . . Plus, I was never worried," Gary said, and Moses hopped off the extra bed and went back to the window to watch and wait.

"Right. Keep telling yourself that, Pop."

They ate quietly and nursed cold bottles of overpriced soda from the small market in the hotel lobby. Grace picked and nibbled on bits of crust from the thick end of her pizza and tossed pieces of pepperoni to Moses, which he ignored.

At one point, all three realized they were watching Moses stare out at the parking lot. It was just after six in the evening, and the hotel had started filling with new guests for the night. "He's not himself, is he?" Troy said.

"No, sure isn't. Poor guy," Gary said.

After another stride of silence and Moses watching, Grace wiped her hands and tossed the tattered remains of her dinner into the box, closed it and pushed it away to the foot of the bed. Then she scooted back and leaned into the headboard. "None of us are."

Gary nodded. "I figure you're right."

Grace rubbed her face, as if trying to wake up everything inside her. "I just don't know why . . . We don't even know that man's name. They threw him in a car and now what . . ."

"Prison," Troy said. "For a long time."

"How long?" Grace asked.

"That depends. If Mark dies? Forever."

Grace closed her eyes. "But why. Why . . . why Mark? An innocent, sweet man. The sweetest."

Troy tossed his empty Mountain Dew bottle at the trash can by the television and missed. "For a few bucks, I guess. He took Mark's wallet but didn't even have time to spend whatever he stole. I know that's really not the answer we want. But stuff happens, right, Pop? Random stuff. Stuff you can't explain. Stuff that's all about a few dollars. But you gotta move on. Recognize some things just . . . happen."

Gary nodded and looked back at Moses.

Grace spoke again, and each word was weaker than the next—like bricks in a dam already leaking. "You guys . . . I liked Mark. So much.

He was such a special man. A friend . . . already. And now he's . . . just gone—"

"—We don't know that yet," Gary clipped. "He was hanging in there. We'll head over later and check. I feel good about it. I do."

They sat in silence for the longest minute of the day.

"It's—I don't really know how to say it—just bizarre," Troy finally said. "That this guy we just met—what, two days ago—became a friend." Troy also looked back toward Moses. "I liked him too. His honesty. His mission."

"And now his best friend, that adorable dog. We never even got the story of her name." Grace's voice cracked again. "They're going to put Beverage down. I just know it."

Neither man corrected her, and another minute of silence passed.

"I've never seen anything like that. Anything so senseless," Grace said. "It was so horrible. So, so horrible."

Gary nodded with his eyes, his head, his memories.

Troy nodded too, then said, "I've been thinking about my mother today."

"Meg?" Grace asked.

Troy shook his head. "Sure, her too. But no, my birth mother."

"Really?" Gary asked.

"Mm-hmm. She's the only person I've ever really known who's died . . . And I didn't even really know her."

Grace smiled at Troy, not with her mouth but with eyes that loved both him and his past. "It's a strange thing, isn't it? Loving someone you barely know. A mother. A hitchhiker. A dog."

Gary looked at Grace, and she saw the question form and fly. "So why not someone you've known almost a lifetime? Why would it be easier to love a stranger than a wife?"

"Pop—" Troy said.

"—No, it's okay," Grace said as she sat up. "That's totally fair. But I wonder the same thing. Why did you stop loving Meg?"

Gary twisted off the cap of his Diet Dr. Pepper, took a sip and replaced it. "I have never, ever said I stopped loving her. It just got . . . harder."

"Why?" Grace asked.

"I didn't make it easy for her. And she chose to leave."

Grace answered Gary, but her eyes drifted to Troy. "Did she?"

"Of course. Yes. She got in her sister's car and never looked back."

"Huh. Well, Pop," Troy said, "she's looking back now."

Gary pointed at Moses with his drink bottle. "She's looking back at him. For him. To see him."

"Oh please," Troy groaned, and he threw a wadded-up napkin at Gary. "Keep telling yourself that too."

When Grace excused herself to go to the bathroom, Gary stood and moved to the window. He scratched Moses's head with one hand and plunged the other into the pocket of his shorts. He looked at the spot in the lot where their trip had turned on its head and then down at Moses. "Mo, I've made a decision . . . It's not going to be easy, but I'm going to leave you with Meg."

Moses looked up at the sweet sound of his name.

"Really?" Troy said.

"Really what?" Grace asked as she emerged from the bathroom.

Gary, still looking out the dirty window, breathed calmly through his nose. "I want Meg to have Moses." He turned to face Grace and Troy. "I want her to have a friend. I figure it might . . . make things better. She can have the dog. Maybe I should have done that when she left. Or right after Sandi died. I don't know."

"Pop, are you sure?" Troy asked.

"Not really. But yes. If it's what she wants. If it fixes things."

Grace walked across the room and put her arms around Gary. While still hugging him, she softly said, "Maybe it's a start, Pop. But she might want more than that. Might need more. But for now, what you're feeling, what you did today for Mark and Beverage." She pulled back from his chest enough to look up into his eyes. "Whether you know it or not, that is what love is."

FIFTY-FOUR

Day Seven

The next time they saw one another, Gary, Grace and Troy were again gathered around food. They'd all slept in and met for a late breakfast in the hotel restaurant.

"How'd you sleep?" Gary asked as Grace slid into her chair.

"Late, but not good. I tossed and turned. Kept seeing Mark and that man. And Beverage. Ahhh. I just want to go."

"Speaking of which, I've got news. I was just telling Troy when you walked up. The Cash guy from the shop called. The windshield came in this morning—quick installation, and we can head over this afternoon and pick up the bus."

"Thank heaven," Grace said. "I'm not cut out for this hotel life."

The server poured orange juice for Grace and Troy and cranberry juice for Gary. "Never thought I'd say I'm ready to get back on the bus," Troy noted. "But I am ready to get out of Macon."

They ordered and discussed their plans for the day. They'd check out at noon, leaving their things at the front desk, and Gary would take a cab back to Ruby's. Troy would walk Moses, and Grace would call the hospital and see what information she could extract about Mark. When Gary returned with the bus, they'd load up, roll out and watch Macon fade in the rearview mirror.

Grace twirled her fork in between her fingers. "I feel sick about Mark. And his things. They'll just toss it all. I bet they do."

A thirty-something-year-old woman passed the table and smiled at Troy with every part of her face. Troy politely nodded, and Grace rolled her eyes. "All we can do is our best," Troy said. "I get that this is all so bizarre, but what else is there?"

"I know," Grace said with a sigh. "I know. Just all they know about him is what we told them and what's in his pockets. What do they do if he passes? Have a service? Have anything?" She asked these and other questions she already knew the answer to. "I just wish there was something more we could do . . ."

Soon the server left their meals and promised to check back. "So, I called Mom. Just wanted everyone to know. Didn't want anyone surprised or anything. She's—"

"—Caught up," Grace said, pushing eggs around her plate.

"Yes," Troy said. After everything they'd been through, he'd decided his mother's scare and trip to the hospital didn't need to be shared just yet. "It was earlier yesterday, before Mark. But she knows what's up with the bus and everything. She's getting excited to see us."

Gary, seeing Troy unintentionally leave a door open, stepped in. "You update her on your shoulder?"

Troy looked up from his Belgian waffle. "What do you mean?"

"I mean she knows you came home to Woodstock injured and you're trying to get better, so I figure she would want to know how her favorite ballplayer's doing."

"Right. Well yeah, sure, we talked about all that," Troy said, and his glance at Grace was anything but subtle.

Not now, Gary thought. The trip, the drama of the day before, the bus, the conflict and seeing Grace cry several times since she'd boarded the bus to Gulf Breeze had taken more of a toll on Gary than he'd realized. *Not now.*

FIFTY-FIVE

Macy walked into Meg's room just after one in the afternoon with Chick-fil-A nuggets and lemonade for two. "I went across the bridge to Pensacola for you," she said as she pulled the curtain aside. "I must really love—oh, whoops. I'm sorry."

"You're fine," a doctor who Macy had never met said, turning and smiling. "We're wrapping up."

"Hallelujah. 'Wrapping up' like 'she can go home'?"

"Not quite," the doctor said. "And you are . . . ?" The doctor looked at Meg, smiled, then turned back to Macy. "A doctor?"

"No, no, no." Macy waved her hands as if to wipe the confusion from an invisible whiteboard. Then she extended her hand. "I'm Macy, Meg's home health aide."

The doctor shook her hand. "Dr. Underhill. Nice to meet you. Though I've heard your name in the hospital a few times already this week."

"Oh really?" Macy's hands went to her hips, and she playfully glared at Meg in bed.

Meg shrugged.

"I'll deal with you later," Macy teased, and she placed their lunch and the cardboard drink carrier on Meg's bedside table. "So what's the holdup, doc?"

Dr. Underhill stole a glance at Meg, and she nodded. "Mrs. Gorton is doing well. We just want to monitor her oxygen and heart another day or two. Though her event was very mild, she's high risk at her age. So . . ." The doctor looked back down at Meg. "Why not be careful? From what I can gather, life's a bit less . . . stressful here than at home." Dr. Underhill looked up at Macy. "Fair to say?"

Macy frowned. "What do you think, Meg? You ready to go home?"

Meg pressed the button on her bed controller and sat up. "I do, yes. I feel better. Slept better last night, in fact."

Dr. Underhill appeared to check the numbers on the monitors on the other side of Meg's bed. "One more day. Maybe tomorrow, later in the day? If things look good."

Meg nodded, thanked the doctor and stuck her straw in her lemonade. When Dr. Underhill said goodbye, Macy followed her into the hallway and let the heavy door close behind them. "Doctor, is there anything we don't know?"

"Excuse me?"

"Anything you're not telling us?"

"Mrs. Gorton knows where she stands. She needs to take it easy. One more day can't hurt."

Macy took a deep breath and let her frustration escape through a long, loud exhale. "Is there a reason she can't just walk out?"

"Excuse me?"

"She could walk out today, right? Without being discharged?"

"Of course, but if you work in healthcare at all, you know it's best to—"

"—Listen to your patients? Yes, it is."

Dr. Underhill, standing several inches taller than Macy, placed her hand on her shoulder. "You care for your client—"

"—Friend."

"Sure. Friend. And you want the best. But we must remember the stakes are high, right?"

"Yes, they are," Macy said. "And because they're high, she needs to be home as soon as possible. It's what she wants . . . It's what we all want."

FIFTY-SIX

It was almost closing time when Gary finally picked up the bus, said goodbye to the crew at Ruby's Repairs and returned to gather up the others. Moses sat in the grass by one of the hotel's side entrances while the adults loaded up. He stared at the road that faced the hotel, the place where it had happened, the place he would never forget. After a full day of trying to convince himself it hadn't really happened, the reality of Mark's attack and Beverage's being taken away was now etched in Moses's mind.

"The gang at Ruby's gave me directions to the hospital," Gary said. "So I stopped, and of course they wouldn't tell me much except that he's hanging pretty tough. Lost a lot of blood, obviously."

"Well, that's something, right?" Grace said. "That he's fighting? That's amazing, actually."

"One of the nurses in the ICU gave me a number to call in a day or two, but no promises. Another lady came over and asked me about a hundred questions about Mark and what we knew. Addresses, next of kin, all that."

"Bet that was a short conversation," Troy said, appearing around the corner of the bus.

"Very," Gary said, and he circled the bus a final time—a pilot in pre-flight. "I don't think we'll get far tonight, I figure."

"Don't even care," Grace said. Just put this place on the map behind us. Ten miles, five miles, who even cares? Just get us closer to Gulf Breeze." She stopped and stooped over to love Moses's back and spot behind his ears. "Right, Moses? Let's get to Meg. Let's get to the beach. You ever seen the beach?"

Moses licked her hand. *Thank you,* he thought. For the first time since Meg had stood on their Woodstock walkway, halfway between the house and the road to Florida, Moses felt a longing and pain. They were leaving, but not everyone was getting back on the bus.

Moses was off his leash when his people all stepped up into the bus, and Troy, last of the three to board, looked at Moses from the bottom step. "Come on, Mo. We can't stay."

Stay, Moses thought.

"We gotta go, Moses. It's time. You wanna nap in the back?"

Stay.

"Let's go. Come on," Troy said. "You can't stay here."

Stay.

"Just go get him, Troy. Let's get going. I want some road under us before we stop for the night."

"Let me," Grace said, and she squeezed by Troy on the bus steps.

Instead of just bending over, Grace sat next to Moses, her tan, bare legs stretched out in front of her on the perfectly cut grass and her feet crossed.

Moses leaned into her and put his head in the nape of her neck. *Stay,* he thought again.

"I know it's not easy," Grace said, and she motioned with a flip of her hand for Troy to back off and give them some privacy. "Moses." She put her hands on his head and placed her forehead against his. "I know this is really hard. I miss him too. Both of them." With their heads still snug together, she began scratching behind both of his thick ears. "They were sweet, weren't they? But we need to go be with your family. The rest of your family. You miss Meg too, don't you, Mo?"

Please stay.

"I promise we'll be okay, Moses. No one will ever take you away. Never. I won't let anything happen to you or those silly boys on the bus. Pop's going to make everything right, you know?" She peeked up at the bus and saw both Gary and Troy watching them through the windows of back-to-back seats. "Pop's got a plan, I promise."

Moses pulled his head back and locked eyes with Grace.

"He does, and I do too . . . But we've got to get on the bus. You've got to choose, Moses, to get on. It's always better when we choose." Grace felt another storm of loss gathering and threatening to stall the moment. She shook it off, hopped to her feet, crossed her arms, closed one eye and tilted her head. "How 'bout a deal?"

Moses stood on all fours, and his ears saluted the sky.

"You hop on board, and at our first stop, you get bacon."

Moses hadn't heard the word. He knew where they were headed and why, and he knew that soon he wouldn't just hear Meg's name—he'd see her face and smell her hands. He'd been happy with Gary in Virginia since she'd left, but it hadn't felt complete, and he'd always known it wouldn't be—couldn't be—until they were a family again.

Go, he finally thought.

FIFTY-SEVEN

After just one pit stop to grab dinner and snacks for Moses—including all the bacon from Troy and Gary's bacon double cheeseburgers—the bus crossed the Georgia-Florida line and stopped near Marianna. No one had said much to each other over the two hundred miles.

Troy reviewed for the second time that day his list of unfinished business in Texas and reminded himself to call the hospital at least one more time to check on the young girl from the crash. Troy hadn't prayed with much energy or heart since high school, but since leaving the Shenandoah Valley, he'd found reason to dig deep every single day. The girl Moses had saved—with some help from Troy—was the frequent subject of what he considered clunky calls to heaven.

Grace read for much of the evening, until the summer sun went to sleep and made it impossible to see the pages of her paperback: Jane Austen's *Mansfield Park*.

Moses had napped, sniffed the spot where Beverage had slept near him and twice ventured over to the seat Mark had claimed during his time on board the bus.

Even though the air was thick and the heat sliceable, none were interested in a hotel, and Gary pulled into an RV park not far from the I-10 interchange. They decided to sleep on the cots at the back of the bus, and Gary reminded Troy again of his foresight when he'd upgraded the bus for the team. "And you thought I was nuts," Gary said, pulling a sheet over himself.

"Still do," Troy said, settling into a cot across from Gary.

Grace rolled onto her side facing the aisle on her cot behind them. "We going to have a sleepover or actually sleep?"

Moses, who'd been on the fourth cot, across from her, stepped down in the darkness, wandered over to visit Beverage's spot again under the emergency door and jumped up next to Grace. "Hey, guy," Grace said, draping an arm over him.

Soon the lights outside began turning off, one at a time, like a stadium powering down, and the inside of the bus was nearly pitch black. "Pop?" Troy said, looking at the bus ceiling.

"Yeah."

"You asleep?"

"Yeah."

"Huh. Seems like you're not."

"I'm dreaming, Son. You should be too."

A minute passed, then two, then three. Troy could hear Moses breathing heavily, on the tipping point of sleep. "Do you think of Mallorie much?"

"Just every day."

"Do you think you and Mom would have stayed together if she . . . you know . . . was here?"

Gary, on his side facing the wall of the bus, turned over to his back and interlocked his fingers on his chest. "Everything changed that day. Everything."

They let their memories speak in silence for another moment. "What about my dad—I mean, my birth father?"

"Robbie Basham?"

"Who else?"

"Troy, he's not your dad or father or anything else."

Troy twisted his head left to view Gary's silhouette. "Sure he is."

Gary's sigh was both audible and intentional. "Son, he bailed so fast after your mother died. How is he your father or dad or anything? He's nothing to you. We've been through this."

Troy looked back up to the ceiling. "But I still think about him. Where he's at. How he's doing. All that."

"Where's this coming from, Son?"

Troy shrugged in the dark—a motion only he saw or felt. "Not sure. This trip. Seeing her again—"

"The name's Grace," she mumbled through sleepy cobwebs from behind him.

"Seeing Grace, almost being in Gulf Breeze. Who knows?"

Gary exhaled again, but this time quietly—a sign to himself. "I figure you remember what we taught you? As you grew up?" He didn't wait for an answer. "No regrets about the life we chose."

"I know."

"We're your parents. We chose that. We chose to put you first."

"I know."

The men heard Grace and Moses shift behind them. Soon all four were on their backs staring up into the unknown night.

As they drifted into sleep, Gary's dreams began where his thoughts pointed them. To an airport. To the lights. To a marriage of metal and pain. To a family that didn't fly that day and to a young woman who did.

To baseball fields. Away games. Nights on the couch. To a broken, battered husband.

To the way things could have been.

FIFTY-EIGHT

Day Eight

Gary and Moses woke first, and they walked half a mile to a donut shop and back. When they returned, Troy and Grace had set up the camp chairs in the weeds and grass behind the bus. Troy had the atlas open on his lap.

"About 150 miles to go?" Gary asked, and he presented the box of donuts and a plastic bottle of orange juice to Grace.

"Maybe fewer," Troy said. "But close enough."

Moses, panting heavily from the morning heat, trotted straight to his water bowl by the rear tires of the bus and drank it dry.

Grace opened the donut box and reached for a Bavarian cream. "There are only ten here," she said.

"Huh. Must have shorted us. Want me to go back?"

"Yeah, why don't you," Grace said, taking a big bite. "But wipe that chocolate off your bottom lip first."

Gary sat, Moses joined them in the middle of their triangle of chairs, and they agreed to make some calls that morning before driving the final stretch to Gulf Breeze. "I want to call the hospital up in Spartanburg—see if she's still there, getting better. I guess just whatever they'll tell me."

"Good, and I'll call and check on Mark again," Gary said. "See if anything changed overnight. And probably call the Macon police too."

"Hmm. I guess a phone would be nice," Troy said. "You know, one that's close, right here, not all the way back at the donut place, if they even have one."

Gary ignored him.

"Grace, wouldn't that be great? Like, if they made a phone that you could have handy anytime? Just, you know, like right here in your hand?"

"Nope." Grace licked frosting off a finger. "I'll pass."

"Well, good news, old man pioneer." Troy ignored Grace's quip and turned back to Gary. "I happen to have just such a device on the bus in my bag. You're welcome to use it."

Gary grunted something and finally looked at his son.

Troy held a strawberry-iced donut in his hand and admired it. "You know what I like about these?"

Even Moses knew what was coming.

"They're bite-sized," Troy said, and he shoved the entire donut in his mouth. "Mmmm."

"Classy," Grace answered, and she crammed the rest of hers into her mouth and followed it with a sloppy smile and a hiccup.

Troy retrieved the phone, powered it on for his dad, and dropped into his chair.

"Couple hours from now we'll be in Gulf Breeze. Seven days—"

"—Eight," Gary corrected.

"Eight days after leaving the valley. I'm not gonna lie, Pop. It's going to be nice to park the bus someplace and forget about it."

Gary punched in the numbers and with his son's help pressed the green "Send" button. As he walked away, phone awkwardly held against his ear, he winked at Troy. "Don't get too excited, champ. We still have to get back home."

FIFTY-NINE

Macy stepped out of the elevator and walked swiftly to Meg's room. The curtain around the bed had already been drawn, and Meg was seated in the chair in the corner with her journal open in her lap.

"Good morning," Macy said. "Ready to escape?"

"From Alcatraz," Meg answered, and she slowly rose to her feet and dropped the journal in the hospital's free canvas gift bag.

"Klepto. You can't keep that if you leave early," Macy jabbed.

They walked out, smiled at the nurses at the nurses' station and waved at Dr. Underhill as she moved from one room to another. "Pretty sure you're not getting a Christmas card from that woman," Macy said.

"She'll be fine. She came by this morning. Said she didn't approve and told me to be careful. I have to come back in a few days for a follow-up."

As they descended in the elevator, Macy confessed some friends were waiting downstairs. "Just Kaitie and Veda. I told them if they showed up at eleven and didn't make a scene, they could see you in the lobby. I thought you might appreciate that more than a house full of people yelling 'surprise' when you get home."

"Wise woman," Meg said. "I'm taking it easy, remember?"

"Says the woman with a particular baseball bus getting closer by the minute."

When the elevator doors opened, the women stepped out and were greeted by whispered cheers from Veda and Kaitie. Veda was dressed in slacks and a blouse fit for a business meeting. Kaitie was dressed in a trench coat and held a beach ball that matched the one hanging in the sky over Pensacola Beach. Before Meg could even say hello, the coat came off, revealing Kaitie in a skimpy swimsuit.

"Oh my!" Meg said.

"Hey, sister," Macy said. "She's *your* friend."

"Yep, she sure is."

A woman's voice from around the corner half-shouted, "We're in a hospital!"

Kaitie and Veda hugged Meg, and Kaitie even kissed her on the cheek. Then she whispered to Macy, "We invited a few others. Hope that's not gonna be a problem."

Every other member of the Letter Writing Club of Gulf Breeze appeared from behind corners, pillars and tall potted plants.

"Lily! Skye! Caleb! Oh, Kaleigh, thank you all." Meg's voice choked and cracked. "Thank you. You didn't need to do this."

Every member of the club approached slowly, spoke softly and one at a time wrapped their arms around her and then released carefully—as if taking a peek at a Christmas present without getting caught.

"Sorry about Kaitie's swimsuit," Skye said as she held Meg close. Meg simply answered, "Don't be. I think we all need one just like it."

The large group sat and chatted in the corner of the hospital lobby for a few minutes—the compromise over bombarding her and lingering at Meg's home—and the club members took turns offering help with the yard, the cleaning, laundry and dishes.

"Speaking of dishes," Kaitie said, "anything new to dish about the boys on the bus?"

"And girl," Macy corrected.

"Whatever." Kaitie dismissed the minor detail with an eye roll, and Meg realized her friend still hadn't put her coat back on.

"They should be here sometime today," Meg said. "That's what we hear."

"And that's why we need to be going," Macy added, and she took Meg's hand and helped her up. "Thank you for coming, all of you."

With the others gone and the two women sitting quietly in the parking lot, Macy put her hands on the wheel, gripped it, turned to face Meg and said, "Let's go home."

SIXTY

The bus and its passengers were quiet as they took the final stretch. They hit I-10 just a few miles after leaving the RV park and drove west across the panhandle. They whizzed past mostly small towns, stopping just once for Moses, and eventually crossed the Escambia Bay Bridge. Then they turned south onto 110 and cut through Pensacola toward the shore. They passed through the historic district, then paid to cross the Pensacola Bay Bridge. When they hit ground on the other side, a sign greeted them: "Welcome to Gulf Breeze."

Gary followed signs to the right and soon pulled the bus into a parking lot under the iconic Pensacola Beach beach ball. "Sorry, guys. I need a restroom."

"You can't wait?" Troy asked.

"I'm popping," Gary said, and he opened the door of the bus and stepped into the salty breeze. A handful of seagulls fought over a shred of soft pretzel. Palm trees stood tall, their leaves dancing—just barely—in the wind. Gary saw a sign for the Pensacola Beach Fishing Pier and considered making the short walk across the park toward the beach, but when he looked over his shoulder, Grace, Troy and Moses were all watching from the windows. Gary surrendered. "Just the men's room, I promise."

He walked to a convenience store on the corner and stepped into a smelly restroom that had been well used by swimmers and beachcombers. He used the urinal, which he hadn't really needed, and washed his hands and face. The dirty mirror studied him, and he studied it back. Gary hadn't shaved since checking out of the hotel, and his stubble was more salt than pepper. His roadside and parking lot adventures had also added some color to his face.

He wet his hands again and fixed his hair, still thick and full for a man his age, though like the beard it was uneven and hadn't been black since long before Meg left. He opened his mouth wide, checked his teeth and spotted a cashew spec in between two bottom teeth. With Gary's jaw wide open an inch from the mirror, a man and a little boy entered the restroom and stepped into a stall. As the boy sat, he jabbered about the beach, the dolphins and the shells he'd collected. "What's that man doing?" the boy asked, and Gary didn't hear the father's hushed reply.

Gary picked the food clear with a toothpick he'd had in his pocket the entire trip, wiped it on his pants and returned it to its place. Then he looked up, flared his nostrils and discovered a long, black hair breaking free from inside his nose. He made at least six attempts to pluck the hair with the nails on his thumb and index finger and grunted and sneezed when it finally pulled free.

"What's that man doing now?" the boy inside the stall asked. "Is he okay? Is that man okay?"

Gary wanted to laugh, but his pulse had quickened since they'd crossed the bridge, and his hands were clammy. He wasn't sure how to react to the boy—or anything. "I'm fine," Gary said. "Thank you."

Gary left the restroom, perused every aisle of the store and picked up gum, mints, two different SPF strengths of suntan lotion, four beach-priced bottles of cold water, a Gulf Breeze dog collar, a city map, a copy of *Sports Illustrated* and a package of three no-bake cookies from a dessert case that the clerk promised were fresh.

He paid and carried three heavy bags back across the street to the waiting bus.

Troy and Grace were standing close to the bus in a sliver of afternoon shadow. "What in the world, Pop? What took so long? We almost called the cops."

"Not funny," Gary said. "I bought a few things. No big deal." He pulled out the city map and found Meg's retirement community and exact street. "Geez, it's close."

"Well yeah, Pop. We're on a peninsula. Nothing's far."

Gary handed a bag to his son and stepped back onto the bus. He sat in the driver's seat, took a long drink of water, popped three mini-mints in his mouth, and checked his hair again in the rearview mirror. "Any other stops?" he asked Troy, who was standing right next to him studying the map.

"I think we've made enough detours, don't you?"

"You sure?"

"Let's roll."

Grace moved to the back of the bus, where Moses stood staring at seagulls out the emergency exit window. "You hear that, Mo? We're going to Meg's." Moses turned, panted, wagged his tail and had just one thought. *Please be real.*

SIXTY-ONE

The bus did not go unnoticed when it rolled into Meg's private retirement community. Gawkers stopped gardening; dog walkers let their mutts get tangled on hydrants and light poles. The yards were perfectly manicured, the streets swept clean—even the bushes and shrubs looked like they'd been put in place by movie-set prop masters.

"That must be the community center Mom told me about," Troy said, pointing at the building on the opposite corner of the four-way stop. A group of mostly women who no one on the bus recognized all stood under the shaded awning. They smiled, and one of them appeared to blow a kiss. "We're close," Troy said.

Moses moved from the back of the bus to the front and climbed onto a seat. Troy lowered the window, and Moses poked his head out. Then his tongue followed, and he soaked in the air, the smells, the anticipation.

Moses was the first to see her, and his bark could have woken all of Gulf Breeze.

He forced his head even farther out the window and barked even louder as Troy directed Gary to slow and park.

Meg, he thought. *Meg, Meg, Meg, Meg, Meg.* Moses pulled his head back into the bus and pushed past both Troy and Grace to the bottom step. *Meg, Meg, Meg.*

Meg was standing on the front walk, wearing an off-white sundress, less than even a hint of makeup and a look of relief.

Gary opened the bus door, and Moses leapt from the bottom step onto the sidewalk. He ran to her, and Meg covered her mouth and began to cry. Just as he approached, he skidded on the sidewalk, stopped, looked up and controlled his panting just long enough to see the entire scene. *Please be real,* he thought.

"Oh, my sweet Moses," Meg said. When she bent down to love him, she fell on her side, and Macy sprinted over from her spot on the front step. "I'm fine. I'm fine," Meg said, laughing as Moses slathered her with proof that he'd never forgotten, had never stopped loving and had never given up. "Sweet boy, I missed you too."

Meg finally looked toward the bus and saw Grace wiping tears from her eyes. Troy and Gary were standing on either side of her with their arms draped across her shoulders. Meg, sitting on her rear, half on the sidewalk and half in the flowerbed, motioned them over. "Well, come over here!" she said with a cry of hope in her voice.

Grace came first, bending slightly to hug her, and then she sat by her side. She pressed her cheek against Meg's and began to cry again—more from the release of emotions than the birth of new ones. "I'm so glad to see you," Grace said. "I've missed you."

"Sweetheart, no need for all this," Meg said, but she was softly weeping too and knew the moment deserved it.

Troy was close behind, and after nudging Moses aside, he knelt in front of her and wrapped his long, athletic arms around her familiar frame. "Hey, Mom."

"You can't possibly know how long I've wanted to hear that again—in person."

He squeezed a little tighter and whispered something in her ear. When he began to stand, she pulled on his hand. "Help me up?"

He did, and Meg wiped loose blades of grass and harmless chunks of flower-bed soil from her skirt. She mouthed "Thank you," and Troy and Grace moved toward the condo, where Macy awaited with a grin, a hug and tears of her own for these strangers.

Meg, again on her feet and standing at the midway point between one home and another, waved awkwardly at her husband and took in his appearance. She'd expected him to have gained a few pounds since she'd left, but he seemed leaner, and his legs and arms were tanned. His hair was thick and so long on the sides it threatened to pull his ears into hibernation. To her surprise, he wasn't wearing a Shenandoah Senators hat. Instead, he wore a light-blue, short-sleeve button-down shirt and khaki shorts.

Meg's knees were trembling, and later she would ask Macy if she could tell. But when she turned around for her best friend's moral support, she saw they'd all gone inside. Even Moses was gone, and Meg smiled when she noticed him watching intently out the front window, snout pressed against the glass.

"You can't stay over there forever," Meg finally said, and she tried to smile, but given her heart rate, the look came out more as a grimace.

Gary strode toward her, each step an admission, until they were face to face. His back was to his bus, and Meg's was to the house she'd called home since the day she left Virginia.

"Hello," she said. "You look good."

He glanced down at his legs, held out his thin arms and ran his fingers through his hair. "Thanks. I'm no younger."

Meg tugged at the sleeves of her dress and blushed. "I don't know why I wore this. Macy's idea."

Gary looked her over, from her freshly painted toes to the top of her head, and finally smiled. "You look good too. Really good."

Meg's face went from blush to flush, and she looked back over her shoulder for help she did not find. "Thank you," she said. Her eyes suggested she wanted him to embrace her, even just a friendly exchange, a taste of what was. Instead he shuffled his feet, and she did the same. From inside, Moses noticed Meg had started swaying ever so slightly, like a nervous prom date.

Then Gary stepped toward her so quickly, he bumped into her and she wobbled on her feet. "Geez, I'm sorry. I was just going to—"

"Hug me?" Meg said, and she opened her arms.

He eased in and put his arms around her. The first woman besides Grace he'd hugged in over three years. "I need to tell you something," Gary whispered, a line he'd rehearsed since standing in the hotel room in Macon.

"Oh, not now, Gary." Meg slowly released him and breathed in the smell she'd missed. "Let's go in. Let's sit. There will be time."

He nodded, even grinned, and his eyes locked on Moses's in the window. "Understood," Gary said. "Later is good."

While Macy poured glasses of cool, filtered water and offered freshly cut fruit to Meg's guests in the kitchen, Moses watched. He breathed on the glass. He narrowed his eyes as he witnessed another scene in Gorton family history that he wished he could hear.

Will he tell her about my friend? he thought. *Will he tell her the truth about our time in Woodstock without her?*

He pressed his nose against the glass.

Please stay.

SIXTY-TWO

Winded—physically and emotionally—Meg sat in her recliner and enjoyed the unusual sounds popping around the condo. Macy gave a tour, and Moses followed along, his long toenails clipping on the floors. When Macy led the others into the kitchen, he stopped next to Meg's chair and rested his head on her lap.

"I'm still here," Meg said, and she ran her thumb tenderly upward on his long snout between his eyes. Moses closed them and breathed deep.

Meg closed her eyes too and listened to Grace's laughter from the kitchen. She'd missed her sass, her unending energy, her love for people and things different from her. *If only,* Meg thought.

Then the carnival of joyful noise moved into the living room. "Please." Macy looked at Gary and motioned to Sandi's recliner. "Have a seat. It was Sandi's."

Gary looked at his wife. "I'm fine. Been sitting all day. All week, actually." He leaned against the mantel.

"It's all right, Gary," said Meg. "Sit. Sandi's not using the chair anymore."

But Gary remained on his feet and pretended to study the framed photos.

Across the small living room, Troy and Grace sat on a leather love-seat, and she lifted and rested her leg on his. Meg grinned at them but said nothing.

"Don't even get started, Mom." Troy sighed like a teenage boy.

"Hey. Meg's house," Grace said as she reached over and tugged on a patch of Troy's leg hair. "Meg's rules."

After a few minutes of small talk, Macy gave Meg a hug from behind and excused herself. "You all enjoy your family time. There's lasagna in the oven, salad in the fridge, plenty of whatever you need . . . Gary, the community center said you're fine to park the bus in the back of their lot while you're here. Better than the street."

Gary nodded. "Thank you."

Macy fought an urge to hug them all again, to kiss their cheeks, to share their grief and regret, to say she's sorry for everything they've endured. "I just have to say . . . this family is really special. I hope you know that. I really do. It's so good to meet you . . . all of you . . . To put names to faces and faces to stories I've heard."

"Uh-oh," Troy said.

"No, no, nothing but good. I swear." Macy raised her right hand and began to back out of the room before the dam broke.

"Join us for breakfast tomorrow?" Meg asked.

"No, I don't want to be underfoot."

"Nonsense," Grace said, and she leapt to her feet and bounded across the room to wrap Macy up in another hug. "You're family. And this dysfunctional group needs you."

"Amen to that," Meg offered. "Come. Maybe the boys can cook."

"Got bacon?" Troy asked, still seated across the room.

"No," Macy said. "But I can bring some?"

"Then, yes, the boys will cook."

Moses lifted his head from his spot in the middle of the floor, perfectly surrounded by family, and looked at Macy.

"See? Even Moses wants you here."

"As long as I bring bacon," Macy replied. She blew a kiss to the room and walked out. After a silence that stretched thin, Grace asked Moses if he wanted to explore the neighborhood. He did, and soon they were also walking down the front walk.

Troy's eyes scanned the room. "This place is nice, Mom. I can see why Sandi liked it so much."

"She sure did," Meg said. "Still feels like hers."

Gary moved across the room and sat on the loveseat with Troy. When he settled in, Troy lifted his leg and rested it on his dad's.

"No thanks," Gary said, and he pushed it off.

"Tough crowd," Troy said, and the room went still.

Meg's eyes followed a routine when words didn't come easily—they went to the urn on the mantel. Troy noticed, stood, walked toward it and carefully picked it up.

Then he looked at Meg.

"That's her. That's our Sandi."

Troy spun the black and burnt-orange urn and admired it. "It's beautiful."

"So was she," Meg offered, and she began rocking back and forth in her recliner. "I miss her. Every single day, I miss her."

The space between them went quiet again, and Troy took his turn studying the photos on the mantel and wall. She'd visited occasionally, but Troy hadn't known his aunt Sandi well. But looking at the photos made the stories of her salty, feisty personality feel more alive than ever. Troy knew much more than Gary about Sandi's final days and passing, but he asked questions anyway for his father's benefit. Troy also asked about life in Gulf Breeze, her neighbors and her friendship with Macy. "Seems you two are pretty close for a . . . what are they called?"

"Home health aide," Meg said.

"Right. I mean don't get me wrong—she seems awesome. Just wouldn't think a nurse or aide would be so close to her client. She seems almost like family."

Meg smiled and stopped rocking. "She is. And she's been through a lot. Mother died of cancer; dad has money and wives and isn't around much."

"Her dad has more than one wife?" Troy poked.

"Not at the same time, mister," Meg said, and she caught Gary smiling from the loveseat.

"So how about you over there? You're quiet."

"I guess," Gary said.

"That's a lie," Troy said, and he flopped back into the loveseat even closer to his dad. "You've had a lot to say on this trip."

Gary shrugged. "Not every day you're trapped on a bus with your family."

Meg hoped Gary hadn't meant for the observation about family to chafe, but it had. She resumed rocking. "Tell me more about the trip."

Troy spoke first, retelling details she'd already heard and adding new splashes of color to each story. He turned to Gary to add commentary, and he dutifully did, but he didn't seem interested in reliving the memories in public.

"My heart breaks for that man and his dog," Meg said, and the men knew she meant it.

Troy lightened the mood by adding the story of their side trip to the library and the quirky, overzealous librarian. "She was something else. Huh, Pop?"

"Something else, for sure," he agreed.

"Maybe you should stop by on your way back—catch her up."

"Maybe we will," Gary said. "Maybe we will."

For another half hour they talked about Grace, Paul and some of the other people they'd met along the way. Meg opened up to Gary about her heart attack scare and her chronic health issues. "Seems I'm always just so tired," Meg said. She also asked about the Shenandoah Senators, a few neighbors at home in Woodstock and Moses's health.

When the conversation waned, Meg smiled at them both. "Thank you. Thank you for coming. Thank you for fulfilling your promise to get Moses here so I could say goodbye. Have another day with him . . . I'm grateful," she added.

I'm so grateful, she thought.

SIXTY-THREE

After dinner and dishes, Meg asked about the others' schedule and plans in Gulf Breeze. Grace and Troy naturally wanted to spend time at the beach, and Gary hoped to visit the nearby National Naval Aviation Museum. "But I figure if we can't, it's all right. I got Moses here—"

"—We," Troy said, and he tossed a throw pillow at his dad.

"Sure," Gary smiled. "Team effort . . . even though I did all the driving."

The banter continued, and Meg let it wash over her. It had been years since they'd sat around and been at ease. *This,* she thought. *This is what I've missed.*

Around eight, Gary asked Troy to join him as he fueled up, cleaned out, and parked the bus at the community center. They left Moses asleep on the cool kitchen floor and the women rocking in the living room. The windows were open, and a summer breeze carried in smells and sounds of the sea.

"It's paradise, isn't it, Meg?" Grace said. She sat in Sandi's recliner, shoes off, ankles crossed, arms resting at her side. "And this chair is a dream. I might steal it when we leave."

"Leave?" Meg said. "You're already thinking about leaving? You just got here."

"No, ma'am. You know what I mean . . . For real, have you ridden on that bus? It bounces and bumps around the road like a pinball. Only comfortable seat is probably Pop's."

"Hmm," Meg sweetly sighed. "Pop. It's nice to hear you call him that. It's been too long."

Grace agreed. "It really has. He insisted, by the way. Sweet old man."

"You got the 'old' right," Meg said, and they giggled like young friends who'd stayed up too late.

"It's so good to catch up, Meg . . . I didn't realize how much I'd missed this family."

As they continued rocking back and forth in recliners just a few feet apart, Meg asked about Grace's family, some mutual friends at home in Woodstock, her nannying job in Rock Hill and her time in Texas.

"Ah, Texas. That's the topic you really want the juice on, isn't it?" Grace asked.

"Excuse me?" Meg said, and she stopped rocking.

"Same ol' Meg Gorton," she said with a laugh. "Bury what you really wanna know in a big batch of small talk."

Meg smiled.

"Not answering is often considered a sign of guilt, you know."

Meg shrugged and resumed rocking.

"I'll spill," Grace said. "Texas was an . . . adventure. I'm glad I went. I actually liked the area and the people more than I imagined. The sky is so beautiful. My heavens, though—it's hot and dry. Sometimes it was so scorching I wondered how they could play. But they did."

"And what about you two . . ."

"As much as I loved Texas, I think we both realized our relationship had, I don't know, run its course? So we went our own ways. And I'm happy in Rock Hill."

"What was it about Texas that stopped working?"

Grace pulled her feet onto the recliner. She hugged her legs and rested her chin on her knees. "I don't know. I guess all of it?"

Meg frowned. "That seems unlikely, doesn't it? After all those years, for it to just . . . cool off. All at once?"

"It didn't happen overnight, so much. We grew distant. More and more Troy chose to spend his off days doing other things. It's like he chose something else . . ."

"Something or someone?" Meg asked.

"I don't think there was anyone else. I really don't. But the longer I was in Texas, the more it seemed he wasn't. Even when we *were* together, it felt like he wasn't there. He became distant from me, even quit hanging with the team as much away from the field. He was just . . . not really there."

Meg nodded. "Don't I know *that* feeling."

They sat quietly, and Moses joined them, plopping on the floor between their recliners.

"Grace?"

"Yeah?"

"Do you still love him?"

Grace smiled. "Troy? Or Troy in Texas?"

"Sure."

"I don't know, Meg. Something is different. Don't get me wrong—being together this week has been so much fun. It's like school all over again. I remember why we fell for each other in the first place. So we're hanging out like old sweethearts, but we're not kids anymore."

Meg rocked again, nodded and agreed with quiet "Mm-hmms."

"Something . . . changed. I assume you know about his shoulder?"

"You mean what's wrong with it?"

"I mean what's *not* wrong with it."

Meg nodded. "I do."

Grace rearranged herself on the chair, crossing her legs and knees on the armrests. "Why wouldn't he tell me? Like months ago? Or years? Or however long it's been?"

"I'm not sure," Meg said. "I suppose he's like Gary. Less is always more."

"I get that," Grace said. "But he didn't trust me? We talked a few days ago, and I don't know if I felt betrayed or lied to or something in between, but I always thought we'd spend our lives together. Like, forever. Why couldn't he just be honest? Tell me he didn't love baseball anymore. Or that he didn't love me anymore. Tell me he's sad, down—struggling with life, with us, with his father never coming back. Whatever. It's like he was . . . acting. Like he was playing the role of star baseball player. I never wanted that. I loved him all the time. Not just on game day."

Meg listened as Grace looped through many of the same feelings and observations.

"I wanted to break down right there when he told me. I mean it broke me. He's been playing all this time just waiting to see his birth father in the stands? Or by the dugout? Or waiting by the bus after a game? It absolutely broke me, Meg." Then the tears came, not in a flood, but in a mist Grace could control.

"I felt the same, sweetheart," Meg said. "He told me about a week before he left the team. It was like he'd circled a date on the calendar and decided that if Robbie hadn't bothered to show up by then, he'd walk away . . ." Her voice had fallen into a sad whisper.

Grace stood and moved to Meg's recliner. She sat on the arm and snuggled against Meg's side, careful to not put too much weight on her.

"You know what I think it was?" Grace said. "I think he gave up. I think he gave up on the idea that his dad would ever choose him. Or choose to love him." Grace put a foot on the floor and gently pushed them back and forth. They listened to one another breathe, think, remember.

"It's not always easy," Meg finally said.

"What isn't?"

"To choose," Meg said.

"To choose?"

"To choose love." As they continued rocking, Meg felt a strange cocktail of regret, anguish and hope.

"It's gonna be hard to go home," Grace said.

"Then don't," Meg answered.

"How nice would that be . . . Hang out with you in Gulf Breeze every day? I'd love it. But my life up there will call me back at some point."

"I know," Meg said. "I know."

"And when it does? I'm still taking that chair with me."

SIXTY-FOUR

An hour later, Gary and Troy returned, and the group passed around Meg's photo albums. They reminisced about the Shenandoah Valley, their childhoods, Grace and Troy's high school hijinks, baseball and all the small-town gossip Meg had missed. But it didn't take her long to realize she hadn't really missed it at all.

Later, even though Troy had heard the story a hundred times, he asked to hear about his mother's crash again. "Dig deep, please. Is there anything you might have ever left out?"

Gary and Meg, sitting but not reclining or rocking, took turns telling the story that had changed their family forever. Gary recalled what they'd had for breakfast that morning and Robbie's last words when he left for work, refusing to watch Mallorie fly.

Meg remembered the onesie Troy had worn that day. Just an infant, he'd grown so fast that it seemed he needed longer clothes every single morning. "Our neighbor, Judy something..."

"Potter," Gary added.

"That's right. Potter. Sweet lady two houses down. She made a dozen cute outfits for you. Most of them had sports patterns. That day you were dressed in a white pair of PJs that had red stitching."

"Like a baseball," Grace said.

"Exactly. Like a baseball."

"I bet you were so cute," Grace said, sitting near him on the loveseat and trying to keep things light by squeezing his left cheek like a baby's.

"He sure was . . . Still is," Meg said, then she closed her eyes as if developing a more colorful image of the day. "The last time your mother saw you, you were in that little baseball onesie. She picked you up from your cradle, kissed your fuzzy head and promised to be right back."

The room became still—like the final moments before a eulogy. "And I didn't go," Meg continued. "I should have. I wish more than anything I'd been there that day to watch her. Support her."

Gary shook his head but said nothing.

"Meg, you were being a mom that day," Grace said. "Caring for Troy when his dad couldn't."

"Or wouldn't," Troy added.

"Regardless, Meg," Grace continued. "You were doing what you needed to be doing. And where you needed to be doing it. An airport isn't a place for a baby. You were smart to stay safely at home. You must know that."

Meg shrugged ever so slightly.

"From what Pop says, you wouldn't have wanted to be there anyway. People still talk about it, and it's been twenty years. I'm glad it's not in your head, Mom."

"Me too." Gary finally spoke. "It was . . . horrific."

Meg turned toward him. "You still think about it?"

"Every single day."

They sat again in peace, remembering what they could and wishing they had more. "But the weather that day?" Gary said. "Geez, it was so beautiful. The sky was perfect. Just the thinnest clouds—much, much higher than Mallorie or the other plane would have ever worried about . . . I remember Pastor Lyddon at the funeral said it was a 'receiving sky.' You remember that?"

"I do," Meg said.

"This is new. What's a receiving sky?" Troy asked, and he leaned forward on the loveseat.

Meg took a long breath and exhaled as she spoke. "Pastor Lyddon, he was so lovely. What a great, godly man. He passed recently. Don't know if you heard . . . Anyway . . . He described receiving skies as the days heaven creates for the great ones to return home. Now we know there's nothing really to it. God takes who God takes, in the rain, in the snow, during storms—whenever He wants. But there was something so kind about the way he spoke about the clear skies and an unimpeded view of heaven. He said if you could see clouds, even one, that was the space between here and there. And someone was waiting on the other side."

Grace shook her head. "That's . . . a gorgeous idea. I can see why you remember it." She looked at Gary. "Did you happen to notice the weather the other day when . . . you know . . . the weather in Macon? It was pretty much perfection."

Gary nodded and let a pure but narrow smile sneak up. Then he retook the wheel of the narrative. "I wish I'd known when we drove down to New Market that we'd never ride together again. Or have lunch together . . ." Gary stopped, and all eyes—even Moses's—were watching. "Yes, I wish I'd known. I wish I'd known Troy wouldn't see her that night . . . or any night." Again he let the words slowly fall out of his mouth, one at a time, like tall dominoes. "The disappointment that hit when we first got there and we didn't think she'd be able to fly. That family was there with money, he was a new member of the club, and everyone wanted him to be happy . . . Why didn't we just leave? Why didn't I tell Mallorie there was something off about the day?"

For the first time in Troy's life, he heard a soft hesitation in Gary's voice. It sounded like fear—not of the memory—but of the possibility he might cry. "It's okay, Pop."

"The girl got sick or afraid or whatever it was, and suddenly we had a choice to make . . . I wish I'd just driven away. Taken Mallorie for lunch or ice cream or on a hike. Anything."

"How could you have known, Pop," Grace said, not as a question but as a shot at comfort.

"So she went. I kept telling her she was ready. 'Do it. Do it,' I said. Weather was perfect." Gary's words were still in the room, filling the air and marking the memory, but his mind was a thousand miles away, and his eyes were wet and distant.

"Pop?" Troy said.

"All I had to do was say no—this is a sign we should go. We should go home, and you can solo another day. I was . . . too afraid maybe. I told her maybe ten times. 'This is your day, your day, your day. I wanted her to have everything. To fly. Then go to space. All the dreams she ever had. I wanted them for her." Gary was sputtering, his words becoming choppy and stunted. "She died. Her dreams died. And I think a part of me . . . a big part . . . died too." Tears were finally visible on his cheeks.

Seeing only his profile, Meg watched the tears roll down and get stuck on his jawline. "Gary, do you know I've never seen this?"

He looked at her but didn't speak.

"Seen what?" Troy asked, and as he waited for a reply, Grace stood and sat on the arm of Gary's recliner the way she had Meg's.

"This," Meg said, gesturing with her eyes. "Gary Gorton is crying."

Gary wiped his eyes with the backs of his hands.

Moses listened from the floor, breathing slowly and fighting sleep to hear every word he might recognize.

"I just . . . I can't . . . I can't believe that after all these years, my Gary is grieving."

He looked at her, his eyes wide. "You don't think I've grieved? You don't think I've been grieving the death of our daughter?"

"I . . . I guess I don't really know. I cried every day for years. In the kitchen. In the shower. In bed at night. On the couch while you were at baseball games. Sometimes I still do, and she's been gone so long her little boy isn't so little anymore. But you . . . you never seemed to grieve. You even watched baseball that very same night on TV. All I wanted was to be held on the couch while I sobbed and to ignore the people coming one after another to the door. And there you were, watching a game."

"Of course you do," Gary said, and the living room again went quiet.

"We should go," Grace said. "Troy? Late-night walk?"

"No, no. I'll go," Gary said. "It's fine. We're all tired. I'm sorry."

"For what?" Troy asked.

Gary stood. "For not grieving her way. And for not grieving out loud."

With that, he excused himself and walked in the blackness to a lonely bus in a dark parking lot.

SIXTY-FIVE

Gary wasn't surprised Moses had chosen to stay in the more comfortable condo, but he hoped for as much time as possible with his best friend before leaving him behind in Gulf Breeze. Gary's act of kindness would be rewarded, he assumed, with a peaceful closing season for all of them. If Meg passed away before Moses, Gary would simply return to Gulf Breeze and bring him home. The more he pondered his plan, the better it felt. He'd tell Meg when the moment was perfect. *Last night,* he thought, *surely hadn't been perfect.*

Gary sat in the driver's seat for over an hour. He could simply start the bus and pull out of the lot, down the road, alone. Over the bridge back to Pensacola, and north until he was parked safely on Water Street. He could apologize to Troy and Grace for leaving them, offer to send them plane tickets and ask them to tell Moses he was sorry for not saying goodbye.

He studied his reflection in the rearview mirror. He couldn't see much—to his surprise the lot behind the community center wasn't well lit. But he could see enough.

His eyes, hopeful just hours ago, were tired and familiar. He squinted and imagined his boys from the Shenandoah Senators spread across the bus, laughing, teasing, recapping a win, listening to music on their expensive portable CD players.

Gary saw himself driving them—like precious cargo—on long hauls to away games and overnighters. He could feel the excitement of pulling back into Woodstock after a long trip, the clock and the engine as tired as they were. He'd slow on the exit ramp, drop his weary players off in the lot by the field and drive the final five minutes to his final destination on Water Street. A road he loved. A home he loved. A family he loved.

With a flip of a switch on the dash, Gary turned on the bus's interior lights and saw himself more clearly. Had the evening been perfect? No chance. But hadn't it been better than he'd imagined on those painfully quiet nights in Virginia? Hadn't his pulse moved from a stroll to a jog, then raced when Meg held him? Hadn't he sat on the couch staring at Sandi's urn on the mantel and allowed himself to wonder if the twins might both board the bus back home?

He turned the lights back off and walked to his cot at the back of the bus. Still fully dressed, Gary lay on his side and stared through the stillness at the cot across the aisle. Then all at once, in a blurry blink, it crushed him. The moment came like an attack, like a vulture cracking glass, like a surprise guest at the door, like a revelation he didn't see coming. Gary knew he'd never been more alone.

Not when Mallorie had died. Not when Troy had left home to chase his dreams. Not even when Meg had left him standing in their front yard.

Then, flat on his back and looking up at a heaven he wasn't sure was watching, the tears came. Salty and stale. They came slowly at first, a few at a time, like harmless sparks. He wiped them away with an index finger under each eye. But he knew the fire was lit, and his chest began to heave. Then Gary covered his face with his sad hands and paid what he knew was the price of caged guilt. Sobs that hid like kindling for so long were loud and free and on fire.

But there was no one to see. No one to reach in and pull him to safety.

Gary wasn't sure if he actually slept, but eventually the sun rose and the neighborhood awoke. He gathered his toiletries and fresh clothes and reluctantly decided he'd take advantage of Meg's offer that they could shower in the condo while in town. Then he waited until eight thirty, when he hoped Macy would have arrived and everyone would be distracted by breakfast. He had no more energy for tension or unexpected family reunions, and he didn't imagine anyone else did either.

Gary walked slowly down the sidewalk and carried Meg's heavy box of journals. He was thankful he'd thought to tape it closed again before loading it onto the bus in Woodstock.

"Gary? Gary Gorton?" He was startled when a woman across the street shouted his name. "Could you help me with this?" Jessie, Meg's neighbor, stood in the middle of her yard pointing at something in her garden.

Confused but curious, Gary crossed the street to take a look. An agitated Jessie was pointing at a small garter snake in her mulch bed. "Can you kill that for me? Please?"

"It's not dangerous, ma'am. It's just a garter snake. Nothing to worry about."

The snake slithered a few inches across the brown mulch, and Jessie jumped. "Please! I don't like snakes. Period. Period, period, period. Would you please kill it or do whatever you like with it? Please? I was gardening when he or she or whatever just appeared." She continued re-telling in emotional detail what she saw, felt and said when she'd first spotted him almost two full minutes before Gary appeared. "I'm Jessie, by the way, Meg's neighbor, and you're her husband."

Gary simply nodded, amused and still somewhat confused.

She seemed to answer the obvious. "Everyone knew you were coming—didn't mean to surprise you . . . Ahhh!" The snake moved again, two more inches toward one of her perfectly manicured bushes, threatening to escape. "Please?"

Gary approached the snake and calmly picked him up just past his head. The snake was less than eighteen inches long, and it seemed as relieved as Jessie to be free of her property. "I'll take care of him," he said. But instead of chopping it in two with the spade Jessie offered, he walked it back to the community center and left him peacefully in a tight grove of trees behind the parking lot. When he returned to view and neared Meg's front walk, he waved to Jessie and called that all was safe.

Jessie looked up, crossed herself and thanked Gary profusely over and over until he finally let himself into Meg's place. He was surprised to see everyone but Macy had been watching from the front window.

"You make a new friend, Pop?" Troy teased.

"Don't ask," he said, and he washed his hands in the bathroom.

Soon they all crammed around Meg's cozy country kitchen table and enjoyed Macy's breakfast. They spoke in rapid fire, making plans for the day and filling the space with enough noise to leave no room for cross-examinations of the night before. Meg and Macy both had endless recommendations for things to do. Fishing on the Pensacola Beach Pier for the boys; eating and souvenir shopping for the girls; more eating at a beachside hot spot and a visit to Fort Pickens for everyone; and ice cream at Macy's favorite shop. Meg agreed to come along for the ride in the morning, but she would return home before the lunch hour, when the heat became unbearable.

For the first time on their trip, the day unfolded exactly as planned. They caravanned in Macy's and Meg's cars—the latter inherited from Sandi—and enjoyed the sites, the smells, the sounds and the company.

They ate fudge, sampled taffy, marveled at dolphins through binoculars and coaxed Meg back out in the evening for a dinner of swordfish and sherbet at a restaurant that sat on a pier, literally overlooking the water.

The next morning they made similar plans, and again to everyone's surprise, the day's agenda went off perfectly. They even took a tour of the community center and met Meg's friends in the Letter Writing Club of Gulf Breeze. Veda, as president, was "greatly honored" to introduce the club members one at a time. Some shook hands, some hugged, and Kaitie pledged to be available any night if anyone wanted a tour of the local nightlife. As they left, Veda invited them to stay and write a letter, as Meg had predicted she would, but the family insisted they didn't want to disrupt the club's important work.

The third day was similarly successful, and Meg had energy for the Gulf Breeze Flea Market. They spent a too-hot afternoon inside playing cards and getting to know Macy. While the others napped or read, Troy called a former teammate in Texas for a favor, and Grace called her cousin Paul in Rock Hill. When the sun finally set and the temperature went from blazing to bearable, Grace and Troy went for a run together and continued to clear the air about Troy's career and what would come next when the bus finally pulled back off I-81 in Woodstock.

Then around eight o'clock in the evening, after a light dinner of sandwiches and potato salad, the doorbell rang. "I got it," Macy said, since she was already on her feet drying her hands at the sink. She moved quickly to the front door, pulled it open and knew the face immediately from photos. "What are you doing here?"

SIXTY-SIX

He pulled a creased envelope from the back pocket of his jeans. "Cause of this," he said, holding it up between them. The middle-aged man wore bootcut jeans, worn tennis shoes that probably hadn't ever seen a court, a red-and-black flannel shirt (an odd choice for Florida in the summer) and a well-loved John Deere cap.

Macy stepped outside and closed the door behind her. "This isn't a good idea, I'm sorry. Meg isn't healthy right now, and this . . . it's just not a good idea."

"Please, ma'am. She sent me the letter. I'm not just showin' up. I'm invited."

Macy tried to make the moment vanish by rubbing her temples. But when she opened her eyes, he was still there.

"Please? I drove straight from Kansas City."

Macy looked out at the street and spotted a pickup truck with Missouri plates. Again she closed her eyes and tried to wish away the scene.

"Please," he said.

Before she could repeat her argument, the front door swung open.

"Everything okay?" The voice was Gary's, but when Macy turned around, she saw everyone standing near the open door.

The man stepped to his right and from behind Macy. His face was worn and tired, and deep, dark lines suggested a hard life more endured than lived.

Gary's eyes flashed wide.

Troy put his hand on Grace's shoulder. Meg's mouth gaped.

Gary had waited years to say so much and so fast. Instead, all he could offer was a single word—"Robbie."

More stunned than welcoming, they stepped aside, and Meg invited him in. When he extended a hand to her, she pushed it down and hugged him. Meanwhile, Troy excused himself and fell into a chair in the kitchen with Grace at his side. Macy offered to take Moses for an evening walk, and the curious dog reluctantly agreed.

Robbie removed his hat and sat on the loveseat. Meg and Gary sat in the recliners and faced him—judge, jury, audience. Robbie looked around the room. "This is really nice, Meg," he finally said.

"Don't," Gary said. "Don't make small talk. Why are you here?"

"I—"

"—I invited him," Meg interrupted. "He's my guest."

"Well so am I. So is Troy. I figure we deserve to know why he's suddenly sitting on our couch—"

"—*My* couch," Meg corrected. "He's here because, as I just said, I invited him. Just as I invited you."

Robbie stood and took four steps across the room, handing Meg's letter to Gary and then backing up and easing into the loveseat in one smooth motion.

Gary took the letter, removed and unfolded the single sheet of paper, then quickly reconsidered and handed both it and the envelope across to Meg. "I don't need to read it," he said. "It's not my letter."

They sat quietly a moment.

"So why is he here?" Gary said, looking at Meg.

"Because it was . . . time," she said.

"For what?"

"For him to be . . . welcomed again."

"Welcomed? No one's kept him away. He chose this. To leave. To forfeit his family."

Robbie looked down at his hands and wrung them over and over—a baker working invisible dough. "I didn't forfeit my family," Robbie said.

Gary cackled. "Oh, really? What do you call disappearing on your son? Leaving a few boxes of diapers and leaving the valley. What is that?"

Meg wanted to intervene, to save Robbie, but she'd always known this reunion would play out like the tense bottom-of-the-ninth scene that Gary thrived on. And she hadn't just expected it; she knew it was necessary.

"I'm sorry. I am. But . . . can I talk to my son?"

"You mean *my* son. I figure that's what you meant, right, Robbie?"

Nothing.

"The ones who raise a child, who buy the clothes, the food, go on field trips, sit through game after game after game. They're the ones that get to call themselves mom and dad. Not you. Not the ones who run, who get afraid. You have no right. No right to call him anything other than what the rest of the world calls him. Troy Gorton."

Robbie didn't look up.

"That's right. Gorton. We changed his name from Basham when you bailed on us. On him. And if she would have let me," Gary pointed at Meg without looking away from Robbie. "I would have changed Mallorie's name too. New headstone. New whatever. The name Mallorie Basham . . . I barely even say it. She'll always be a Gorton to us. Always. Living or not. Always a Gorton."

Robbie looked up, first at Meg, then at Gary. "I know. And you're right. I'm not here to argue nothin'. Nothin' you said is off base. Not a single word."

"Then why?" Gary said. "Why are you here?"

Robbie looked at Meg, and Meg held the letter up again into the air. "My, Gary, you can't be this slow. Again, he's here because I invited him. Because it's time . . . Troy?" She called, hoping her voice would easily land in the kitchen. "Please come in here. Come join us. Grace, you come too."

It took a full minute, but eventually Troy appeared and stood behind Meg's recliner. He rested his large hands on her shoulders. Meg couldn't see his face, but his eyes were already red. Grace stayed in the kitchen but kept tuned in from around the corner.

"Troy," Meg said. "This is Robbie Basham. He's your birth father."

"I know who he is."

Robbie stood and extended a hand, but Troy remained anchored behind Meg's recliner and didn't even acknowledge the gesture with his eyes. Robbie sat again, this time deeper in the loveseat, and nervously lifted his left leg and rested his foot on his right knee.

"Troy, listen to me," Meg said, but her eyes were fixed on no one but Robbie. "Your father—"

"—Stop calling him that," Gary said.

Neither Meg's eyes nor her voice flinched. "Look, your life allowed you two fathers. It's a blessing, not a punishment. Your birth father, Robbie, is here because I wrote him and asked him to come and to come soon. And he did. Just like I invited you and your dad. This . . . whatever it is . . . ends here in Gulf Breeze."

"How can you end what never started?" Gary said, and he started rocking aggressively in Sandi's recliner.

"Gary, please," Meg said. "You're a guest too."

Gary mumbled something only Grace heard, and she moved next to him, reached up and took Gary's hand.

"First, Robbie, you should meet Grace. She's Troy's . . . high school sweetheart."

Robbie stood and shook her hand. As he sat again, he said, "I know who you are. It's nice to meet you."

"And the woman at the door, Macy Chrisman—she's my aide. And really my best friend."

Robbie nodded, Gary rolled his eyes and mumbled something else, Grace squeezed his hand tighter, Troy let loose a deep breath he'd held hostage for too long, and Meg began rocking slowly back and forth.

"Okay, intros are done . . . Robbie, I'm glad you got the letter. I wasn't sure I even had the right address. But grateful I did and grateful you came. Obviously you didn't take long to decide." She stole a glance at Gary, and he pretended not to notice. "How long have you been in Kansas City?"

Robbie sat straighter. "A couple of years. I moved there after these kids graduated from high school." He motioned to Grace and Troy.

"And where were you all those other years?" Gary asked.

"Gary—"

"—No, it's okay," Robbie said. "I was close. Winchester, mostly. Working. Taking care of my parents. They got sick, and I ended up living with them for a while. A long while."

"We're sorry to hear that," Meg said.

"After Mallorie . . . I didn't know what to say. What to do. I was . . ." He let a long silence develop that swallowed up the room. Then he said all the words that came to him. "I was scared. Terrified, more like. And alone. And lonely . . . Not ready—not even a little bit—to be a dad by myself. Mallorie was everything to me. And to you all. She was a dreamer, and she dreamed of being the world's best mom. Then she was gone. And . . . I was . . . lost. Leaving was the hardest thing. I wanted to come back about a million times. But each time I drove down to your place, it got even harder to knock on the door. I was . . . ashamed. Maybe that's the best way to say it."

Gary stopped rocking. "I agree, Robbie. Ashamed feels like the best word for you."

"No. We won't do that, Gary. Not anymore," Meg said. "We've wondered and judged for a long time. Not anymore."

Another lengthy silence came and went before Meg nudged the conversation along. "Troy. You've wanted to ask Robbie something for a long time. For twenty years. So ask him, sweetheart."

Troy inhaled, pulled his hands from Meg's shoulders and gripped the back of her recliner. "Son, it's okay," Meg said.

Troy looked at Robbie across the room and took in the surreal scene. A man he knew only through family photos—photos that ended just before Mallorie's crash—was sitting feet away. His eyes were Troy's, along with his big hands and lean, athletic frame. For a moment, Troy allowed himself to picture his mother sitting next to Robbie. If she'd never flown, never dreamed, if that family hadn't given up their spot in the plane that day.

"Why?" Troy said.

When Robbie didn't immediately answer, Meg interjected. "Why what, Troy?"

Troy locked eyes with Robbie. "Why not . . . show up. Somewhere. Even once."

Robbie stood and took a short, single step toward him. "I did."

"When?" Gary said. "When did you show up? Did I miss you at one of his birthday parties? When we went to the airport on the anniversary of Mallorie's crash every year? At a game?"

Troy let his dad's questions stand, and he continued staring Robbie down.

"Actually, I've seen a lot of games," Robbie said.

"How do you figure?" Gary asked, leaning forward.

"Please, Gary," Meg pled. "Let him speak."

"I went to your Little League games, and when the crowd was small, I watched from the parking lot. When the crowds were bigger in high school, I mixed in with the visiting team's friends and families. I was there at games in Front Royal, Strasburg, Winchester.

When you went to the state championship in Richmond, I was there. Then when you signed your minor league deal and started playing in Texas, I was there. I've probably seen more games than I've missed."

Grace stood, put her arm around Troy's waist, and her eyes found Robbie's. "That's why you moved to the Midwest."

Robbie nodded. "I knew my son—I knew Troy—would likely be playing in St. Louis, Dallas, Omaha—all those cities with solid double-A and triple-A teams."

Grace looked up at Troy and saw his eyes start to glisten.

"I took a job with a small trucking company," Robbie continued. "I bought my own rig, told them I would make my own rules. Drive the routes I wanted when I wanted. Mostly it's worked out." He took one more step toward Robbie. "I saw you win; I saw you lose—though you haven't done much of that with that arm. And I cheered for you. I just did it from a distance."

Gary stood and stepped toward Robbie. "Guess what? The joke's on you, Robbie Basham. Turns out Troy hates it. Hates baseball. Hates you."

Troy's face flushed. "Pop, stop. Please."

"Why? You afraid to tell him? Afraid to tell me?"

Nothing.

"Afraid to tell you mother?"

Nothing.

"Or maybe she knew?" Gary said, looking down at his wife.

"Pop, please," Troy said.

"It's all right," Meg said, and with Troy and Grace each taking a hand, she stood and faced her husband. His arms were tense and his chest proud and puffed out. "I've known for a while, Gary. Troy told me."

Gary shook his head. "Of course he did."

"You're not injured?" Robbie asked.

Troy shook his head.

"Is it true?" Robbie continued. "You don't love it anymore? You're done?"

Troy nodded, and Grace put her arm around him again. After weighing his words, he looked at Robbie and let the confession flow. "I haven't loved it for a long time. Since I gave up . . ."

"Gave up?" Robbie asked.

"On you coming home. I would jog out to the mound, step up and look out. I thought I saw you a couple times in high school. I really did. But when you didn't stick around or find me after the games, I convinced myself it wasn't you . . ."

"I'm sorry, Troy," he said, and for the first time his own tears came and his voice trembled.

"There was a game in Fort Worth last year. I came up in the eight inning to save a game when our closer was out with a bug or something. I looked up in the stands and saw Grace. And I was so sure I saw you about ten rows behind her. I was so sure . . ."

Grace put her other arm around him and hugged him sideways.

"You struck out five in a row to end the game," Robbie said.

Both men stifled cries.

"I'm sorry, Troy. I'm sorry I didn't know how to be a dad without your mom in our life. I'm sorry I didn't know how to grieve. I didn't even know what it was back then. Didn't know what I was feeling. Didn't know anything. So I just . . . didn't. And these people, this family—they were all you needed. They did what I couldn't."

Troy stepped forward and hugged his birth father. Two tall men, embracing, crying. "I'm sorry," Robbie whispered. Then he said it again and again and again. "I'm so sorry."

Gary quietly excused himself, and though it was close to midnight, he went for a long walk that took him all the way to the Pensacola Beach Pier. *Figures*, he thought, realizing the attraction was closed for the night. So instead of standing on the pier, he sat in the cool sand beneath it. The hours rolled by, and his memories came and went with the tide. Then when the first signs of light began peeking over the horizon, Gary began the long walk back to both his baseball bus and the past.

SIXTY-SEVEN

It was almost 7:30 a.m. when Gary stepped back onto the bus. Feeling his age and the effects of his first all-nighter in decades, he crawled onto one of the cots at the back of the bus and dosed off. Just before sleep hit, he decided that when he woke he'd walk all the back to the pier alone to rent a pole and fish.

Back in the condo, Grace and Troy ate a late breakfast and borrowed Meg's car to drive across the bridge toward downtown Pensacola. They parked on a street they didn't know, window shopped at stores they'd never enter and ate a long lunch at a buzzing restaurant with dollar bills stapled to the walls and ceiling.

Robbie returned to Meg's condo but just missed seeing Troy and Grace before they left. Meg offered him toast and fruit, which he ate quietly on the loveseat. In time, she joined him and shared her family albums. She described in colorful strokes the highlights of Troy's life. She laughed, she cried, she listened, she cried more, she forgave.

After returning from her walk with Moses the night before, Macy had let him back in the front door and left without being noticed. She'd driven home to her small, lonely apartment and spent a restless night wondering how the Gortons' story would end. She loved the entire family, even Robbie, for reasons that would be hard to explain.

The day moved slowly, and just before six, the hour she'd promised to return and meet the family for dinner, Macy's phone rang. As she often did, she let the answering machine pick up. After her greeting and the standard beep, she heard a familiar voice.

"Hey, Macy. It's Dad. Don't know if you're there or not. Pick up if you are . . . Okay . . . Look honey, I'm still in Stockholm, but I've been thinking a lot about you, about our last call. Can't stop thinking about it, actually."

Macy stood and put her hand on the phone, but hesitated.

"I know. I know. We've talked it through. And I know my advice isn't worth much. And I know if your mom were alive, you'd be getting advice from her. You wouldn't be waiting for it—you'd be asking for it. Begging for it even. That's just one of the things she was good at . . . But Macy, I'm still your dad, and even though I'm not around as much you'd like . . . or everything I should have been since mom died, I'm still the one person who never gives up on you. Who always believes in you . . ."

Knowing what was next, Macy gripped the phone and nearly picked it up again to end the message and short circuit what was about to come. But instead, she released the phone and placed both hands flat on the Formica countertop near the answering machine.

"It's time, Macy. Time to tell her. Time to tell the truth . . . It's hard, but it's right . . . I love you."

SIXTY-EIGHT

With tension still thick, the family met back at the condo a few minutes after six. Earlier, Meg had called the community center and been given permission for the family to use one of the activity rooms for dinner. With six adults, the condo's kitchen was getting tight, and they'd appreciate the opportunity to spread out. Not everyone was sure they'd even survive the night, but they'd all agreed to try.

Macy arrived at the condo with four white paper bags of tacos, rice, refried beans, salsa and lime from Welty's. Grace and Troy each took a bag to ease her load, and the entire group paraded down the sidewalk. It was the farthest Meg had walked unassisted since her hospital stay, and Robbie walked slowly with her at the back of the pack.

They set up in Activity Room 2, the home of the LWCOGB, and Meg invited Macy to grab a case of bottled water from the perpetually unlocked kitchen. Once settled around the large table, they passed around paper products, divided up enough tacos for twenty and began eating.

What am I doing? Macy thought, and she looked at the faces of the family around her. The mood was still heavy—a wool coat in winter—but at least it felt lighter and more upbeat than it had when she and Moses had disappeared for their long walk.

She barely knew Gary, but she'd heard the stories and could tell he was moody. Still, Macy believed he had a right to be protective and defensive about Robbie's arrival. Gary had said little on their walk from the condo, and she didn't expect that to change much as the evening wore on. She imagined the moment he had stood without saying goodbye and walked outside to the parking lot and to the safe oasis of his baseball bus.

Macy watched Robbie squeeze lime on top of a soft corn-tortilla taco, his flannel shirtsleeves rolled up and unbuttoned one button lower than might have been normal. He was tentative, careful, quiet and observant. Macy wondered what kind of dad he would have been. *A good one,* she thought. *Maybe a great one . . . If only.*

Grace and Troy sat near one another, alone on one side of the square table. She watched and wondered what might become of them—if anything—and it was impossible for her to not imagine Mallorie and Robbie in the same setting decades earlier.

Meg was sitting to her left. She'd worn a light sweater because the community center air-conditioning had a history of "blowing like Antarctica," as Meg liked to say. She was right—Activity Room 2 felt a bit like the grocery store freezer section.

When all that was left were chip shards and the smells of salsa and cilantro, Macy sat forward in her chair. "This was really nice," Macy said to the group. "I know the circumstances are . . . unusual. To say the least. None of us will probably ever have a day or a dinner like this again."

The group nodded and sighed like a quiet choir.

Macy reached over and took Meg's hand. "If it's okay, I'd like to tell you something. About me . . ."

"Of course," Meg said.

Macy dove in before her courage was digested. "I haven't always been honest with you." The room, already quiet, dipped into utter silence. "I knew Sandi a long time before she died."

"Oh, we knew that, sweetheart. She talked about you. Made me promise to hire you after she died."

"Right, but I'd known her even before that. Before you were in Florida . . . We'd been penpals."

Meg smiled and patted Macy's hand. "That's sweet. Everyone knows how much Sandi liked her letters. She probably wrote you right here at this table, with the letter-writing group."

Macy exhaled. "Probably . . . The truth is, I started writing to her when I was a child, very young, before I even knew what a penpal really was . . ." Macy waited for a comment or question, then continued. "I'd wanted to write you, Meg. And you, Gary. And even you, Troy and Robbie. But my parents wouldn't allow it. In time they agreed I could write Sandi, and we exchanged many letters over the years until I moved here to Gulf Breeze, not long after you."

Troy wiped his mouth and said, "Why would you write us? Or even know of us back then?"

Macy stood and walked around the table. She stood inches from Troy, and he studied her eyes until she spoke again. "Troy, I grew up in DC. Don't know if I ever got that specific with Meg or not. But it's true. I was raised in the DC suburbs, plenty of money, a father that had everything and wasn't afraid to spend . . . One day . . . " Macy's voice broke, and she covered her mouth and took a long breath before continuing. "One day we went for a long drive. I was as excited and nervous as I'd ever been. I didn't know what euphoria was back then, but that was what I felt. We drove out early one morning to this lovely little town . . . New Market . . ."

The room fell so quiet—they could all hear the low hum of a tired overhead fluorescent light.

"I was so scared," Macy said. "More so the closer we got. I ate my snacks for the drive out and the drive back all at once. My stomach was spinning and spinning and . . ." Macy began to cry, and her breath was labored and short. "We were going to the airport, the tiniest one I'd seen then or even since."

Macy took several long breaths and wiped her nose. "We were going to fly that day. It was a gift. A gift to me. We were going to fly over the valley. I was just a girl, Troy. A child."

Macy finally turned to look at Meg. The looks she'd long expected— betrayal, shock, grief reborn—were nowhere. Instead Meg simply listened with love in her eyes.

"I don't know why or how it happened, Troy. I don't. But the nerves, the anxiety, the excitement all got to me, and I got so sick inside the plane. Before we even took off. My dad yelled, my mother comforted me, and I remember walking away from the plane feeling so . . . small. Like a little child."

"You *were* a little child," Meg assured her, and the room seemed braced for what they already knew.

"My mother cleaned me up inside a small, little restroom in the air-port office. I remember how it looked and felt. How it smelled. Then we walked back to the car. My dad was so upset. We'd driven so far, spent money, made plans, and I'd ruined it all. And we could have waited, gone later in the day, but he wanted to make a point, I think. So we sat in the car and dad pulled out into the open field so we could watch the plane take off with a new pilot."

Troy's cheeks were wet, and Grace's hands covered most of her face. Gary was stunned—too winded for emotion. Robbie had pulled his hat down to cover most of his face.

"Meg, Gary . . ." Macy looked at them both. "She looked so beauti-ful walking out to the plane. I watched her and wanted to *be* her. Even though I didn't know a thing about her. Only that my father had been told it was her first solo flight and she had flown a lot with others. But here she was on her own. Making history. Her own history."

Macy moved toward Gary. "We watched. We watched her board. We watched her roll to the runway, speed up, take off into the sky. And climb and climb . . ." Macy's narrative was smoother than it should have been, and later she'd privately admit that she had spent years rehearsing.

"We watched it all. The flight, the turns, the dips. I thought to myself that one day I would be that high in the sky, that close to heaven . . . Then we watched another plane come into view. I'll never forget it. I'll never forget my dad saying. 'What's he doing? Why's the other guy up there?' Then . . . it happened."

Macy's voice collapsed, and so did she. She had made her way back to her seat near Meg and slumped back into it. She held her face in her hands and sobbed at what her mind's eye could see, remember and never forget. "I was watching both planes, my eyes darting back and forth. I remember it like I was watching a game. A cartoon. Something that wasn't real . . . Then the space between them shrank and shrank until there wasn't any . . ."

Meg leaned over and gently rubbed Macy's back. "It's okay. Shhh. We're not going anywhere."

Macy sat up, her face a wet mess of tears, her nose running, her cheeks red. "And every time I close my eyes, every time I try to see anything else, I see that pile of fire and metal. I see you, Gary, watching not far from us. And I know that because of me . . ." Macy looked at Troy. "Because of me, your mother is dead."

SIXTY-NINE

When the emotional storm ebbed, Robbie hugged Macy and Meg, nodded politely at the others and returned to his hotel for the night. Soon, Grace, Meg and Macy made their way back to the condo while Gary and Troy quietly cleaned up the trash, wiped down the table and turned off the lights. Gary said he'd be back shortly and climbed into the bus while Troy walked back alone.

Moses noticed that Gary hadn't returned. *Where'd he go?* He thought.

Inside the condo's living room, Troy dropped into Sandi's recliner, Meg into her own, and Macy and Grace sat close on the loveseat. Macy's eyes were still wet, and every few minutes she apologized.

"Don't be silly," Meg said. "You're allowed to feel everything you're feeling."

Moses heard the discussion behind him, read the body language, felt the emotions, but he kept his eyes on the sidewalk and his nose near the window.

"I'll just say it," Grace began. "I know I'm not a Gorton. I mean seriously, why am I even here for this? I get it. But Macy, you have nothing to feel sorry for. You were a child. And even if you weren't, even if you were there to fly all by yourself—like Mallorie—you would have every right to say, 'Not today.'"

At the sound of Grace's voice, Moses turned away from the window, trotted to the loveseat and wedged himself up and in between them.

"I'll say this," Troy offered. "Obviously you knew, right, Mom? I mean the rest of us are sitting here like we're stuck in a movie or something, and you're . . ."

"Aware," Meg said.

"Sure. Aware," Troy agreed.

Meg smiled at Macy, who once again was shaking with the weight of the revelation. "I've known a long time," Meg said. "My sister, my twin, she kept nothing from me. You could have guessed that. I wasn't thrilled—no, that's not the right word. I wasn't pleased when Sandi first told me about the letters and your friendship. But what was I to do? Cut you off? Call your family? Then the years passed, and Sandi told me about your parents' divorce. I was sick about it. Sandi told me that morning haunted you, and she was the only one you could really talk to. And then when your mother died, I wanted to reach out, but I didn't know how. What's it been? Three or four years?"

Macy nodded.

"By then my marriage was hanging by a thread. Gary and I were just enduring the days, and I was miserable and depressed."

Macy began again to weep silently, and when she let her guard down, Moses licked her face.

"How could I say anything? Sweetheart, I know how hard this was for you too. So when Sandi invited me down for about the . . . millionth time . . . I came and promised Sandi that if anything ever happened to her, I'd be there for you. A friend. A mother. A home."

Macy smiled through more tears. "That was *my* job," she said. "I told

Sandi I'd take care of you when she got sick. I promised I'd be a friend, a daughter, a nurse, whatever you needed."

"And you have been all that and so much more," Meg assured.

Troy watched Grace stand and move behind the loveseat. As Macy spoke, Grace ran her fingers through her new friend's hair and began braiding it.

Moses also watched. He loved when fingers ran through his hair too.

"I feel so relieved." Macy looked up at Grace and then at Meg and Troy. "This has been a heavy thing to carry around. And I just kept telling myself that the more I loved you, Meg, and stayed close, the more I'd move on from that morning."

Troy leaned forward in the recliner and rested his arms on his thighs. "We're glad too, but again, as much as I missed not having her growing up, this wasn't your fault any more than it was mine or Mom's." Troy stretched across, took Meg's hand and rested their hands on her armrest. "This beautiful woman was my mother in every single way. I knew about the crash for—well, I guess I don't remember not knowing. It was part of growing up. I knew I was the weirdo in school being raised by my grandparents. And so what . . ."

Moses watched Troy and admired his devotion to Meg. He had the urge to walk up and lick Troy's face, to lick every face, but the day had worn him out too.

"As for Robbie," Troy said, "the dad that I always wanted to know, I guess I don't know yet. I don't know what happens next with him . . . He grieved his way, I guess. And we all grieved ours. I don't know what happens from here, other than I'm open. Open to keep listening."

With that, they heard a knock at the front door, and Moses made his way to the window. A moment later, Gary appeared in the living room. With Grace still on her feet braiding Macy's hair from behind, he slipped into her spot on the loveseat.

When Meg began to catch him up, he began loving Moses with one hand and raised the other. "Wait," he said. "Just wait."

Moses scanned the room and saw all eyes settling on Gary, so his did too.

"Meg. I figure this whole trip. This . . . reunion or whatever you want to call it. It's mostly my fault—"

"—Hold on, Pop," Troy said.

"It's true. I've thought about that day every day since it happened. When I've gotten up, gone to work, gone to games. When I've slept. When I've dreamt. When I fought with you, Meg. I thought of it. Why I didn't stop her. Then why I didn't confront Macy's parents and shout my head off. Then why I didn't chase down Robbie when he walked out. I figure I have more what ifs and whys than anyone."

Moses flopped down on Gary's lap and began watching Meg.

"I figure you all grieved your way, and I did mine. Which probably wasn't the best." Gary paused, seemed to study Moses's face and scratched his head. "I guess what I most want to say is that while I don't think I can fix the past or go back in time and take different roads, all I can do is try to make today better. It's hard, maybe the hardest thing I've done. And I know it's not perfect, and it might not even be what I really want. But I'm afraid it might be the best I've got." Gary leaned down and kissed Moses's head. "I've made a decision."

When he paused too long, Macy touched Gary's arm. "Should I go? I should go."

"No," Gary insisted. "Stay. It's good. You're good." Gary looked at Meg and grinned. "These guys already know. Well, I figure Macy wouldn't, but here's the thing. I want you to have Moses."

Meg's brow furrowed. "I'm sorry, what?"

Moses wanted to sigh. He sensed this moment was coming, had read the signs, but the reality that his life was changing forever had taken his breath. He lifted his head and watched and waited.

"You heard me. I want Moses to stay. I'm giving him to you. I want you to have him, to have my best friend."

Best friend, Moses thought.

"This is my way of saying . . . I want you to be happy. And to not be alone."

"Wait, Gary. Are you being serious? With me? With us?"

"Nothing but," Gary said, and he stiffened his back.

Moses read the room.

Troy awaited Meg's move.

Grace was more interested than ever in Macy's hair.

Moses thought Macy's face looked as if she wished she hadn't asked if she should stay. That perhaps she should have simply jumped through the window and run.

Meg sat forward and looked sideways at Troy. "Was this your idea?"

Troy shook his head. "Absolutely not. "

"Grace?" Meg said. "So what is it? You all decided the best way to fix things was to leave an old dog and ride that dumb bus back to Virginia?"

Moses snorted. He didn't know all their words, but he surely knew what "old dog" and "dumb bus" meant.

"No, definitely not," Gary said. "This was my idea. My suggestion. I don't want you to be alone, and I regret the last couple of years."

"You regret."

"I do."

"Just the last couple years?"

Moses looked at Gary and didn't know whether his dad was supposed to nod or shrug or both.

"Well, yeah, Meg. I do."

Meg looked at Troy but gestured to Gary with her left hand. "So he's demonstrating his . . . regret. With Moses."

"Mom, keep hearing him out. He's trying."

Meg slowly stood, shook off Troy's help and began to walk out of the room toward the back bedroom. "Yes, you're right. He's trying," she said. "To apologize with a dog."

SEVENTY

Troy gave up the comfort and air-conditioning of Meg's place for a cot in the back of the bus. He and Gary said little as they readied for bed, and neither slept well. When the sun woke up Gulf Breeze, both men were already on their backs staring at the ceiling.

They folded up their sheets, tidied the rear of the bus, and Troy made the short walk to Meg's for a shower. "Son, we need to get on the road. Don't be long."

There was so much to say but no energy to say it. Troy simply stepped off the bus and disappeared across the parking lot. While he was gone, Gary drove the bus to a gas station with an island large enough for trucks and buses, filled the coolers with ice and scraped bugs off the windshield. He also washed his face, brushed his teeth, used the restroom and bought himself a Diet Dr. Pepper and a package of six powdered mini-donuts.

Back in the community center lot, he packed up Moses's things into a Senators drawstring shoulder bag. Then he slung the bag over his shoulder and made the walk back to Meg's to face both the past and present.

As expected, Moses was watching through the window when Gary appeared in view. Gary waved at Jessie, in her yard as always, and took heavy steps down the walk toward the front door. He was relieved to see Macy's car in the driveway. She surely deserved a thank-you and a warm goodbye. Gary knocked, waited and looked to his right at Moses—the witness to everything.

Grace opened the door and welcomed him. "You don't need to knock," she said, and she hugged him tightly.

He stepped in and didn't need to look to know Meg was sitting in her recliner in the living room. He breezed past the entry and into the kitchen.

"Good morning," Macy said. "Breakfast?"

Gary shook his head. "No thanks."

Macy glided across the kitchen and hugged him. "I'm sorry, and thank you. Both."

"For what?" he said. She was still hanging on him.

"For not being honest, more quickly, for all of that. And . . . thank you. For forgiving me."

"None of that is necessary, but . . . I understand."

She finally let him go and pulled away but then grabbed his hands. "Troy says you're leaving today."

"This morning."

"Can we talk you into one more day? A trip to the beach? Fishing the pier one last time? More tacos?"

Gary answered with a tight smile. "No, but thank you. It's time to get on the road. Get home. Get back to things."

Macy kissed him on the cheek, whispered, "Talk to her," and began clearing the table.

Gary exhaled breath he didn't really have to give and walked into the living room. Troy was sitting in Sandi's recliner, and Grace was sideways on the loveseat, her feet hanging over the edge. When she saw him enter, she quickly slid her feet off, sat up and placed her hand on the spot next to her.

Gary hesitated, but finally sat. When he did, Moses lumbered over and jumped onto the loveseat between them. "He's not going to leave you," Meg said. "Look at him."

Gary scratched Moses behind the ears. "Sure he is. He's saying good-bye."

Gary saw Meg sneak a peek at Troy, but he pretended not to notice and continued giving Moses just what he wanted.

"Gary, I want Moses to go with you. For Moses. It's best for him."

Gary looked everywhere but at Meg. "No, it's not. He wants to be here. And it's what I want."

Moses looked up at Gary, and his ears perked.

"Moses, hop down. Go on. Go."

Moses was obedient. Loyal. Confused. Willing. He stepped down off the couch, suddenly sore and older. When all four paws hit the floor, he looked back at Gary over his shoulder. *I will,* he thought. *For you. For her.* Then he sat by Meg, and she loved the top of his head.

"This is ridiculous, Gary. He doesn't want to stay."

Moses turned to face Meg and licked her hand again and again until she pulled it away. Moses could see her eyes growing moist and glossy.

"Looks like he does," Troy said.

Grace put both arms around Gary. "That is the saddest and most beautiful thing I've ever seen."

Gary wiped his eyes too and hoped no one noticed.

"Grace, you sure you can't stay too?" Meg asked.

"I wish I could. Really, I wish I could stay forever. But I need to get back to Rock Hill and figure out what's next for me."

"What about Robbie?" Meg asked. "What will you tell him?"

"He knows we're leaving," Gary said. "He has our number at the house. Same as it's always been. I'm sure he'll call or something when he's ready."

"Will we ever be together again?" Grace asked, scanning the faces of everyone in the room.

Please stay, Moses thought.

Soon the group was gathered in the front yard. Gary, Grace and Troy said goodbye to Moses inside, and all fought back tears as they closed the door behind him. He went right to the window and, like a soldier on duty, solemnly watched his protectees.

Macy hugged everyone—twice—and promised to take care of Meg.

Troy hugged his mother and insisted on buying her a cellular phone when he got home. "You'll never have to wonder where I am. And same for me." Then he pecked her on her cheek a final time and backed away.

Meg stood with her back to her home and her dog watching through the window. "Goodbye, Gary."

Gary looked at Moses and waved. "Please take care of Moses," he said. "*Please.*"

Then he turned and walked away. But when he got to the sidewalk, he looked back up at her again. "And yourself."

Inside the house, still hanging on every moment, Moses watched Gary, Troy and his beloved Grace walk away.

Please stay.

SEVENTY-ONE

Meg, Macy and Moses spent the first few hours after the bus left Gulf Breeze inside the condo. The temperature was approaching ninety-five degrees, a rarity for Pensacola. The breeze seemed to have followed the bus back across the bridge, and the remaining stale air was a punishment.

Moses explored the nooks and corners he'd missed when he was just a guest and eventually helped himself to Sandi's recliner. Meg watched him circle on the seat cushion as the chair started to rock, and he quickly fell into a ball. Meg was happy to have a connection to home, but she also pictured Gary alone. Alone in the house. Alone at games. Alone at the river. Alone when his evening game shows began. Alone.

As she pushed the thoughts aside, the doorbell rang. "Come in," Meg said. Robbie appeared over Meg's shoulder. "Okay to visit?"

"Please," Meg said, and he sat on the loveseat.

"Here alone?"

"No," Meg said. "Macy's cleaning the bathrooms. Turns out guests, even family, leave messes behind."

Robbie nodded, and Meg noticed he'd swapped his jeans and

flannel for shorts and a T-shirt bearing the logo of a band called Hot Tub Dolphins. On his feet he boasted fluorescent green flip-flops. "All they had left," he said, lifting his feet slightly off the floor in confession.

"The rest took off," Meg said and set her recliner in motion.

"I saw that. Saw the bus gone and wondered if that's what was up."

She smiled at Moses. "But not everyone. Moses stayed behind."

"Huh," Robbie half-grunted. "Must've been hard."

"For who?"

"For Pop—sorry—Gary."

"Robbie, I don't think anyone cares if you want to call him Pop. Just call him."

"I will."

For a full hour, with a short break for Macy's fresh limeade, Robbie continued filling in the gaps of his life. He'd survived a crash in his first semi, the result of another overzealous truck on the interstate, and a handful of relationships that stopped somewhere between "I think I love you" and "I do."

"But you never tied the knot again?"

"No, just couldn't. Felt like I was cheatin' on Mallorie. On Troy. Really pretty much on all of you."

Robbie cried when Meg asked if he'd ever returned to New Market to see the memorial they'd placed in Mallorie's honor. "I wanted to," he stuttered. "But didn't think I should. Didn't really feel like I deserved it." Robbie held his head in his hands, and when he looked up, there was something different in his eyes. "You know what, Meg? If I could, I'd walk from here to New Market to see her again. Even if just for a second. To watch her fly. To apologize. Shoot, some days I think I'd even watch her fly and die that day if it meant I got to see her another morning."

Meg smiled. "That's why she loved you, Robbie Basham."

They enjoyed the quiet, and Macy passed through the room with a basket of bath towels.

"Meg, can I ask ya something?" Robbie said.

"Of course."

"Why'd ya write me?"

Meg stopped rocking. "What do you mean? You read the letter."

"I know I did. You wanted me here. To say goodbye . . . But seems . . . I don't know. Like me comin' here is just . . . for more."

"Robbie, this can only be the beginning for everyone. It's going to take time. Maybe a lot of it. Your son headed home, and he's still a stranger to you. That won't change with a visit to Gulf Breeze or a birthday card. Your visit isn't the end—it's the beginning. It's the start of your 'I'm sorry.'"

Macy appeared in the entry between the living room and kitchen, as if hiding behind a sand dune. "It's interesting, isn't it, Meg?"

"What is?"

"Apologies. They're beginnings, not really endings. And everyone does it their own way, don't they?"

Meg resumed her gentle rocking, back and forth, a few inches in the past, a few in the present, a few forward into the future. "And sometimes it's the hardest thing they ever have to do." Meg looked at Sandi on the mantel. First at her urn, then at her face in the photo.

"Robbie has work to do," Macy said. "We all do. But he's here. I'm here. Moses is here."

Moses lifted his head and looked at Meg.

"Some come from Missouri. Some come from an apartment just across the bridge."

"And others?" Meg asked without looking up from whatever memory had captured her vacant eyes.

"And others come on a bus."

SEVENTY-TWO

If they stuck to the interstate, Grace's home in Rock Hill was less than ten hours away. After almost two weeks of adventures, they were all ready to shower in their own bathrooms, sleep in their own beds and change into something other than the three or four options they'd packed along.

Gary sat in the driver's seat and kept the bus steady and straight. They hit Montgomery, Alabama, just after lunchtime and stopped for pulled-pork sandwiches and fries at Demers Drive-In on the northside of the city limits. They'd already traveled 160 miles, but Gary still saw Gulf Breeze in the rearview mirror.

A forgiving breeze blew through a collection of old picnic tables in the gravel-and-dirt parking lot. "Great. Another picnic table," Grace said. "I'll be just fine if I never sit and eat at another one of these things after this trip. Some things are hard to unsee. Unlive."

Gary finished his lunch first and walked alone to a convenience store a hundred yards away with—he hoped—a working restroom. Grace and Troy dipped their remaining fries in the drive-in's allegedly famous homemade ketchup. When Troy stood up to refill their paper cups with more ice water, Grace watched every step. His smile at an older couple eating barbeque chicken. His hat tip to a friendly toddler who waved first. His smile—wholesome, authentic, bright—when the owner stopped him at the orange water cooler strapped to a table with bungee cords. "I'm Denise. The owner. Y'all enjoy your lunches?"

"So good," Troy said, and she asked for and got a high five.

He sauntered back to the table. So cool. So confident. So complicated. "Nice lady," he said, sitting back down at the table and facing Grace.

"Too old for you, champ," Grace said, and she fished an ice cube from her cup and munched on it.

"No such thing."

"Mm-hmm. Right." She craned her head to see the convenience store and saw that Gary hadn't yet begun the short walk back. "Can I ask you something? Before this ends?"

"Lunch?"

Grace dipped two fingers in her ice water and flicked them in his face. "No." Then with the same wet fingers, she pointed at the bus parked at the far side of the lot.

"At this point? Sure," he said. "But the trip has pretty much been flawless so far. So, you know, be careful."

Another wet flick. "Just feels to me like we should finish . . . clearing the air. Before my stop on the . . . Shenandoah Senators Express."

"Dang. That's not bad, actually. We shoulda been using that."

"Seriously, Troy." She leaned in. "Texas. You. Me. This." She waved her hands back and forth between them. "The end of it all happened pretty quick, don't you think?"

Troy shrugged, dipped his pinkie in the ketchup and began sketching some strange abstract art on his flattened sandwich wrapper.

"Couple of silly arguments. What, like three games in a row canceled for all that rain? Then a road trip . . . By the time you came back, things felt . . . I don't know. I guess, different. And then they were different. You became distant. So I did the same."

Troy wiped his pinkie off on a dirty napkin. "Sounds about right," he said. "Just felt like we'd . . . drifted?"

"Are you *asking* if we drifted? Or are you telling me?"

"Both?"

Grace crossed her arms, closed an eye for her trademark heavy wink and exhaled through her loose lips like a horse in the gate. "You can do better than that."

Troy balled up his trash and in one fluid motion tossed it fifteen feet away into the bottom of a tall metal trash can.

"Maybe that's your problem," Grace said. "Wrong sport."

Troy groaned, and Grace reached across the table to take his hands. "I just want to understand. What changed?"

Troy looked her in the eyes. "I did?"

"Okay. Tell me how."

Troy pulled his hands away and tucked his hair back behind his ears. "I was . . . falling out of love with baseball. I think that's the best way to put it. My whole life had been baseball. My personality. My friends. Everyone in my life was there because of baseball."

"Whoa now. Everyone in your life was there because of baseball? Really?"

"That's what I figure."

"First of all, you sound just like Pop. And second, you're an idiot . . . You think people love you because of baseball?"

"That's not what I said."

"Uh, kinda is, Troy."

"I just mean that Pop, you, the guys in high school, they knew me as the kid who was going to play in the majors. I was the golden boy. Put Woodstock on the map—all that junk."

"You can't be serious, Troy. You can't be. Haven't we covered this? You think I loved you since the eighth grade because you could throw a baseball really fast?" Her volume rose enough that the entire Demers Drive-In crew had tuned into their domestic drama.

Troy took off his hat and vigorously scratched his scalp—just like he might have scratched Moses's.

"Troy. Did you push me away to make life easier?"

Troy shrugged.

"Did we . . . 'drift' . . . your words . . . because you'd given up on Robbie? On your grandparents?"

Troy felt a fat frog crawl from his gut to his throat, and he pushed it down with everything he had.

"Did we drift because you were afraid? Afraid that if you were just Troy, a boy from Woodstock, that we wouldn't work?"

Troy looked toward the gawking Demers family and smiled sheepishly.

So Grace stood up, stepped on top of the picnic table, then stepped down on his side and straddled the bench. "Troy, I learned to love baseball because you did. It made you happy, and if it made you happy, it made me happy. I chose that. And if you told me right now you loved . . . I don't know . . . finger painting with condiments . . . I'd love that too. And I'd love you even more."

Troy's eyes were wet—he'd lost the war, and Grace had noticed.

"We don't love each other because of what we do—we love each other because of who we are. I never chose baseball, or a big career, or money, or your ridiculous good looks. I *chose* you. I *chose* to love you."

Troy looked up at her and deadpanned, "Well . . . you're right about the looks thing."

They stared at one another and drew close.

Troy saw the woman he'd secretly cried over in Texas.

Grace saw the middle schooler, the high schooler and the unfinished man with unfinished grief sprawled across his face.

SEVENTY-THREE

Gary stood alone at the sink in the convenience-store restroom. He studied his face in the cracked mirror and noted how much sun he'd gotten in Gulf Breeze. His hair was thick and unruly, and he promised himself he'd visit his barber when he made it home to Woodstock.

He opened his mouth, examined his teeth and pulled from his front pocket the same toothpick that had survived the entire trip. He poked and scraped, rinsed off the tired pick and tucked it back into its place.

Gary turned on the faucet, closed his eyes and splashed cold water on his face. But instead of quickly wiping it dry, he nodded down at the sink and let the drops race along his cheekbones and drip into the dirty drain. He breathed in the moment and picked up the distant scent of salt, suntan lotion and a warm ocean breeze.

As the water ran, his mind wandered into history. To Washington, DC, and New Year's Eve. To the most beautiful woman he'd ever seen. To fireworks and a hotel lobby. To a first kiss he could still taste.

Gary heard the faint buzz of a plane overhead, saw smoke and lights, heard tears and fights. He felt the weight of a black suit, a white church and a brown casket. He could suddenly smell Moses's feet, Meg's lemonade and freshly cut infield grass.

He looked back up to see his reflection. The deep lines mapping the decades of his life. Marking birthdays, baseball and buses. River bends and Shenandoah sunsets.

Then a moment in the street. Meg and Sandi climbing into a packed car. The look in Meg's exhausted eyes. Sadness. Regret.

But there was something else, Gary remembered. A flicker of something. Hope. Desire. A step into the road. Some heart. Some fight.

Gary dried his face in a wad of paper towels, and when he finally unlocked and pulled open the restroom door, he saw that a father and his young son had been waiting patiently for their turn. Gary apologized, held the door, then meandered down the aisles. Five minutes later he bought gum he didn't really need and, out of habit, the most recent *Sports Illustrated*.

Back outside he walked toward Grace and Troy. Some fifty yards from their picnic table, still out of earshot, Gary stopped and plunked a piece of Big Red into his mouth. He tossed the wrapper in a tall trash can chained to a parking lot light pole and imagined Troy and Grace's overdue discussions.

He questioned how they'd recover, if they'd climb out of whatever potholes they'd dug and landed in. He could almost hear the whispers about the painful past and their uncertain future.

Mostly, he wondered if they'd take their own advice. Would they forgive? Would they fight for one another? Would they choose love?

Though he could not hear her clearly, Gary smiled when Grace climbed over the top of the picnic table and seemed to make a speech. But he didn't have to hear her to know what was unfolding. Their smiles would have been visible from Gulf Breeze.

Gary looked at the cover of his magazine, rolled it up into one hand, tapped his other palm with it like a mini baseball bat, then shoved it into the trash can. When he arrived back at the bus, he pulled Grace and Troy in close. "How would you feel about a detour?"

SEVENTY-FOUR

Within thirty minutes of their pit stop, Troy was napping on one of the cots in the back of the bus and Grace was sitting in the front row opposite Gary reorganizing his glove box and sharing more untold stories about her time in Texas and the unexpected move to Rock Hill.

Gary pretended to listen, but his mind was rehearsing. He looked in the rearview mirror and saw Moses's dried nose, paw and tongue marks on the emergency-door window. His best friend had spent years of his life in that spot. He'd cheered the team after wins and moped with them after losses on those excruciatingly long rides home. But in that moment, Gary imagined him cheering.

Gary hit the gas a little harder—a mile whizzed by, then another. He checked the speedometer and couldn't believe he was actually going thirteen miles per hour over the speed limit. *I don't think she's ever gone this fast*, he thought.

As they crested a hill, Gary spotted a state trooper heading the opposite direction. He tapped the brakes, but it was too late. The cruiser slowed and pulled through an emergency crossover in the median. When its lights flashed, Gary pressed the gas.

"No, no, no, Pop," Grace said. "You gotta pull over. Were you speeding?"

Gary groaned. "Hardly."

He checked the mirror and saw the familiar lights flashing behind him. "You've got to be kidding me."

He signaled right, pulled well off the road, and with his head resting on the steering wheel, waited for the inevitable.

Grace yelled to wake Troy and handed Gary the registration and insurance card she'd just fished from the messy glove box. "Here you go, lead foot," she teased. "Coulda been worse, right? Vulture anyone?"

Gary finally lifted his head when the trooper knocked on the bus's side door. Gary pulled the heavy horizontal handle, and the door swung open. "Good afternoon," the trooper said. "Everything okay?"

"It was," Gary said.

Gary thought the trooper's eyes were already writing a ticket. "You know how fast you were going?"

"Not very. This thing barely does the speed limit."

"Right," the trooper said. "Well my radar says otherwise."

"Look, I'm sure it did. But this old beast barely runs. Maybe a malfunction on its part. It happens."

"Again, my speed gun would disagree."

"Well, sir, you know what they say—speed guns don't write tickets; troopers do."

"Pop!" Troy called from the back of the bus. "Be nice."

The trooper stepped up into the bus, looked back at Troy and Grace and narrowed his eyes. "You two all right back there?"

"Oh, come on, man. What do you think is happening here? A hijacking on a baseball bus?"

"Stop it—seriously, Pop," Grace said.

"How about you step off the bus for a moment?" the trooper said.

"Are you kidding?"

"Hardly."

Gary grunted and unbuckled. As he stood, he looked back at Troy and Grace, and both were glued to the rear window. Gary took the steps down to the ground and found himself in weeds up to his knees. "All this for a speeding ticket?"

The trooper took Gary by the arm and led him to the cruiser parked behind the bus. "Get in, please."

"Seriously?" Gary said, and he didn't notice it then, but another vehicle had also pulled over.

"Just while I sort this out," the trooper said, and he opened the rear door.

Gary eased in but didn't take his eyes off the trooper as he walked back toward the bus. Then a voice from the other side of the back seat raised the hair on his neck. "So, what are you in for?"

"Meg?" Gary said, and his breath and heart were swept up in her smile. "What are you doing here?"

Meg laughed. "I was about to ask you the same thing."

"Well, I was southbound. Back on the bus to Gulf Breeze. Until I got busted for speeding."

Meg put one hand on his and another over her mouth. "You were coming back? For Moses?"

Gary leaned in. "No, not for Moses." He lifted and kissed the back of her hand. "For you."

She wrapped her arms around him, and instantly the cruiser, the highway and the world disappeared.

"Wait, what about Moses?" Gary asked when they finally pulled apart.

"Look behind you." Meg said, and as if rehearsed, the door of an animal control van opened and Moses appeared with a deputy. "He's heading home," Meg added. A moment later the deputy opened the cruiser door, and Gary stopped him.

"Nope, not ready. Don't let me go yet. Just one more minute."

The deputy, aware of the magic of the moment, smiled. "Consider yourself still in custody." Then he shut the door and stepped away.

"Meg, I'm sorry."

Her eyes said, *Thank you.*

"I am so sorry I chose baseball over you. I did. I know I did. And I went for baseball over talking. Over crying. I'm sorry I gave so much to Troy, to the team, to that job, to everything and everyone but you. You got what I had left, and it wasn't much." Gary's voice was wispy, and he held and rubbed Meg's hands tightly, as if to ensure the moment was happening—at last.

"Meg, I miss her. I miss her so much. I have missed our Mallorie every day. Every single day. I see her in my dreams, I see her when I drive, when I watch games. And every plane, every single one I see in the sky or on a field or on a stupid TV show is hers. And I'm just so sorry. Sorry I let her fly. Sorry I didn't drive us away from that airport."

Meg pulled him into her arms and whispered, "Shhh. It's not your fault, my love. It never has been. Shhh."

Gary composed himself, eased out of the embrace and put his forehead against hers.

"I love you," she said.

"I love you too. I just want my family back."

Meg didn't need to answer.

Gary hugged her again and knocked on the glass. The trooper quickly returned, and they stepped back into the highway air. When Moses saw the couple, he broke free from the leash and barreled toward them. He gave Gary a swift lick on the leg and then raced toward the bus. They heard Moses's happy barks travel from the front of the bus all the way down the aisle to the back.

"Now what?" Gary said.

"We go home." Meg wrapped her arms around Gary one more time and rested her head on his chest. "Thank you."

Gary looked up at the bus, and three sets of eyes looked back through the same small window. "For what?"

"For coming. For being you. For choosing."

Gary breathed in her hair and the perfume he'd missed. He began swaying, gently—an overdue dance.

"And . . ." Meg looked up at him. His hair was blowing in the highway breeze. "I'm sorry. For hanging on to so many things and for not hanging on to so many others."

Gary looked back at the trooper and the animal control deputy. They were standing in front of the cruiser, cheering and gesturing for them to get on with it.

"Watch your speed, sir," the trooper called with a grin and a wave.

With that, they boarded the bus, and all together they began the long road home.

SEVENTY-FIVE

Moses was exhausted when the bus pulled into Rock Hill just before eight at night. *I need a bed*, he thought. When he realized they were parking on the same street as Grace's townhouse, he barked three thank-yous to Gary. *I am definitely getting a bed.*

All five stepped off the bus like weary ballplayers and crossed the street. Grace, Meg and Moses were set to spend the night in Grace's townhouse, and the boys would either crash on the bus or find a motel back by the freeway. They slowly approached the townhouse, and Grace was greeted as usual by her friendly and nosy next-door neighbors.

Come on, people, Moses thought. *I also need a drink and a belly rub.*

Grace and the group stood in the driveway trying to pry themselves away from the neighbors' game of twenty questions. When the door opened and Paul appeared, Grace excused the entire group. "Oh whoops, gotta run. Good to see you."

Was it? Moses groused, now both hungry and grumpy.

Paul stepped out the door, hugged Grace and Meg and reintroduced himself to the guys. "You made it back," Paul said. "Sounds like your bunch had quite the adventure."

You can say that again, Moses thought.

Then Paul bent down and grabbed Moses's head. "Hey, pal, I got a surprise for you."

Bacon?

But Moses instantly knew he was wrong. Paul stepped aside from the open door, and a dog came racing down the hardwood floor.

Beverage?

"You did it!" Grace said, and she hugged Paul again and kissed him on the cheek.

"Gross," he teased.

"Best. Cousin. Ever."

Troy and Gary both got on their knees and let Beverage thank their hands, their faces, their ears. Then Grace bent down and did the same, and Beverage licked Grace's wet cheeks.

Please be real, Moses thought.

Gary stared at Meg. "Like I said," she smiled. "Grace knows people."

"And I've got news about your friend, Mark Richards. I called in a couple of favors, and he's fine—excellent actually. He's out of ICU, healing up, getting strength back. Could be out in a week."

Grace covered her face and exhaled out the memory. "Thank you, thank you."

"We'll get you back home soon," Gary said, still petting Beverage. "Sound good, girl?"

Moses didn't know what home would look like for wanderers like Mark and Beverage, but he felt peace. And that's all that mattered.

Later they gathered around a large dining room table and snacked on a veggie tray. "I'm glad you called when you did," Paul told Grace. "Another half-day and that girl was almost certain to be put down . . .

We've had fun the last couple days. Haven't we, girl?" But Beverage wasn't listening. She was on the couch in the other room, legs and paws intertwined with Moses's.

One by one they thanked Paul. Even Meg became emotional even though her tie to Mark's dog was purely through the travel log of the others. "I can't believe they've both survived this."

For fifteen minutes, Troy and Gary told Mark's story. By the time they were done, Meg and Grace were in tears—again. "I feel like I'll be living that story for the rest of my life," Grace said.

"We all will," Gary said. "Even Mark. Not just that detour, but every mile." As he spoke, he reached into his pocket and produced Mark's pocket-sized blue Moleskine notebook from his lap.

Grace's eyes and mouth both shot wide open. "How? Why?"

"Maybe best to not share too much. I figure we didn't know, for sure, whether he'd make it. So just in case, I wanted to know it was . . . safe. And now Paul here, who probably has handcuffs handy—well, let me just say they left me unattended in that Macon police car a little too long."

The room erupted in laughter, and Moses and Beverage both lumbered off the couch, stood side by side and served as witnesses in the doorway.

Gary handed Mark's well-loved journal to Meg and smiled. "We better get this back to him. Looks like he's still got work to do." He breathed, smiled and looked at Meg. "Because love is a choice."

Then, for the first time since long before the day she said goodbye in Virginia, Gary put his lips near hers. "Should I count down from ten before kissing you?" But there would be no more waiting.

On the other side of the table, Troy pulled Grace down off her feet and onto his lap. Then, for the first time since long before she'd said goodbye in Texas, Troy kissed Grace.

In the doorway, Moses watched the happy ending play out just as he'd hoped. Then, for the first time since—the couch in the other room—Moses leaned over and licked Beverage's paw.

SEVENTY-SIX

One Year Later

"Seven-zip." Troy tossed the keys on the chipped edge of the Formica countertop. "Seven. To. Zero." He punched the air with the numbers. "Did you hear me? We won! Game one of the playoffs is in the books."

Troy and Grace smiled at Gary and Meg snuggling like teens on the couch. They were sitting smack in the middle, leaning into one another, holding hands, as if any movement by one would sink the other.

"Where are they?" Troy asked, and Grace sat on the couch and leaned her head on Meg's shoulder. Troy was still wearing his Shenandoah Senators uniform as he walked down the long hallway of his parents' newly painted pastel-yellow ranch home. "Moses? Beverage?" The geriatric canine couple was asleep, as they often were by nine in the evening, in the guest bedroom. The dogs wheezed, snored and smiled. "Guess you'll have to wait 'til tomorrow for the news," Troy said, and he quietly pulled the door shut.

Troy sat in his mom's reading chair in the corner of the living room and recapped the highlights. The hits, the tension, the stolen bases, the opposing manager getting tossed for arguing a blown call. "All the usual stuff. You guys coming to the next game?"

"Maybe?" Meg and Gary said in harmony. Then Gary added with a wink, "There's always stuff to do here."

"Oh. My. Gross." Troy said, and he pretended to lose his dinner in his hat.

"Moving on . . ." Gary said. "And you? How'd you do?"

"Well, Grace says I'm the best pitching coach slash bus driver slash cheerleader in the league, but who knows? She's biased."

"True," Grace said, her eyes closed and her voice sleepy.

"Agreed. Always thought you were overrated as a player," Gary teased. "And now as a coach? I'm surprised they keep you around."

"You kidding? They call me 'the man.' As in, the man who finally took your sorry old place. I dropped the median age in the dugout by like fifty years."

"It never ends," Meg said, shaking her head.

"And how's my Grace?" Meg turned just enough to kiss the side of her head.

"Asleep, evidently," Troy said.

"Not asleep," she corrected and raised a finger as if scoring a point.

"She's toast. I should get her back to her place. The state police academy has really been kicking her fanny the last couple weeks."

"Maybe so, but this kid can do anything," Meg said.

"Nah," Troy answered. "Always thought she was overrated."

Meg and Gary both giggled. "Put *that* line in your vows," Meg said, raising her eyebrows for emphasis.

"Still not asleep," Grace said, and she opened one eye and snarled at her fiancé.

"Oh, Troy," Gary said. "Don't forget to call your father back. Robbie said you'd help set him up with that cellular phone."

"How many times I gotta tell you, Pop. It's just . . . *cell* phone."

"I'll call it a paperweight if I want. Point is he's driving down 81 to . . ."

"Knoxville," Meg finished Gary's sentence.

"Right, Knoxville. And he wants to say hey and get help. Cool?"

"Please don't say cool, Pop."

As nine thirty approached, Meg elbowed her husband and motioned with her eyes toward Troy.

"What?" Troy said.

"You sure?" Gary asked, and his forehead collapsed into a wave of wrinkles.

Meg nodded, lifted their held hands and kissed the back of his.

"We've been waiting to tell you that we've decided on our next trip," Gary said.

"What? Already? You just did one a few months ago. March, right?"

"Time's not slowing down for us, Troy. We're healthy, and we're going."

"Where to?" Troy asked.

Meg and Gary looked at one another, smiled, smiled wider, then wider, and both began cackling. "That's the good news, actually. Macy is going to join us on this one."

"Awesome!" Troy said.

His dad rolled his eyes and shared a dramatic sigh. "Please don't say awesome, Troy."

Meg groaned and shook her head.

"Seriously, where to?"

"Do you remember where Mark was headed to when you and your dad first met him last year?" Meg asked.

Grace sat up and yawned. "Wait. What's happening?"

"Uh, hold on . . ." Troy took off his Senators cap and scratched his head. "Yes, yes. I do remember. Orlando. Disney. That was one of his wife's places from the journal."

"Nice work, Son." Gary said. "Mark asked for some help, a little moral support, with this particular trip. So we're picking him up and heading to Orlando together for a few days."

"You've got to be kidding. So you're going to Mark's new place? To pick him up?" Grace asked.

"Yep," Gary said.

All four looked at one another and smiled from the inside out.

"It's true," Meg said with a grin. "We're heading back to Gulf Breeze."

"Sweet," Troy said. "Let's take the bus . . . I'll drive."

ACKNOWLEDGMENTS

Like so many other writers, I used the quiet and quarantines of the COVID-19 pandemic to create. During the spring and early summer of 2020, I wrote a manuscript using Google Docs online at a public link. Every day readers would peek behind the curtain of the writing process as I wrote every single word with an audience. It was a process and a journey I'll never forget.

That manuscript's working title was *The Bus to Gulf Breeze,* and it later became *Even the Dog Knows*.

I must thank my talented daughter, Oakli Wright Van Meter, who served as my first draft editor. As I wrote with the world watching, she edited in real time. Her candor, keen eye and endless encouragement were invaluable. I cannot wait until her debut novel releases.

Thanks also to my wonderful wife, Kodi, and our other children: Jadi, Kason and Koleson. I'm also immensely grateful for our son-in-law, Troy, and our grandchildren, Gary and Annie. They're the real stars of the family, and they make our lives a big, beautiful adventure. Gratitude also goes to Lobby, Gary's friend in the tree. He knows why.

ACKNOWLEDGMENTS

I'm also grateful for the guidance and creative instincts of our powerful publishing team at Shadow Mountain: Chris Schoebinger, Heidi Taylor, Alison Palmer, Troy Butcher and Ilise Levine, among many others.

No novel gets from an author's imagination to a published project without the assistance of beta readers. Because I wrote online with readers following along, I can't possibly name them all. But I do express my sincere thanks to every single one of you who read as I wrote and cheered for me and our quirky cast of characters.

A few friends provided critical counsel and extraordinary encouragement. They are Matt Birch, Eric Farnsworth, Stephen Funk, Aaron "Al" Lee, David McConnell, Laurie Reynolds Tinsley and Ron Zirkle.

My deepest thanks to my business partners. Many of them own pieces of my novels, and their support of the books and their development into films has been critical. An extra dash of thanks to David Williams and Janice Fleming for their friendship in recent years. Without them, this novel might have been written in a tent by the Shenandoah River.

I owe my career and an endless debt of gratitude to book clubs. Thank you to the big clubs in big cities and the tiny clubs in tiny towns. Your passion for storytelling and your love of good old-fashioned printed books is the fuel that keeps my writing fire burning bright.

Finally, three thank-you barks to the fictional Moses and to real dogs everywhere. We love you for your friendship, forgiveness and loyalty. Yes, you know things.

DISCUSSION QUESTIONS

1. *Even the Dog Knows* is a story about love, family and forgiveness. Why is forgiveness an essential part of maintaining good relationships? Is it easier or harder to forgive family members as opposed to other people? Why?

2. Some characters eventually recognize that they were wrong. Why is it so hard to admit that we could have done something better? How do we forgive ourselves?

3. Both Meg and Gary experience long-term grief over the death of their only daughter, Mallorie. What are different ways of dealing with grief? How can grief help or harm relationships?

4. Moses helps bring the Gorton family back together, and Mark relies on his dog, Beverage, as a companion. Do you think beloved pets can help individuals and families through difficult times? How?

5. Troy has a hard time admitting that he doesn't want to play baseball anymore. Why? Why do a person's job or interests sometimes become a core part of their identity? Is that okay?

6. Troy and Grace are high school sweethearts who drifted apart for a

season. Do you know a similar young couple who remained together years later? Why do couples sometimes grow apart? What can be done to prevent that from happening?

7. Macy carries guilt about inadvertently causing Mallorie's death. How does she manage that guilt? Why do we sometimes feel guilty for things outside our control?

8. After being estranged for almost all of his son's life, Robbie attempts to reconnect with Troy. Why did he stay away for so long? How does a person forgive someone who has done something that seems unforgivable?

9. What does true love mean to you? Where in the story do you see characters express moments of true love?

10. Woodstock, Virginia, and Gulf Breeze, Florida, take on such prominent roles in the story, they nearly become characters in the book. Have you been to either place? Would you be interested in taking such a long road trip by bus?

11. In the acknowledgments, the author specifically thanks and warmly recognizes the role of book clubs. Why are book clubs so important in today's literary landscape? If your group had a theme or motto, what would it be?